I0817614

Ice Nine Kills

Welcome to Horrorwood

PRAISE FOR ROY MERKIN

"Nobody exposes the bald truth like Roy Merkin."

—*The Nude York Times*

"A sharp razor couldn't shave Merkin off this story."

—*American Case File*

"Merkin goes below the belt and pulls the rug off the Ice Nine Kills conspiracy."

—Sethley Ferber

Ice Nine Kills

Welcome to Horrorwood

ROY MERKIN

RARE BIRD

THIS IS A GENUINE RARE BIRD BOOK

Rare Bird Books
6044 North Figueroa Street
Los Angeles, California 90042
rarebirdbooks.com

FIRST TRADE HARDCOVER EDITION

For more information, address:
Rare Bird Books Subsidiary Rights Department
6044 North Figueroa Street
Los Angeles, California 90042

Set in Dante
Printed in the United States

Distributed by Simon & Schuster

Standard Trade Hardcover Edition: 9781644284964
Deluxe Limited Hardcover Edition (Signed): 9781644285619

10 9 8 7 6 5 4 3 2 1

Library of Congress Cataloging-in-Publication Data available upon request

I
Opening Night

The fourteen chapters you are about to read were hidden away long ago, deemed too grotesque for public consumption by a federal judge. Recently, however, they were unearthed by journalist Roy Merkin. These pages will soon gain infamy as key evidence confirming that Ice Nine Kills frontman, Spencer Charnas, was brutally slain by the District Attorney prosecuting him for the murder of his twenty-eight-year-old fiancée. Though the original title of the book penned by the DA herself remains unknown, Roy Merkin would make sure that it forever be remembered as Welcome to Horrorwood.

Spencer is dead and The Silence has killed him. As far as I can surmise, this fact reaches an indisputable level of certainty. It is beyond fathomable for the general public to be so oblivious. While hordes of screaming fans of the horror-metal band Ice Nine Kills (Psychos, as they are known within their inner circle) continue to listen to his music, attend his concerts, and meet him at conventions, the man they are interacting with is not Spencer Charnas, the band's frontman, but a clever—albeit talented—imposter. Perhaps this new "Spencer" is driven by intelligence of an artificial nature. Or he could simply be a well made-up lookalike. Maybe it even comes down to some form of witchcraft; in this,

I cannot be certain. But as I pen this book, what I do know for certain is that he is no longer himself.

I am going to reveal to you, dear readers, the true story of how it has come to be that Spencer is no longer Spencer, the story of how he died. All I ask is for an audience that is willing to read between the headlines. Are you ready for the unvarnished truth? Can you put aside what you think you know? Are you open?

Before we begin, a note: Much like the real Spencer Charnas, many of the following chapters were dead, so to speak. They are, in a way, a zombified text. Originally penned by Los Angeles County District Attorney Marcie Kent, much of this book was part of another book, once shelved for reasons that will become obvious in the later chapters. I have taken many of these passages and added my own details and embellishments—factual only, of course. Undoubtedly, readers remember the news bulletins from the time. But Spencer's trial (and the aftermath) will go down in history as one of the greatest legal blunders of our century. Marcia Clark may have butchered the O.J. Simpson case but, unlike Kent, she wasn't the one wielding the knife.

The bloodied postscript to the trial has left many unanswered questions. Some of these answers had been locked away in DA Marcie Kent's book as she described what happened up to and during the trial.

Before we get there, however, I would like to address the rooster in the henhouse, as we say in my native Texas. I am aware that I would never be accused of being Spencer's biggest fan; we have, in fact, often been portrayed by various mainstream media outlets as "enemies." However, over the course of reading and adapting Marcie Kent's original writing, I have developed a certain sympathy for Spencer. Now, do not let that sympathy be confused for an endorsement of his lifestyle and past actions; I do not condone his rockstar way of life. But, in this case, he has proven to be a victim himself, a man who was framed as being something he was not based purely on his art and nothing more. Like a West Memphis One, if you will.

The new Spencer, by contrast, is much more sinister, much more dangerous than the musical frontman adored by millions of fans. After sustaining a horrific set of injuries, Spencer famously went into a coma; but the Spencer that "woke up" is hardly Spencer at all. In that regard, let this book be a warning. Spencer is, yet again, NOT TO BE TRUSTED. This new version wears Spencer like a skin, parading him around for all to see. I hope to peel back the layers of flesh and reveal the true nature of this beast, so that perhaps next time you rub elbows with this imposter-Spencer at one of his "Meat and Greets," you think twice before you get too close.

—Roy Merkin

II
Welcome to Horrorwood

Ink fills the page…

"Shit," Assistant District Attorney Marcie Kent whispered under her breath before snatching the offending pen away from her legal pad. The stain had seeped through the first five pages of her meticulously crafted opening statement, and it took her a split second to realize that her small outburst was in full view of the judge, the jury, court onlookers, and the defendant, Spencer Orenthal Charnas.[1] She looked around sheepishly as she blotted the mess. Not a good first day of trial impression.

DA Kent's assignment to this case was not by any accident of random chance. No, she very much chose this for herself. Always a believer of creating destiny, rather than waiting for it to strike, Kent was a go-getter, type-A, DA's office all-star. And Spencer? Well, he was just recently accused of killing his fiancée, Hollywood starlet Nadia Teichmann, a beautiful young girl with a lot of potential. The DA had watched her own star rise over the past few years and this case was just the ticket she needed for admission to celebrity status in the legal world. She outmaneuvered, outgunned, and outmanned everyone in the central office to get a crack at this

1 As a note here, I was also present on this day of the trial. This is Roy Merkin, by the way, and I'll be talking to you here, annotating much of the book with my little Merkinisms from the depths of the footnotes section of these pages as we progress deeper on our descent into hell, madness, darkness, what have you…

defendant. She had been with the case since day one, was even the first to the courthouse for his surprise arraignment. Chalk it up to first day jitters, but here she was with a page full of ink, the first blemish in what would soon become a botched trial.

Kent quickly composed herself and apologized. She looked over to the defense table where she spotted Spencer's lawyer, Carlos Cochran, and the defendant himself, a smug look on his face. On this day (as on most days), Spencer was "rockstar" incarnate. Slicked back hair, California-tanned skin, and a fitted suit that covered up two full sleeves of tattoos. He had a certain magnetism that could easily have a chilling effect on getting a conviction, and she knew that she would have to get ahead of that charm as soon as humanly possible. Kent made eye contact with a couple members of the jury, then took a breath before launching into her initial statements.

Suffice it to say, Kent handily recovered from the earlier mishap, delivering what could only be viewed as total perfection in her conveyance of the facts of the case. Like the scalpel of a seasoned rhinoplastician in nearby Beverly Hills, she cut through the jury's doubts, dexterously molding them into the shape and size that suited her argument, all while removing the distractions that could mar an otherwise beautiful case.[2]

He did it.

This is how he did it.

Acquittal is not an option.

And then her final blow: a set of videotapes that would become the lynchpin of the case. She had the whole room eating out of the palm of her hand and used that momentum to build up these pieces of evidence. The jury would practically believe they had witnessed

2 Much of this speech is available online and can be seen in both the dramatization format, as well as the real thing. It is also worth noting here that while her book notes and some of her court notes were used in the writing of this book, Marcie Kent was unable to be interviewed and in no way endorsed the publication of this volume.

Spencer commit murder in real life. Even if they were alleged to be merely works of fiction.

As she came to a close, Kent wanted to give her audience, the jury, a taste of what this trial would bring. "Give them just enough rope and they'll hang him with it," she thought. Thus, she used her remaining time to allow Spencer to introduce himself—on her terms, of course.

"Ladies and Gentlemen," she began. "We're asking you to consider whether the defendant brutally murdered his fiancée in cold blood. I could go on all day about the defendant's depravity. But let's hear who he really is, in his own words..."

†

[It should be noted here that large chunks of italicized text are the actual video tapes put out by Ice Nine Kills. These tapes would be used as evidence against the singer and, thus, are described in full detail, depicting the plots and visuals of these vital artifacts. These videos are available online, wherever music videos may be streamed, with the QR links provided. But, be warned: many of them are graphic in nature and are not for the faint of heart.]

Lights up on the deserted streets of Horrorwood, illuminated only by pale street lamps and the orange glow of a burning vehicle, a relic of recent destruction. High up in the hills, a large, white-lettered sign displays "HORRORWOOD" against a backdrop of lush green. But we're down on the streets below. There, in the middle of the madness, a movie theater

previously prepared to premiere a film that has since gone unshown. The marquee remains unlit, suggesting the theater's idle state. Cutting through the black, one lone klieg light strikes the night sky, as if to alert the universe to the source of chaos, the eye of the storm. Bodies lie strewn about the front of the theater. Someone—or something—very dangerous has been here. Standing amidst a sea of bodies and bedlam is, perhaps the danger himself, Spencer. He wears a blood-stained yet well-tailored tuxedo and stares down at his crimsoned hands. What have they done?

With a loud POP, the marquee behind Spencer illuminates, casting light onto the massacre surrounding him, a sea so red it's hard to know where the carpet ends and the blood begins. The marquee for the Silver Scream theater announces the picture: Welcome to Horrorwood.

A phone rings. It is quickly answered by Spencer, now riding in a limo, unbloodied and unburdened by the actions of the evening. It is a time before the mayhem—hours, minutes—it's hard to tell. In this otherwise quiet limousine, Spencer screams into the receiver of the rotary phone. He is surrounded by three gorgeous women, none more so than his beautiful fiancée, Nadia, whose red dress evokes the color of the bloody mess soon to come. As the limo sharply rounds the corners of the streets, Spencer and his female guests are thrown around the bench leather seats, their champagne reaching the rims of their glass and sometimes spilling over.

The limo swerves past neon signs and art deco-style buildings. Finally, it reaches its destination: a well-lit, well-attended movie premiere, night-and-day from the previous iteration of the theater. For starters, no one has been killed. The crowd screams as Spencer exits the limo, donning his black wayfarer sunglasses and taking his place at the edge of the red carpet, where he joins the other members of Ice Nine Kills. A woman on each arm, Spencer is thereafter flanked by Ricky Armellino and Dan Sugarman, his two guitarists. On either side of Ricky and Dan: drummer Patrick Galante and bassist Joe Occhiuti. The band moves forward in unison as camera flashes flicker and fans fawn over their fame and fortitude.

The scene at the movie premiere continues, intercut with shots of the band playing on top of bullet-riddled cop cars and burned-out vehicles on the havoc-ridden streets of Horrorwood. Spencer sings from the center.

Back at the premiere, Ice Nine Kills is treated to the cheering of fans, dressed up in various horror costumes and band t-shirts and memorabilia, including a mask called "The Silence."[3] *The night is not without its detractors, though. Dozens of protestors also line the red carpet, chanting and holding up handmade carboard placards emblazened with "IX=666," "Death to INK," and "Die Devil Worshippers."*

Notoriety is not without its naysayers.

Spencer extends both middle fingers to the protesters, who now flank the pathway into the theater and are held back only by velvet ropes. Journalists and camera crews crowd the band, blocking their swift entrance as they seek to grab an exclusive about the band's big plans for the night, for the future. One particularly dim-witted journalist with a cheap haircut and an even cheaper tan steps in front of the rest to ask a question. Spencer politely listens as the man asks, "Spencer, now that the Halloween franchise is over, do you think Michael Myers will make another Austin Powers sequel?"

Spencer pauses for a brief second, lost in thought, before removing his sunglasses and placing his arm slowly by his side. Suddenly, his pace quickens. He reaches up, pushes aside the man's microphone, and grabs him by the back of the head, slamming him toward the ground. Once the man falls to his knees, Spencer carefully places his hands inside the man's mouth—one on the maxilla, one on the mandible—and brusquely pulls the two apart. Once the cheeks are torn from the teeth and bone, the head gives way and the top half is separated from the bottom. Reporters, fans, and protestors alike scream in horror as pieces of the reporter's previously intact skull fall on the red carpet. Spencer's bandmates and

3 This mask will become tremendously important as the investigation and trial of Spencer Charnas moves forward. It will perhaps go down in history alongside Ted Kaczynski's Unabomber Manifesto, Ed Gein's human skin lampshade, or even Monica Lewinsky's Blue Dress.

their dates laugh and cheer the frontman on as he beams with delight at what he has done.

Chaos erupts through the crowd as various parties scatter for safety. In direct contrast, Spencer calmly strolls through the fleeing masses and toward Nadia. On arrival, she hands him a gold-wrapped present box, which he receives in stride, as he marches toward the protesters at the other side of the red carpet. Although this group maintains their distance from behind a rope, they stand their ground amidst the mass exodus. When Spencer is just a few steps away, he opens the box and drops it to the ground, revealing a pump-action shotgun. He raises the gun and aims before asking, "How's this for an establishing shot?"

He pumps the gun and fires into the crowd, blowing a hole the size of a grapefruit in the face of an awaiting protester. A melee erupts. The band and their fans rush the protesters and reporters. The opposing sides clash, an explosion of anger and violence.

Spencer lowers his weapon slowly, a smug look crossing his face. He likes what he is seeing. From out of the crowd, Channel 9 entertainment reporter Diane Saw-Yer runs toward Spencer, her cameraman in tow, trying to catch the man at the heart of this insanity. Spencer casually asks to borrow the shoe of a nearby female moviegoer dressed to the nines. Diane's story-first mentality and bouncy personality, summed up neatly in the way her blonde hair catches the air as she runs, causes her to misinterpret Spencer's current state of mind. He rises from removing the moviegoers pump and points the shoe directly at Diane, catching her mid-stride and embedding the stiletto heel in her eye socket. The squish of the hard shoe in the soft orifice echoes louder than it should, as blood pools around the gaping hole left in the front of her face. Spencer pulls back the heel, allowing Diane's instantly lifeless body to fall backward, away from the offending object.

Seconds later, a large police response arrives. The crowd scatters wider until only Spencer and his bandmates are left. Weapons are drawn on both sides—the police and the band—and a standoff ensues. Firing round after round, the police duck behind their vehicles. The band finds refuge in the theater's vestibule as they mow down one officer at a time, stopping only to reload their weapons. Officer's heads and bodies explode as they are hit by the members of the band, who seem to be winning, until reinforcements are called in.

Before the group of new officers can fully arrive on the scene, it seems as if time stands still. Something is awakened in the form of a large man in a tattered coat. With one hand he struggles to affix on his head a Silence mask, a pale white face and dark black lips both of which are marred by numerous scars, including the largest one across the front that takes the shape of the roman numeral nine. The wild mane of the large, unkempt man flows out the back—the rest of his identity otherwise shielded by the mask. More terrifying is what occupies his other hand: a large chainsaw.

He is just the type of savage this town attracts.

Two police reinforcements, a beefy man and a smaller woman, approach with arms drawn, ordering him to the ground.

"Drop your fucking weapon!" the female officer shouts.

The masked man does not comply. Rather, he raises the chainsaw over his head, revving the blade and waving it around. Just as quickly as the officers are upon him, he swings the chainsaw in their direction, first impaling the woman, then continuing through her and toward the beefy officer, skewering them like a shish kebab. He then proceeds to ram them into their own police cruiser, sending sparks flying and a grinding sound that echoes through the streets. Satisfied that they are dead, he parades his newly minted, double-bodied trophy down the streets of Horrorwood and into the darkness whence he came.

Meanwhile, the band holds their position in front of the theater firmly, despite an onslaught of police-issued rounds. Just as the band relaxes in their advantage, police SWAT vehicles arrive in droves. Heavily armored officers pour out of the vans and into the streets to take up a fortified position against the group of assailants. From behind flimsy glass, the gun-toting, tuxedoed members of Ice Nine Kills step forward, arms raised in surrender. Mouthing words that in no way express regret and remorse, the band appears to be waving to their fans just as much as surrendering to officers. Harmless and misunderstood. The whole scene is a large joke, mass murder its punchline.

While the extreme gore of the violence against ordinary citizens and police officers plays out, the band continues to perform from atop the bullet-riddled police cruisers and vans. Lit primarily by the neon lights of Horrorwood, they bask in the lawlessness of the deserted city. The blood-splattered tuxedos of the band members flap in the wind as they wail guitars and bang drums, Spencer commanding it all with a conductor-like presence at the center of the brutality. Police sirens draw the song to a close as the unmistakable metal pattern of the double bass echoes like bullets in the air.

PAUSE.

With the click of a button by District Attorney Marcie Kent, the video stopped. Not one to miss an opportunity for potential impact, she allowed the grainy image to remain on the screen, a reminder to the jury of the horrors they had just witnessed. She had them right where she wanted them, now it was time to go in for the kill. While the jury had watched the horrific violence of the music video, DA Kent had been watching the jury. Juror 3, a retired school bus driver named Al,[4] had followed along stoically; he'd seen worse, one could easily conclude. But Juror 10, a part-time baker and suburban mother named Sam (Samantha), had been unable to watch for more than a few seconds at a time. Others had a mix of reactions. Juror 1, a young man named Eli who had been elected foreman, even fell asleep. Kent knew that if she wanted to

4 Little information is known about most of the jurors in this case. We do, often, know their first names and occupations, but some of the names had to be changed or invented for the sake of clarity. This is only to protect the innocent and, by association, the guilty as well...unfortunately.

get through to someone like Eli, she would need to heighten the theatrics. It was, of course, a balancing act. For example, Jurors 1 and 3 would need to be confronted with all of the gore—all of the brutality—in order to move them, while 12, the suburban mom, would need to be led along slowly, when she was ready.

Not one to be deterred by complicated jury pools, the DA dove in.

"There you have it," she began. "Violence against women. Violence against law enforcement. Violence against mankind."

Spencer snored loudly in his seat. It was clear to those present that he wasn't sleeping, but merely mocking the entire proceedings. Whether the jest was at Kent's expense or that of the sleepy juror, one couldn't tell, but Kent certainly took notice. She made a quick gesture to Spencer's lawyer, Carlos Cochran, who almost as swiftly nudged Spencer awake, embarrassed by his client's behavior.

The DA continued.

"Now, the defense is going to try to convince you that it was all an act. Shock value to sell music, T-shirts, concert tickets. But I answer that with Spencer's own words from this very video's lyrics: 'This is not an act.' "

The jurors were nodding along with her now. Like the syncopated head movements of Ice Nine Kills fans during a catchy breakdown, they seemed to be saying "yes, we believe you," all in rhythm. The power would be intoxicating for anyone, and certainly for the DA.

She thought, "This must be how Spencer feels in an arena full of fans."

"So, ladies and gentlemen of the jury," she continued. "I submit that this was an act. An act of murder."

"This is ridiculous, your honor!" Carlos' voice echoed off the rich oak panels and the marble-floor of the courtroom as he stood up. "And I object to this opening statement and its flimsy narrative.

The idea of a music video foreshadowing a real life killing? What is this? A Wes Craven film?" Carlos' voice shook slightly as he addressed the room. At 5'6", he was slightly shorter than his client and had a smaller build but clearly hoped to punch above his weight in this all-important case.

DA Kent looked immediately at the jury. No need to waste time focusing on the opposing counsel—or the judge, for that matter. Her concern was reserved for those who would ultimately decide Spencer's fate. Fortunately for her, they weren't buying what Spencer's shyster lawyer was selling.

Had she looked to Spencer's lawyer, however, she might have seen the sweat on his brow coming down from his curly brown hair and onto the large-framed, square glasses that slipped down his nose when he got upset. Nerves were getting the best of Carlos. He had defended similar cases, even some as first chair, but this was bigger. Earlier in his career, he had been very close to sitting as assistant counsel on the second trial of the Menendez Brothers, but a last-minute replacement spared him that humiliation. He also worked on the Gibson divorce, even uncovering the infamous "green dress" tapes, but this was another level. This was murder and celebrity. Camera crews everywhere. A team of lawyers working under him. This was the "big time," and he had to act like it. He hoped the jury wouldn't notice his suit that was slightly too large for his smaller frame or his fake Rolex watch. He wanted them to focus on the facts of the case—or the "lacks" of the case, as he was prone to call them. Regardless of what he had planned, here he was, objecting to an opening statement. While not often done, he knew he had to get it into the record that the whole case was an overreach. If he lost, he would always have grounds for appeal, but only if he got everything entered into the record. His mentor and third cousin twice removed, a more famous lawyer with the Cochran name, had taught him that. He continued in his plea, "I move for an immediate dismissal of this case, your honor! With prejudice!"

Judge Harlan Reinhold didn't respond immediately to Carlos' outburst. For a moment, the DA was concerned he might actually consider silencing her opening statement, but that was just his way. Judge Reinhold was an old southern gentleman, a relic of a bygone era. He had sat on the Los Angeles County bench for the better part of three decades, never losing his country boy sense of style. The silver buckle of a bolo tie peeked out from the collar of his robe and his hair still had the matting of a man who had earlier donned a cowboy hat on top of a head still wet from the shower. When Reinhold did respond, he began with a slow look at the two lawyers. "Your objection is noted. But overruled."

The DA breathed a sigh of relief. Carlos sat back down as Spencer tapped him on the forearm, a gesture of thanks for his attempt.

"I'm inclined to keep this thing going," the Judge continued. "The only sin of a case, in my opinion, is to be boring." Judge Reinhold displayed the signature colorfulness that had made him well-known in Los Angeles legal circles, while managing to bristle both prosecution and defense by preventing them from getting a good read on what he was thinking. Contrary to whatever was in the opposing counsels' minds, Reinhold didn't seem particularly focused on the case at all. It was unclear what was preoccupying his mind, but as it was almost five o'clock on a Thursday, perhaps it was dinner. The case had started later in the day than was typical and Reinhold seemed like the type that was itching to get home and trade his robe and gavel for an apron and tongs to sear a steak on the grill.

He paused before continuing, quickly glancing at the files before him. "And we got a lively one here, folks. Court is adjourned until tomorrow." He banged the gavel. If he didn't break it up between the two lawyers, he might be there all night. And Reinhold was certainly not the type of judge to ever let his courtroom run over for time. At least not unless it was absolutely necessary.

Carlos wanted to object to the abrupt ending of the day, wishing he had time for his own opening statement, but he knew it would be in vain and would only further incense the judge. The good news for Carlos was that he would get the jury with fresh eyes and alert ears the next morning. He would have to make sure to hit the DA back point-by-point, slicing away each accusation like he was carving a wax sculpture. After this first day, Kent appeared to be winning, but only because Carlos hadn't had the chance to even begin to present his case. This ultimately would work in Carlos' favor, as he didn't seem his usual theatrical self during this first day of the trial. A good night's sleep would be necessary for him to dial up his energy and bring the fireworks for the next day's opening statement.

The bang of the gavel had electrified the room into movement. Bailiff Bosco, a stern, no-nonsense type with a thick mustache asked all present to rise as the judge left for his chambers. The jury were escorted out of their box and into their sequestered assembly room until it was deemed safe to leave the courthouse. Spencer and Carlos huddled up to whisper over what had just partaken and to strategize for the next day. DA Kent confidently sat back down at her table next to Captain Leopold Harris, the lead investigator on the case who, for some unknown reason, insisted that he be allowed to sit at the prosecution's table.

Captain Harris was an angry prick who liked to get his way. It was obvious that Kent had hoped he would have concluded the investigation and moved onto another case at the start of the trial. Harris, however, held other ideas. He had previously written to her in an email that he wanted to "ride this thing all the way to the end." She had failed to object, most likely because of the evidence that was missing even as the trial commenced. Evidence that would be necessary if they were to have any chance at a conviction.

Harris had a demeanor that could annoy anybody, but especially the DA. Their personalities could not have been less similar. Harris was cocky. Careless, maybe. He investigated with an ever-present chip on his shoulder, as if the crime had been done to him rather than to the victim. But he got results. One way or another, whether legal or not (most of the DAs he worked with didn't want to know), Harris would get his man. Or woman. So, in this case, Kent must have given him the benefit of the doubt that he would be able to get Spencer. She had little choice but to trust him and, with her brilliant opening to the trial, she must have won his trust as well. Now, whether she wanted him to or not, Harris sat beside her, ready to take down Spencer Charnas.

Harris was tall and lanky with a gaunt face and thin brown hair that fell straight down around all the sides of his head. Today, he wore a loud patterned shirt and tie coupled with a brown corduroy jacket that would fit better on the set of the Merv Griffin Show rather than a modern-day LA courthouse. This would have been enough to make Kent wish he had shown up looking less ridiculous, but the beard he was sporting was a bridge too far. For reasons beyond comprehension, Harris had shown up to this trial with a bushy growth of facial hair. Kent scribbled a note on her pad to tell him to shave before he had to testify; she had no interest in putting Grizzly Adams on the stand.

DA Kent and Captain Harris spoke in hushed tones while the courtroom emptied out. Spencer and Carlos continued their conversation as well. During those few minutes of dueling discussions, the DA kept looking over at Spencer, perhaps trying to deduce what was going on in his twisted mind. Did he think he would get off scot-free for killing his fiancée? Sure, the evidence wasn't all there, but he clearly did it and knew he did it. Maybe that would be enough. The media was abuzz with whether or not Spencer would take the stand, but no one could have been more hopeful than Kent. If Spencer did act as a witness in his own defense, Kent would ceremoniously bury him with her cross-examination. She was right on the cusp of getting that Perry Mason moment any attorney would kill for. Just her and Spencer. One-on-one. She frequently stole glances at him during her discussion with Harris. Killer or not, she would later write that she felt his presence was "magnetic". Everyone felt that way. People were drawn to him. Perhaps this would later contribute to what was regarded in the media as her reluctance to examine him effectively. As you will see, there were far greater reasons for this than just the rules of attraction.

Toward the end of the inaudible discussion between Kent and Harris, he made a gesture toward the awaiting reporters in the lobby of the courthouse. The DA groaned, knowing full well that the only way out of the building was through the corridor where the press was already gathering. She would try to get in and out of there as fast as possible; rip the band-aid off. She could give them what they want—or more likely, dodge their questions—and then go home to a glass of wine and a night alone with her case files and takeout. This was how DA Kent frequently spent her evenings.

††

Kent walked out of the courtroom to find the lobby of the Los Angeles County Superior Courthouse swarming with journalists. Her case files would have to linger unattended at home for her inevitably delayed return. She strode in toward the press conference podium, begrudgingly approaching it with Harris by her side. Harris almost always had a smug look splashed across his face when the lights from the news cameras first lit it up. One could easily tell that out of all the things he hated in the world, having the spotlight on him wasn't one of them. He relished in it, even despite a marked distaste for celebrity. Kent, by contrast, acted as if journalism were a necessary evil, there to be used when convenient, and ignored when not. Her strategy in this particular case would begin by preventing Spencer from remaining in the ever-shifting news cycle for too long. The more people talked about him, the more speculation and reasonable doubt might arise. She would lose the trial-by-media before she had a chance to even question him on the stand. She was not about to let that happen. Once enough evidence was found against Spencer, she would make sure to slowly leak this out to the press so that ordinary citizens would be easily led to the conclusion that he was guilty. Moving from suppressing the narrative to controlling it would be Kent's core media strategy. If only she had time to consult with Harris about the plan.[5]

Upon reaching the podium, Kent's face met the flickering of the hot lights as her slight frame all but disappeared behind the wall of microphones that extended out from the arms of reporters who shouted over each other to get their question answered. Kent immediately moved Captain Harris aside, not wishing him to get the first word; it was her case at this point, and she wanted to make sure he and everybody else knew. Unfortunately for her, Veronika Korningstone[6] shouted her question over the others, addressing it to Harris. "Captain Harris, after such a long investigation, what led to Spencer's indictment?"

5 Kent's repeated tactic of withholding evidence from the press until as late as possible has been looked back on less than favorably, and even sometimes as borderline illegal. She would often invent some kind of crime or stage a leak, thereby creating enough of a spectacle that her case would be widely reported on. Three separate bomb threats in the Los Angeles County DAs office were later attributed to her. Each, however, resulted in her getting what she desired.

6 My fellow journalist, Veronika Korningstone, is allegedly the basis for the character later known as Veronica Corningstone (with a pair of Cs) from a certain hit film about on-air news anchors. While this is very obviously the greatest film of all time, I do not condone the misuse of any very real journalist's name.

Before Harris could respond, Kent grabbed the microphone offering, "The DA's office has no comment at this time." She was playing it close to the vest while also neutralizing Harris, but the press wasn't satisfied and silence remained as they waited for a more complete answer. Kent didn't speak, hoping to wait out the awkward pause for the next question to begin. At some point soon, she would have enough solid evidence to show Spencer was guilty, but for now, strategy was everything.

Not one for silence, Harris grabbed the microphone. "Well, we've got some new evidence," he began.

The DA bristled at his remark, knowing full well he was instructed that morning to make no mention of this ace-in-the-hole they were working on. It was promising but hadn't been finalized yet. To her dismay, he continued, "And I'm very happy to say, it's made this case no longer a stab in the dark." He gave a little chuckle at his play on words. Kent couldn't help rolling her eyes, immediately hoping it wasn't picked up on camera. The joke was dad-joke bad, but no one else would have understood the truth behind the attempt at comedy. Only the DA would have been aware that he was referring to their recent discoveries of the stab patterns found on the victim's body. If Harris had told the press, it might give the defense too much time to refute the evidence, not to mention the trouble she might have for not disclosing their findings to opposing counsel in a timely manner.

"Captain Harris, can you speak to the evidence?" stammered journalist Scott "Stretch" Armstrong, his eyes crossing as they often did when he was nervous. Stretch had been a reporter for years but never got used to these public press conferences, and with a case as high-profile as this one, he could barely get his words out. DA Kent tried to step in front of Harris and answer the question, but he leaned in toward the reporter first and she was not afforded that opportunity.

"It'll come out in due time, and uh…" Harris clapped back. He trailed off as something caught his eye from behind the reporters. The DA had to crane her neck to see and a few members of the press pool turned toward Harris' gaze as well. What Harris had locked eyes on was Spencer being led away in handcuffs by Bailiff Bosco. Once reporters realized this fact, the cameras turned toward the famous defendant. Harris yelled over the bustle of the crowd, "Speaking of doing time." He cackled at his turn of phrase. "You're going to do time! Tighten those handcuffs, Bailiff!"

The DA cringed. This was the kind of cocky showboating that could blow the whole case. And here was this idiot cop doing it on camera.

"Sorry." Harris returned to the reporter after Spencer was led away. "Actually, we're under a need-to-know gag order right now."

The DA relaxed; he had stopped short of divulging anything that was highly confidential at that time. Regardless, she tried to step toward the microphone to prevent this charade from continuing, but questions kept being directed to the detective.

"Captain Harris, can you comment on the disappearance of Officer Dunbar and the murder of Detective Ophelia. Weren't they working directly on this investigation?" posed Sean Clark, a local homicide reporter with a taste for the most macabre of cases.

Kent shifted nervously.

"Well you're a Chatty Cathy," Harris chuckled. "Um, I don't know where you heard that rumor, but it just reminds me maybe we should be a little more tight-lipped around here." He looked toward the DA, as if to accuse her of the leak. Anyone watching the press conference would have to have picked up on the DA's body language. She tried to hold her disdain inside, as she always did, but she was not as successful as her usually tactful self. Her eyes darted left and right, looking around as if trying to find some way out before they landed on Harris, forming themselves into a death glare in his direction. With so many cameras trained on Kent, she couldn't simply slip away. She had to move this briefing along. Maybe it was the heat from the fluorescent lights or Captain Harris' demeanor, but her body tensed up as she reached her breaking point. With tight fists and a clenched jaw, she moved toward the microphone, bumping Harris out of the way and leaning in. She was going to use the favorite tool in any District Attorney's office toolbox. She uttered those three magical words: "No further questions." The press let out a collective moan. It was over.

The reporters grumbled as the DA and her team strode off down the marble-floored hallway, Harris in tow. "Come on, sweetheart, I was just getting warmed up," he called after her.

She snapped around, pivoting on one heel and moving toward Harris. Despite being a good six inches shorter than the detective, even in heels, she stood her ground, shoving a finger in his face. "Call me sweetheart again and I'll have your badge, gun, and balls sitting in the top drawer of my desk."

"Easy. I was being polite…Feisty."

"You haven't seen feisty," she clapped back. "Now you better get something more on Charnas before this trial ends or I'll show you what Horrorwood really looks like. I have a perfect record in cases like these and I'm not about to lose it to some half-wit has-been with a detective squad he can't even find half the time."

"I'm sure that's just—"

"As far as I can see, you're not sure of shit."

The DA had him right where she wanted. He was a good warm-up act to the case. A rehearsal for how she was going to bite the head off of the defendant in the days to come. "Find your people, find the evidence, or find yourself another job, Detective."

Harris stood open-mouthed. A rare example of this usually verbose individual being rendered speechless.

"Have a good night." The DA flashed a saccharine smile that would be the last image Harris had of her for the evening. She turned around and walked out of the building.

The detective knew he had nothing else to add. His people were missing. He had already found out what fate had befallen Ophelia,[7] but Dunbar being missing was new to him. Surely this was beyond coincidence. Spencer was in handcuffs, so he couldn't have done anything. But maybe someone around him? Anyone in the situation would have to be worried that Dunbar had gone the way of Ophelia and Spencer's fiancée, Nadia. But, had Harris feared the worst fate he could think of, it wouldn't even begin to describe the truth of the situation happening to Dunbar that very minute across town. It was Dunbar, alongside Ophelia, who had first brought him Spencer's case, and it was Dunbar who had helped to confirm the stab patterns of Nadia's killer. The evidence Harris had almost leaked to the press was not as concrete as Kent would have liked for her case and Dunbar held the information they both desperately needed. But, for now, Harris remained in the dark, with nothing from his subordinates but Silence.

---

7 Detective Ophelia and Dunbar will be covered in-depth later in this work, for now, suffice it to say, their tale is as gruesome as one can imagine. Well, I should say, "as gruesome as a typical individual can imagine." It's been confirmed that some of Spencer's so-called "Psychos" have darker imaginations than most.

III

A Rash Decision

Three Months Earlier…

It was eight o'clock on a December Thursday morning, and Captain Harris was finishing his usual vacation routine. First, a quick dip in the nearby lake to rejuvenate himself followed by a hearty breakfast. Today it consisted of three eggs, baked beans, a few strips of bacon, and two slices of toast. And plenty of coffee. He had a habit of logging his meals after he ate them, yet he rarely improved his diet habits, something that showed both his meticulous eye for detail and also his habit of missing the forest for the trees. After a shit / shower / shave (he always said it as one word), he would begin the full day he had planned, which was hardly full at all given how he spent his days at his reclusive, rural cabin. He would, however, have to start preparing for his inevitable return to civilization. This meant knocking down the healthy, gray-tinged beard that he had grown over the past couple of weeks. After that, his day would be filled with reading, perhaps some fishing, anything but police work. He had another ninety-six hours of vacation left and would make sure to use every one of them before returning to the city on Sunday.[8]

8 We are leaving Marcie Kent, our primary subject, because in her own book she discussed the series of events that led up to the trial of Spencer Charnas and began with the detectives who investigated this viscous felony. This is their story.

Harris had always used this cabin as a way to get away from the ills of the world. Or as he referred to those ills collectively, "The City of Los Angeles." He often referred to his hometown as a "cesspool"—both a dry desert and a moist swamp. He preferred the great outdoors, and so a couple of decades back he'd purchased this remote patch of land, and the simple cabin that sat on top of it; he had since made use of it whenever possible. With retirement coming up in a few years, Harris was planning to make this his year-round home. He was getting to that age and could feel the urge to hang it all up. Perhaps he was waiting for some major case to serve as a feather in the cap of his years of service; he had always wanted some notoriety for the hard work he put in. He clearly felt it was owed to him. Without such a case to hang his career on, this cabin would have to be his only reward for all those hours of overtime and years of slaving away for the LAPD.

Only three hours north and just outside Bakersfield, Bunyan Mountain couldn't have felt more different. Today, the area was awash in bright yellow and orange colors, even some deep reds. Early winter was in full flourish as the leaves changed color, something seldom seen just a few hours south by the ocean. The cycle of life, death, and rebirth as the seasons changed was always happening here in Kern County, something Los Angeles would never know with its stagnant summer.

The cabin itself was small and quaint, but it felt more like home to Captain Harris than LA ever did. A makeshift kitchen shared the same room as a living area and faced the front door. Through a short hallway to the back was the lone bedroom and a bathroom, each on opposite sides of the hall. Harris had been up here more often during the COVID-19 pandemic, choosing fresh air over the stifling city. Whether it was pestilence itself, or the fear that hung in that air, one cannot be too sure but, either way, Harris left Los Angeles as often as he could.

Never one for being told what to do, Harris' escapes often coincided with whatever new ordinance was being created by the department, preventing him from railing against his superiors to the point that he may have been let go before a typical retirement age.[9]

Thus, the cabin served as a bastion of freedom that he could go to on weekends or when cases were slow. Given that a lot more of the department business was handled online, even in spite of the "essential worker" status of detectives, he installed satellite internet so that he could stay connected. Prior to this upgrade, he was off-the-grid, and often kept it that way. For his last few days here, he had shut off his phone and computer, only checking each of them once per day. So far, nothing in his email or voice messages had reached a status of importance that he needed to spend his precious vacation by offering any kind of response.

He was, however, by no means always alone. The nearby towns held a steady supply of women with whom he could contract companionship, if even just for one evening. One such lady of the night was still lingering in his bed on this crisp December morning. He had meant to kick her out but figured, as long as he wasn't paying for the time, it was nice to look at somebody other than himself in the mirror for a change.

Harris was mid-routine and had just stepped out of his 1970s-era, pink shower (he was meaning to repaint but never got around to it) when his day took an abrupt shift. As he began lathering up for his shave, a breeze caught him from the open window to his right and he turned to shut out the cold air. Before he could move his hands

---

9 Harris was briefly shifted to street duty during the first days of the pandemic and almost left the department because of it. After years as a detective, he had practically forgotten how to go out on calls or directly help citizens and he certainly resented the one time he was asked to direct traffic. Fortunately for him, he was soon moved back to his detective work and could do some of his investigations from home.

onto the sash, he heard a snapping sound coming from outside, toward the front of his house. He listened again. Footsteps. It was unmistakable. Someone traipsing across his property, but not toward the front door. Seemingly, they were approaching the window right next to him. He looked out the open bathroom door and across the hall into the bedroom. There, his eyes landed on the mass of tangled, dirty-blonde hair, allowing him to deduce that his paid-for guest was not the one outside. As if on cue, the woman, Karen, turned over, revealing a face of smeared makeup. "What time is it?" she asked him, groggily.[10]

Harris spoke with a violent whisper. "Shut the fuck up," he said, leaning toward the bathroom door.

"So-rry," blared Karen, ignoring any sense of danger. She then rolled back and pushed her face into the pillow.

Harris ducked back against the wall toward the shower and listened again. His face was full of lathered shaving cream and he had on nothing but a towel, so he was already in a compromised position, but would not go down without a fight. There was a curtain over the window, but it billowed in the wind and he couldn't take any chances to be seen. Thus, he maintained his position against the wall. He looked down at the safety razor in his hand. His gun was all the way across the hall in the bedroom. He would never be able to get to it fast enough if this was an armed assailant and Karen couldn't be trusted with such a job either. Not yet out of options, Harris stealthily snuck himself down under the window and back across toward the sink. From his crouched position, Harris used his fingers to feel around inside the Dopp kit that sat on the sink's edge until he found what he was looking for. He extracted a

10 Karen Tate was instrumental in piecing together what happened during this day at Captain Harris' cabin. When I located her, she had fallen on particularly hard times. Born Shilane Benes, Karen was better known by her stage name, which she initially used on the lesser-known adult website, LonelyMans. Following this case, she would see her fame bubble grow and eventually pop like a bad boob job at altitude.

larger shaving knife, old school. While never used by him, it had belonged to his father, and he felt a connection to him in keeping it there. Perhaps now it would save his life.

Harris moved back toward the shower and raised himself up. Not a second later, a shadow covered the window and what looked like the figure of a man peered in. In one swift motion Harris reached through the open window, grabbed the back of the man's neck, and spun him around so that he was facing away from the cabin. With his other hand, Harris put the knife blade across the man's neck only to hear a familiar scream.

"Harris! It's me!"

"Dunbar?" Harris eased up his grip on both the knife and the younger man's neck. "What the fuck are you doing sneaking around my house?"

"I've been calling! You didn't answer," Officer Grant Dunbar forced in response. His heart was racing so fast that he was out of breath. "You could've killed me."

"Damn right I could have. And if you're about to interrupt the last days of my vacation, you're going to wish I did," Harris said. He let go of his subordinate, turning him around as he did. Despite their similar heights, Harris stood about six inches above Dunbar due to the foundation being slightly elevated above the ground. In the daylight, he could easily see Dunbar with his medium-length, coiffed light brown hair, his neatly trimmed beard, and a look of pure terror on his face.

"Yeah…" began Dunbar, unsure of himself. "But you're going to want to hear about this one. Ophelia's here too. In the car."

Harris was intrigued, perhaps in response to the way Dunbar's face lit up as he spoke about whatever it was they were working on. Or maybe it was because Detective Ophelia Crane would never bring anything to him that wasn't solid—unlike Dunbar, who was, in his own words, the office clown. Much like the fishing Harris had planned to do later that day, he must have known he would catch a whopper with this case.

"Well, shit. Let me get some pants on and I'll come around and open up the front door," Harris said, attempting to close the window, which was still blocked by Dunbar's head poking through.

Dunbar spotted the woman through the open door of the bedroom. "Who's that?"

"Don't worry about her, just meet me out front," Harris responded, shoving Dunbar's head out and slamming the window shut immediately after.

Dunbar chuckled from outside the window, yelling through, "Party man! Nice..." before he walked back toward the front of the house, occasionally glancing curiously back over his shoulder.

When he first graduated from college, Officer Grant Dunbar hadn't set out to do police work. Instead, he eventually landed on it after a series of unfulfilling odd jobs and some gentle prodding from his uncle, who had served on the force in nearby Pasadena. Dunbar's sense of humor wasn't lacking (depending on who you talked to) and he was always quick with a dad joke or a clever quip following almost anything anybody said. His investigative work, however, certainly wasn't up to par, and he had yet to pass his detective's exam. Many in the department often wondered what Dunbar brought to the table, but Dunbar was nepotism in its finest sense. Harris never would have hired Dunbar had he not known his uncle from their days at the academy. This was further coupled with a feeling of indebtedness stemming from a coverup after Harris was almost caught cheating on an ethics exam. Dunbar's uncle had helped him out of a jam, and he later returned the favor by hiring his ne'er-do-well nephew.[11]

11 Harris' ethics exam cheating isn't well documented but is often spoken about around the LAPD and has contributed to a significant amount of department lore. There is even,

After briefly watching Dunbar walk toward the front of the cabin, Harris stepped back from the window and toward the hallway. Before he could exit the bathroom, he caught a glimpse of himself in the mirror and remembered he was mid-shave. He grumbled as he made his way to the sink, splashed some water on his face, and wiped off the now-unneeded shaving cream.

A few minutes later, Harris opened the front door. He was fully dressed in jeans and a plaid shirt, which was not fortifying enough against the cool air of the impending winter, but he had been in a rush and his coat was still inside.

Dunbar stood on the front porch accompanied by Detective Crane, who almost always preferred going by her first name, Ophelia. This preference stemmed not only from her distaste for ceremony and titles, but primarily because using a first name alone fostered stronger connections to victims and their families. She had been in a sex crimes unit prior to joining homicide. In stark contrast to Dunbar, she was smart, capable, and serious—everything one would look for in an officer of the law. Nevertheless, she still had trouble commanding any kind of respect in the boys' club of the homicide division. Harris tried to stand up for out of respect for her talents and contributions, but he was just as much a part of that world as anyone else. One thing was undeniable, though: he trusted her.

"Nice place you got here," offered Ophelia.

Ruining the compliment with his usual buffoonery, Dunbar chimed in saying, "Good for…entertaining." He laughed.

Harris stared at Dunbar, forcing the smile from his face before turning back to Ophelia. "Thanks, yeah. Still meaning to fix up that fence in the front." He gestured to a broken wooden fence just down the slight slope of the driveway that eventually led back to

---

in some squad rooms, an unofficial "least ethical" award given out dubbed the "Leopold," in honor of Captain Harris.

a main road. Harris saw Dunbar's black, unmarked, department-issued cruiser parked just beyond the fence. It was an older model with a big engine and Harris became momentarily worried for his security here at the cabin if he could fail to hear that behemoth lumbering up the hill and into the driveway. He hoped it was only due to the noise of the shower he just took but resolved to fix the fence over the weekend before returning back to LA. If this didn't force him to return even sooner.

Harris gestured to the two rocking chairs beside the front door, and Ophelia and Dunbar followed his offering and took a seat. Harris himself posted up on the railing that ran across the front of the porch, simultaneously leaning and sitting as he awaited their report.

"Two chairs? Isn't it just you up here?" questioned Dunbar.

"It's reserved for when some smartass shows up unannounced with bad news," Harris returned.

In a display of perfect timing, Karen chose that exact second to stumble her way out of the house. Her hair and clothing were disheveled, her makeup smeared, and she clutched a purse and her shoes in her thin arms. The smell of alcohol permeated the entire porch despite the light breeze that ushered in the cooler air from the mountains. Ophelia turned away, as if trying to give Harris some sense of privacy, but she couldn't hold off for long. All three of the officers watched as Karen hobbled her way to her beat-up Toyota that was parked on the side of the house.

"Just some, uh...local flavor," said Harris.

Karen's car started with a bang and lurched down the driveway.

"So what's up? Better be good," said Harris.

"Rockstar. Killed his fiancée," Dunbar said.

"Well, that's not exactly everything," Ophelia chimed in. "It was particularly brutal and there's a decent trail of evidence."

"Burned alive. It was fucking gross," added Dunbar, stopping himself before he seemed like too much a wuss in front of his boss.

Harris looked intrigued as he responded. "Jesus fucking Christ. Some people..."

"We could barely identify the body, but believe it's a young woman named Nadia Teichmann," continued Ophelia. "Actress, influencer, beautiful girl. In the prime of her life. To see someone brutalized like that, it's horrible."

"We got called in too quickly, if you ask me," interrupted Dunbar. "I'll never get that smell out of my head."

"So what else you got?" Harris stood up and twisted to his left to pick up a small stick that had wound its way around the top rail near where he had been sitting. "Some rockstar suspect, you said?"

"They were engaged," offered Ophelia. "It's usually the closest person, right?"

"Damn straight," answered Harris. He was pacing now and breaking apart the stick he had picked up. "What kind of guy are we talking about here?"

Dunbar checked his notes. "Well known musician from a metal group called Ice Nine Kills. 'Kills,' I mean. It's right there, you know?"

"Hiding in plain sight. Shifty fucker," commented Harris.

Dunbar continued, "Name is Spencer Charnas. Not much is known about him before he burst onto the scene here in LA a few years ago. Kind of a shady past, if you ask me. He was previously investigated for some crime back east where he's from, but the records are sealed."[12]

"We're going to wanna get a look at those," added Harris.

12 While these records were sealed at the time, Captain Harris was able to put a release on them. The most prominent record, that of a case involving Spencer in his earlier days in Massachusetts, has been documented in my first book, The Silver Scream, available wherever books are sold.

"Of course," Dunbar said, returning to his notes.

Harris continued, "These celebrity types really get under my skin. Prancing around in fancy outfits at their cocktail parties. It's enough to make your stomach crawl." Harris turned around, staring out at the red and orange tinted landscape in front of him. "Maybe it's something in the water, but it's like some kind of sickness. And it's spreading. Maybe even out here someday."

"Captain?" asked Ophelia, pulling Harris out of his trance.

Harris turned back around. "Los Angeles ain't what it used to be. We've lost that...grit. You know? Bunch of so-called 'artists' coming in from the East Coast, making us soft. And they all have their little quirks. I'm sure this guy has his thing. We just need to zero in on it and cut him out of decent society..." Harris paused, waiting for some kind of response, he wasn't sure what.

"Charnas and Ice Nine Kills do a lot of horror tie-ins with their music," Dunbar said, snapping Harris back to reality. "Like, it's all kind of based on these iconic films. I'm not really a fan, to be honest. I don't like the killing parts."

"Yeah? Well, probably better off. Sometimes these movies turn people into real psychos," Harris said, turning back around.

"It's funny you say that," Ophelia cut in. "The fans of his band call themselves 'psychos.' There's a whole army of them."

"I don't like the sound of that," Harris responded, already convinced of Spencer's guilt. "But I'm starting to like this guy for a murder. What else you got? Any hard evidence?"

He would need to make sure it was enough to force him back to the city and not something that could wait a couple more days. He looked out at the land around him. The mountains loomed over the backdrop of leaves changing. It would be a hard place to leave, but he would surely assume he would be back someday soon.

Ophelia answered after a moment. "No real murder weapon. Although he does have this horror character that he's created called The Silence."

"Got a mask and everything," Dunbar offered, backing her up. "Real legit horror movie stuff...It's really pale with scars and has an 'I' and an 'X' carved into it, like the number nine in Roman numerals. Kinda clever—"

"The character also carries an ice pick," Ophelia continued, ignoring Dunbar. "Which, and here's the kicker, we located something similar near the body we found at the bottom of a canyon up near Runyon."

"I thought you said she was burned alive?" Harris questioned.

"She was, but as to what actually caused her death? We're not too sure." Ophelia shrugged as she spoke. "M.E. was still taking a look, but initial reports suggested stab wounds, burning, maybe even some animal bites."

"Motherfucker, this is a juicy one! Might get a lot of press!" exclaimed Harris, suddenly excited by the prospect of a high-profile case.

Dunbar nodded along, not understanding the enthusiasm but appreciating his boss being in a slightly better mood than when he recently held a knife to his throat.

Ophelia continued, "Now, I think it's really nothing, but there's also one more thing we recovered from Charnas' house—"

"Videotapes," Dunbar interrupted, rocking back and forth in his chair as he said it.

"Of the crime?" questioned Harris. "Ooh boy. Sounds pretty open and shut to me!"

"Not exactly," began Ophelia. "They aren't videos of an actual crime, but music videos."

"Music videos? Like from his I Sign Kills band?

"Ice Nine Kills," responded Dunbar.

"Whatever," shot back Harris. "Why would we care about his music videos?"

"We only watched one so far. Pretty fucked if you ask me," Dunbar said.

Ophelia rolled her eyes. "The videos depict gruesome acts, or, at least from what we've seen so far. We pulled a bunch out of the home but are waiting on a warrant for the rest. Again, it feels like a dead end."

Despite her dismissal, Harris leaned in, interested to hear more. "Why didn't you just take all the videos? Shoot first and figure out the paperwork later. Isn't that what I'm always telling you people?!"

"Even the first ones we got were a stretch. We said they were in plain sight, but...well, you know." Dunbar was pleased with his ability to procure evidence under dubious circumstances.

"Gotta do what you gotta do," Harris said, approvingly. "So what's on these things? What kind of sick shit are we talking about here? Snuff stuff?"

"Nothing illegal," responded Ophelia. "It's art...if you could call it that. It almost goes too far, though. He kills his fiancée in the video we saw, and even though it's just fiction, it almost feels like a confession."

There was a brief pause as Harris got the sense that he was about to be asked for something. He turned away looking back toward his tranquil property.

"So we hate to ask," Dunbar interjected. "But...we wanted you to come back and see if we have enough on this guy to make the arrest. Nordberg should have already picked him up—"

"Are you fucking kidding me?!" Harris interrupted, raising his voice.

"We know it's your vacation," responded Ophelia.

"No! The vacation's already fucked," bellowed Harris. "Nordberg! That goddamn idiot. He knows the rules. And you should, too. You pick a guy up, you got forty-eight hours to charge him or you let him back on the streets. You can't pick somebody up who's got celebrity status and expect it to not leak to the press!" Harris turned on them as they both leaned back in their chairs, wishing they could increase the distance between them and their angry boss. "And I don't need an army of psychotics, or whatever the fuck this deranged lunatic calls his 'fans,' coming down to our station and demanding the guy's release. Fuck Nordberg and his quick decisions! And fuck you both, too!"

Silence hung in the air until Dunbar broke it. He asked sheepishly, "So, is that a 'yes'?"

"I think it goddamn has to be, thanks to you idiots. I'll get my stuff and shut this place down. Gotta turn off the water in case it freezes out here. Give me twenty." Harris walked inside the cabin without another word.

Dunbar and Ophelia got up from their rocking chairs and made their way back to the car in silence.

True to his word, Harris emerged about twenty minutes later. He vowed to himself that he would return as soon as the investigation was over but wasn't sure when that would be. It sounded like an easy case, but he was more than ready to sink his teeth into something. As much as he'd grown to hate his job and the city he served over the years, he loved sticking it to celebrities and showing the world who they really were in their deepest and darkest places.

†††

Just over three hours later, the sun had started to set over Los Angeles and the western sky was a deep orange and red. Harris pulled his tan 1995 Mercedes Diesel-run E-class into his spot at the station. He had about forty-four hours left to get enough evidence to charge Spencer Charnas. So much for R and R. A day that had begun by counting down the hours left of relaxing quickly became a day stressfully watching the minutes fall away before having to let a clear criminal back on the streets.

Harris looked around before taking the elevator up to his squad room. Although it was only on the second floor, he often avoided the stairs out of habit. Also waiting for the elevator was Officer Justin Roth of the K-9 unit and his dog, Mambo.

"Hey, Captain Harris!" he said in a friendly manner. "I thought you weren't coming back yet—"

"Change of plans," Harris interrupted, not at all in the mood for pleasantries.

He headed for the stairs, where Ophelia and Dunbar caught up with him.

"I'm going to need you two to get out there right away. We gotta search this asshole's house before he can have somebody hide evidence. These musician types, they all have assistants and hanger-ons."

"You got it," offered Ophelia, trying to keep up with Harris' swift pace on the stairs as his longer legs took them two at a time.

They quickly reached the squad room and turned in through the double glass doors that separated the homicide division from the hallway. Upon entry, they passed the high front desk where Officer Janet Perkins was tucked in behind in a low chair. "Captain Harris," she warmly shouted over the high desk, "we didn't expect you so soon." Not one to desert her post, Officer Perkins was a kind old woman who predated even Harris in the homicide squad with her nearly forty years on the force. She and Harris had a mutual affinity—and she was, perhaps, the only person whom he treated with a degree of decency.

"No, I didn't expect so, either. But duty calls," Harris said with a forced smile. He turned away from Officer Perkins and toward the rest of the squad room, with mostly empty desks save for a few odd officers and detectives working away. "Now, can somebody tell me where the fuck Nordberg is?!" he shouted.

A heavier-set detective, DeBello, looked up from his desk and used his pen to gesture toward the back corner. "Interrogation room two," he said, before returning to his work.

Harris stormed through the squad room as Ophelia and Dunbar followed behind. He entered the hallway that housed the interrogation rooms and immediately looked in through the two-way mirror on one of the walls. There, he saw Officer Shelley Nordberg pushing across what looked to be some kind of Halloween mask to what must be their rockstar suspect. It was the first time Harris would lay eyes on Spencer Charnas, but by no means the last.

Spencer looked down at the floor, ignoring Nordberg, which also made the suspect look somehow smaller. Harris could have reasoned here that this non-threatening appearance could be the essence of Spencer's underlying danger. Instead, he simply stood at the window for a few seconds until, suddenly, Spencer's gaze shot up toward the mirror, as if he could see through it. He continued to glare in Harris' direction seeming to sense the presence of the detective. This caused Dunbar, now beside Harris, to shudder. Spencer said something to Nordberg that Harris couldn't hear because the speaker that fed into the hallway was not yet turned on. The detective could, however, witness Nordberg sigh in response. Harris banged on the glass, and Nordberg looked at the mirror as well before gesturing to Spencer with a raised finger, as if to signify he would be right back.

Nordberg came out into the hallway, where he immediately spotted Harris. "Captain! Good to have you back!" he said, jovially. Nordberg was eager to please and thus often found himself serving as Harris' errand boy, despite being close in age. He had been passed over for promotion twice in the last two years but never let it get to him. Afterall, he was still a lieutenant in a detective division, and that seemed to be enough. He was not the most brilliant of legal minds, although he sometimes surprised the rest of the squad with an occasional bit of police code obscura. Regardless of ability, this lapse in judgment during the detainment of Spencer Charnas was out of character for any detective in the LAPD, let alone someone on Captain Harris' squad.

"Are you fucking kidding me with that? 'Good to have me back'?!" Harris shouted in disbelief. "What kind of a candy-ass response—you know what? Nevermind. What the fuck is going on here, Nordberg?"

"What do you mean? I got a murder suspect and—"

"You didn't think to call me?" shot back Harris.

"We tried. You were off the grid," offered Nordberg.

"We did try," Dunbar added timidly. He had almost continued his thought, but Harris spun around to glare at him, stifling any further discussion.

"So that's it? You tried and just figured you'd pick the guy up without my say-so?"

"I know. Forty-eight hours. We're on it," responded Nordberg, attempting to show his competence. "And don't worry, I didn't forget the Miranda rights this time."

"You wouldn't know Miranda if she walked in here with Samantha, Charlotte, and Carrie," Harris replied, surprising the others with his reference.

"It's fine. We've got officers working on the warrant right now and I was trying to talk to him, but he just lawyered up."

"Fuck that," Harris retorted. "I'll call in the damn warrant. Got a judge owes me a favor. After that, you're all going to this guy's house and the crime scene immediately. From here on, nobody sleeps, nobody eats...Christ, nobody even takes a shit without me knowing about it until we get enough on this guy to charge him."

"Uh, Captain?" Dunbar started. "That drive was long, so I was kind of hoping to..." he pointed toward the men's room down the hallway.

"You know what I mean!" shouted Harris. "Get everybody in here first thing tomorrow morning. I'm also going to need that videotape and a VCR, it sounds like. I want to see this shit for myself, ASAP."

"It's all set up in the conference room," said Ophelia.

"And put that guy back in his cell," Harris continued. "Let's see how he does being away from the rockstar lifestyle for a night."

"On it," responded Dunbar, moving immediately toward the interrogation room.

Harris peered again through the two-way mirror as Spencer continued to stare straight ahead. "Now let's rock this metalhead's world..."

IV
Assault & Batteries

Captain Harris gathered every detective and officer under his command early that Friday morning. From his wrinkled shirt and rumpled suit pants, it didn't take a seasoned investigator to reason that he had spent the night getting up to speed. It would follow, then, that he was trying to show his team just where they stood in terms of evidence against murder suspect Spencer Charnas. Detailed notes from both Harris and Detective Ophelia Crane show that the unit was far from being able to charge Spencer with what little they had gathered. And now that Nordberg had started the clock on holding the potentially dangerous metal frontman, they only had until Saturday night or Monday morning if they had to wait for the courts to open. Harris was about to attempt to lay all his toys out in the sandbox in hopes that it might kick his fellow detectives into gear. This would also be the first time he played the videotape recovered at Spencer's home for the entire squad.

Upon viewing the videotape, Ophelia and Dunbar had realized that it was a previously lost and unreleased Ice Nine Kills music video, in which Spencer was shown murdering Nadia. It was a work of fiction, of course, but despite not being real, maybe it telegraphed something lurking beneath the surface of Spencer's rockstar façade. They could only hope.

But an artist's work being used as proof that a crime was committed?

While certainly not unheard of, this kind of accusation would take a special kind of finesse.[13]

Further complicating things, each music video was also based on a well-known, widely released horror film; it would be a lot easier to convict if the alleged crime were plagiarism. Murder, however, felt like an overreach. Regardless, Harris was now going to try to rally his team around the "art imitates life" theory of the case. If successful, he could perhaps move on to convincing the District Attorney's office, and they, in turn, would convince a jury.

What little Harris could have known about Spencer must also have been the exact character traits that usually irked him. He would have seen him as some smug rockstar who (rather than just shutting up and playing music) decided to murder his fiancée in cold blood. To add insult to mortal injury, Spencer was now taunting law enforcement and the institution of justice by bragging about it through the release of a series of music videos made while Nadia was still alive. It was as if he had acted out the murder over and over again on screen, only to have it down pat when it came time to do the real deed in real life.

This case may have seemed flimsy to some, but Harris had pushed cases to trial with less, although usually against some youthful public defender fresh out of law school and not whatever seasoned professional Spencer would find to represent him. It must have felt at this moment that Harris' entire career was leading toward this point. This would be the perfect homicide to serve as his swan song before retirement—end with a bang, he must have

13 There are a number of well-known serial killers who themselves were artists, but typically this art has been unnecessary to garner a conviction. Of note is John Wayne Gacy, whose portraits of clowns have been sold at auction where they have fetched large sums. I myself was tragically outbid in one such auction where Gacy's painting "Pogo the Clown" eventually sold for over $10,000.

thought. And,what better way to do that than to investigate a high-profile murder by a high-profile musician? He always wished he had found his way onto the Phil Spector case, having instead been thwarted by a crosstown rival for the job. Perhaps they would make a movie about this Charnas case someday. Despite hating Hollywood, it still must have consumed some area deep in the recesses of Harris' mind; for anybody living in LA, the film industry was an inescapable prison. In his journals and case notes, he often mused about who would play him in the movie of his life. Willem Defoe seemed to be a frequent answer. Harris clearly took a liking to Defoe, particularly when he played an officer of the law. But if Harris were to have any chance of filmic immortality, he would have to push this case forward.

Harris stared at the big board of evidence in front of him in the detective unit's conference room. He and a couple other detectives had hastily constructed it overnight. It may have had a stereotypical layout, straight out of the movies, but it was a layout that worked to brief everyone effectively. The board connected various aspects of the case and contained images and pinned up evidence that he, or other detectives, felt were pertinent to finding the killer. The potential murder weapon, a decorative ice pick with a skull on the handle hung in a bag. It had been recovered from near Nadia's body, but they needed to figure out how to retroactively place it in Spencer's hand. There was also a mask, known to Ice Nine Kills fans as "The Silence." It was the band's own creation, and here was the original version, or so the detectives suspected. Spencer's personal copy of the mask, taken from his home. Witnesses had placed a person wearing such a mask at the scene of the crime, but that still wasn't enough to go on.

Toward the top of the board was the deceased: Nadia Teichmann, Spencer's fiancée. She graced the board in two forms.

The first, a photograph from long before the incident, beautiful, full of life. The second essence of Nadia was the crime scene photo with her charred body, unrecognizable save for a set of teeth.[14]

Careful trial watchers would remember that another set of teeth would later emerge into importance in this case, but Harris and his team were still operating partially in the dark, as they had not gotten the full report from the Medical Examiner yet. Harris remained silent as the detectives entered, staring at what little they had pinned to the big board: A barely recognizable body, a potential weapon that had no connection back to its owner, and a mask that may have been spotted by witnesses near the crime scene, but the witnesses couldn't be sure. Harris quietly waited until the final detectives and officers filed in.

Harris had convened a whole squad room full of his best—or more accurately, his only—detectives. Ophelia, Dunbar, and Nordberg were there, joined by Detectives Dallon, Pasteur, Movery, Van Ung, and a few uniformed officers all around one large table in the center of a metal-dominated room. The cool, blue-gray of the steel and concrete walls and metal table gave everything a sterile look, but Harris liked it that way. Less distractions. All work. He briefly looked around at his detectives, all of whom had worked with him before in some capacity. As this was a big case, the higher-ups were putting a lot of bodies on it, but not exactly the city's finest. Deep down Harris must have known that he would need to rely on his own mind to get results. The concern with this specific group of less-impressive colleagues caused him to shift uneasily, something the other officers and detectives undoubtedly noticed, despite not being the most observant set of investigators the department could have assigned him.

14 The dental records in this case were so damaged that there was little to go on, but as keen followers of the proceedings will remember, even that little bit proved to be nothing more than a hen's tooth.

Harris dispatched with the usual pleasantries, something he was not typically known for anyway, and dove right in. He picked the VHS tape off its spot at the center of the table and briefly held it in silence. Like a priest waiting for the divine intervention of transubstantiation, maybe if he wished for it to be so, the evidence would become a more solid depiction of Spencer's involvement in the crime. It was all he had. For now. If this group of detectives could be convinced that the tapes could be used to affirm Spencer's guilt, maybe the District Attorney's office and, eventually, even the public could.

"Time's ticking, people. Now, I got something I want to show you." As he spoke, Harris waved the tape around like an old cowboy of the wild west, fitting because he had wanted it to become the smoking gun that he needed it to be. "I think it'll let you all see what kind of sick son-of-a-bitch we're up against here. He's left a paper trail. Or video trail, more like. So he's a stupid fucker as well. We just need to use all this against him." Harris turned toward an old Barclay brand television set with a built-in VCR. "So, without further ado..." he said with a flourish. A couple of seconds went by as the internal pieces clicked and popped before static flickered on the screen...

Lightning strikes across an otherwise black sky, temporarily illuminating the bleak landscape below. It's a rural area with a few scattered trees and bushes being battered by the rainstorm. In a lonely

corner of an otherwise empty horizon, dead trees and gnarled vines surround a singular white farmhouse, strangling it with their bent branches and curled stems. The wooden siding is made of rotting boards and chipped paint. Nevertheless, the home remains standing. The peaked roof takes a beating from the wind and rain, but the house refuses to sway in even the strongest of gusts. Overgrown grass and weeds spring up in all directions, and a solitary light shines from a second-floor bedroom, casting a warm glow onto the yard below.

"Andy?" a motherly voice calls out, searching for her son.

"In a minute, ma," comes the response from a child running through a darkened hallway and toward the lit room. He's a boy, about twelve-years-old, wearing a red and white striped shirt and denim overalls.

"I have a present for you," calls the boy's mother, trying to lure him away from his intended destination. Unrelenting, the boy enters, revealing a playroom filled with toys of ages past, cast aside for newer distractions.

"After my show!" the boy yells back, plopping himself down in front of a 1980s television set.

The boy flicks the television on with the touch of a remote to reveal WDOL News Channel 9's six o'clock report. The news theme begins as a clean-cut male newscaster starts in on his broadcast. "Breaking news," he begins. "A deadly shootout at a local toy store has left one police officer wounded and a wanted serial-killer, dead—"

The boy changes the channel. Cheering is heard. Unbeknownst to the boy, his mother, played by Nadia in this video, enters the room behind him. She carries a large box with polka dot wrapping and a clear plastic front, allowing a viewer to see the life-sized doll it contains. From the TV there's more cheering as a female talk show host introduces her segment. "Our next guest claims her son's doll is possessed by the spirit of a dead masked murderer—"

Before the host continues, the boy flips one more time, landing on a child's program. A familiar jingle picks up and the boy smiles. He has found exactly what he was looking for. His mother tries to interject so she can present him with his newest toy but is interrupted by the phone ringing from an adjacent room. Lost in the magic on television, the boy never looks away from what he is watching. His mother leaves to answer the phone.

The jingle continues, but inside the box two eyes glow red, pulsating with anticipation. Sensing some danger, the boy looks around, only to meet the unnatural gaze of his new toy. The doll raises a knife and slashes its way out of the box, calling "Hey, Andy" as he does. The doll is played by Spencer, and having come to life he exits the box and walks stiffly toward the boy. He shouts, "It's time to play, motherfucker!"

And the song begins.

The Spencer Doll's face bears numerous scars and a bulging mass on his right temple. His outfit is similar to the boy's, only his shirt is black-and-white striped and his overalls are embroidered with a "IX" symbol along with icons of knives. In direct reference to the stitching, the Spencer Doll also carries a very real, very sharp-looking kitchen knife in his right hand. He stalks his prey, chasing him down the previously darkened hallway and toward the room where his mother left to answer the phone. The boy runs, but like any classic horror film victim, he can't outrun what appears to be a much slower predator. Finally, the boy reaches his mother. He grabs onto her, desperate for salvation. She puts down the phone and points to the doll at the end of the hall, saying "Isn't he cute?"

The doll is, once again, just a doll.

A lightning strike lights up the end of the hallway, showing that Spencer is once again returned to an inanimate state.

The boy's mother walks out of the room, phone in hand, while the boy turns back toward his doll. Just as the mother is out of sight, the doll lifts its head and raises his knife, reinitiating his pursuit of the boy. The Spencer Doll strolls the hallway, stabbing his knife through the air with each step, all in rhythmic succession. The boy runs to the other end of the hall, away from the doll and toward another room, hopefully one of safety. Instead, he finds the full Ice Nine Kills band playing and a choir of ghostly children creepily singing along to the song's chorus. The lyrics taunt the boy and further drive him toward madness, and maybe murder. The band members are dressed similarly to Spencer, with black and white striped shirts and symbol-clad black overalls depicting weapons and the Roman numeral IX. Their bright white faces are also covered in scars and they play their instruments with the mechanical movements of the dolls they inhabit…or who inhabit them.

The haunting melody of the chorus is reminiscent of toy ads from years past and teases the boy as he attempts to escape certain death at the hands of this possessed doll. Running from the room, the boy reenters the hallway, avoiding the Spencer Doll as he does. He once again finds his mother, who still refuses to listen to his plight, despite his cries of "Mommy, mommy, my doll is alive!

However, after an initial protestation, the mother takes a closer look at the doll and sees it moving on its own. She then clocks the knife in its hand and grabs her son, pulling him forcefully down the hall and away from the danger.

The mother and son enter the playroom again, where the TV now displays an advertisement: a mustachioed Spencer with the on-screen text announcing, "The Carnage Continues!"

The fearful family lock the door behind them. Almost immediately, the knob jiggles. As they back toward the wall, the mother clutches her son, attempting to shield him from whatever lurks beyond the door. They both breathe heavily, bracing themselves for the doll's next move. The lights flicker and when they come back on, as if by some magic, the doll is suddenly in the same room. Doors are no match for the evil they are facing. This time, Spencer has also brought along other doll friends. The entire Ice Nine Kills band stands in their doll outfits, brandishing weapons and forming a V-shape, Spencer in front. The television continues its commercial, which boasts, ""Assault & Batteries" Included!"

The mother holds her son, hoping to save her life and his, and Spencer continues singing, threatening them with his words.

Within seconds, the mother and son both faint.

In another, larger wooden room, Spencer stands over the boy and hovers his hand above the boy's head. "Ade due damballa," he mutters, the words a demonic-sounding incantation. "Ade due damballa." Over and over again. His refrain causes the boy to rise to a seated position, his hair blown back from an unnatural wind. He opens his eyes, showing they are glazed over with a white sheen. He is ready to do some evil entity's bidding.

The mother wakes from her fainting spell only to see the shadow of her son emerge from the hallway and enter the playroom.

There is a brief moment of relief. He is okay.

But then the boy reaches his mother, towers over her. He hits her over the head with a toy bat and drags her lifeless body into the larger wooden room, where he ties his mother to a set of toy train tracks. She's the damsel in distress of a Saturday morning cartoon. Only in this instance there is no hero to save her.

At the Spencer Doll's bidding, the boy presses a button on a remote control, awakening the toy train that inhabits the tracks. A large fireman's ax that is affixed to the front of the train moves up and down as the toy engine lumbers forward. When it finally reaches the mother, one swift blow severs her head from her body. The blank, emotionless look on her face remains in the center of the frame as her detached head flies upwards and hangs in the air for a long second. When the head lands at the boy's feet, the mother winks. The Spencer Doll picks up its head and strokes the mother's hair lovingly. He kisses the lips of the severed head before throwing it away as the choir of creepy children laugh…

The video ended, static overtaking the screen of the old television. Captain Harris pulled the VHS tape from the slot and slammed it down on the squad room table.

"Jesus Christ," he hollered. "Not only did this piece of shit kill his fiancée, he doesn't have an original thought in his fucking head. I mean...Kid Play and Chuckie Norris doll. What a fucking hack!"

The malapropisms could be attributed to the detective's relative anger at the situation, or to his ignorance of horror films. Either way, Harris was rattled and perhaps out of his depth with this case. Whether or not the detectives acknowledged it at that time, they had to be thinking there was something important in these videotapes—even if they seemed somewhat hack-ish.

"Original or not, he definitely hacked the hell out of his fiancée on there," joked Officer Dunbar.

The entire room filled with laughter, further incensing Captain Harris.

He needed to make them understand the severity of the situation. Time was ticking.

"Hey!" bellowed Harris. "That's not funny. Now, you guys know the drill. We've got forty-eight hours to get something on this asshole or he walks!"

The case would get a whole lot harder if Spencer were allowed back on the streets. They had already begun from a position of weakness, and Spencer lawyering up would set them back further. Today they would most likely hear from the DA's office. Harris' hatred for celebrities was well established, but it paled in comparison to his hatred of lawyers. Lawyers were the ones who always managed to ruin his cases, made him out to be the bad guy. Harris was a law-and-order kind of guy—as long as he could bend the law to his own order.

The lead detective had another problem, too. If Spencer was able to rally his impressive fanbase, it could cause a minor stir and a major problem for the LAPD. This would be blamed on Harris, who had to avoid any complications in this case. He was already in hot water over previous misconduct and knew he was well past his nine lives and likely running out of chances to keep his job.[15] A gag order against Spencer was out of the question, given that the trial had yet to begin.

Harris turned back toward the evidence board before addressing the group again. "Thanks to Nordberg, we're looking at about thirty hours left. And according to Mrs. Perkins, this guy's lawyer is apparently on his way."

Nordberg shifted his weight nervously.

Sitting at the table, Detective Ophelia picked up the tape and turned it over in her hand. "What are we supposed to do with this?" she asked. "Originally I thought it was something, but it's really just a music video, not a confession. It's not like he's killing her for real here."

"It's a loose end," shot back Captain Harris. "I don't like letting go of loose ends and this is a loose end."

"This whole thing is full of loose ends," chimed in Officer Movery, gesturing to the board. "We can't connect him to the murder weapon or that mask or anything."

"Are you sure we have enough to go on here?" added Dunbar, dejectedly.

"Of course I'm fucking sure we have enough to go on. It's right here," Harris said, tapping his gut. "That's enough for me and it damn well better be enough for you. I didn't bring you here to bitch and moan about having to do your fucking jobs. I brought you

15 Captain Harris' dubious law enforcement career has been the subject of numerous articles over the years, but suffice it to say, you'd have a better chance at mopping the ocean than cleaning up a cop this dirty.

here to be detectives, not a bunch of talking heads with nothing between the ears!"

The group was silent for a minute.

Harris looked at each one of them as if sizing up their fitness for the task. "Now, instead of worrying about what we don't have, let's worry about what we do have. We got a whole board of evidence—we just have to connect it all. We're the ones in control. Now let's go out and find something on this piece of shit."

The group nodded along with him, some of their eyes glazed over. They looked like a bunch of zombie puppets, bobbing their heads in unison. If Harris wanted them to operate effectively, he would have to pull the strings and lead them to the obvious conclusion: Spencer was guilty.

"I want everybody here to talk to every goddamn employee on every one of these videos, 'cause somebody must have seen something…" He paused, giving them a chance to think about the logical next step. After determining they were clearly unable to come up with anything and needed more prodding. "Okay, Go! Go! Go! Everybody!" Then, remembering something, he continued, "except you, Nordberg."

Nordberg turned, clearly hoping for an important assignment.

"I need a cup of coffee," Harris said.

Norberg sighed. "You got it, chief." He turned back toward the door, his shoulders slumping more forward than before.

Harris called after him, "Decaf. Two Splendas." He clutched his heart, as if suddenly remembering how caffeine always raised his anxiety and made his heart race. He hoped to avoid further exacerbating the tachycardic response this case was already having on him. It would be a long night poring over the evidence. He would have to stay awake out of sheer will, and not with the use of his beloved coffee.

He took one long look at the photograph pinned to the top of the board: a headshot of Spencer. Obviously taken by a professional, the photograph depicted a devilish person with dark, disturbed eyes. As if whispering it into the universe would make it come true, Harris said, "You're going down, Mister Horrorwood…"

Harris was startled when he heard the door to the room open. He spun around and was confronted with a horrific sight for any officer: a suspect's lawyer. In this case, Carlos Cochran. While he had not been on cases as large as this one, his firm was known for keeping high-profile killers out of jail. Within the halls of justice, it was said that Cochran's firm was solely responsible for Los Angeles' high murder rate. Carlos was shorter and more slender than Harris with tight-cropped, slightly curly, salt-and-pepper hair. The glasses he wore only for reading were slightly too big for his face.

He thrust a pile of paperwork in Harris' direction. "You Harris?"

"Yeah," responded Harris. "Who's asking?"

He knew damn well who was asking, but he wasn't going to give Carlos that satisfaction.

"Carlos Cochran. I believe you have my client, Spencer Charnas."

"Well, that does sound like one of our murder suspects, Mister Cochran—"

"Carlos is fine. Let's cut the formalities and cut the shit," Carlos interrupted. "You either charge him or you let him go."

"You really want to force our hand here?" Harris got closer to Carlos, staring him right in the eyes. "I have a mind to go ahead and get him all arraigned this afternoon. How's that sit with you?"

"Pretty well, actually. It'll be thrown out in a heartbeat, and you know it." Carlos looked down at the file in his hands, holding it up to Harris. "I've seen what you think you have on him, and it looks pretty thin to me."

"We're only just getting started. It's only been eighteen hours, and from what I can tell, your client is going to fry."

"I admire your confidence, Captain. But either you arraign him this afternoon, or you release him. None of this internal forty-eight-hour bullshit rule you guys go by."

Harris stared at him, incredulously.

Carlos continued, "Yeah, I know how you guys all wish there was no fourth amendment, but sorry to break it to you, there is. So you gotta shit or get off the pot."

Harris remembered the evidence board behind him. He quickly turned around and ushered Carlos out of the conference room. "I got a whole board of evidence up here that I can't let you see just yet. But suffice it to say, it's enough to fill a whole lotta pots," Harris said, unconvincingly. Outside, in the main squad room, Harris shut the door before continuing. "Why don't we both go get your client and we can take a little ride over to the courthouse. It's a beautiful fucking afternoon for an arrest, wouldn't you say?"

V

The Shower Scene

It was Friday, December 11, around 2:43 PM, and the soon-to-be-venerable Carlos Cochran had forced the hand of Captain Harris, who was now arraigning his client. Carlos had the hotheaded detective right where he wanted him: on his back heels with nothing to show a judge.

Entering the courtroom lobby, Harris showed his badge and walked through the security checkpoint followed by Spencer in handcuffs, led by Nordberg. Harris motioned to the security guard and made sure that Carlos was stopped and forced to put his wallet and phone through the X-ray machine before submitting to a full-body frisk by who had to have been the most hands-on guard Harris saw working that shift.

It was late in the day and most judges had already departed for the weekend. Harris checked the schedule posted on a board in the front lobby, only to find nothing on the docket in the entire building. Twelve courtrooms, twelve vacancies. He spent a few minutes looking around for whomever it was that would be meeting him from the District Attorney's office. Given the short timeframe between the decision to arraign and the close of business, it would most likely be whoever was sitting in the office with little to do on a Friday afternoon.

Enter: DA Marcie Kent, just the type of attorney to be putting in hours on a Friday afternoon before the holidays. All business in her black pantsuit and white top, she closed in on Harris with a purposeful gait, her ombre hair bouncing with each stride. She was attractive in a conventional sense, which she often used to her advantage when dealing with police officers, particularly the males. For Harris, however, she would have come off as too professional. Too perfect. Too principled. Maybe it was the way that she looked down on law enforcement, as if she were somehow superior to Harris and his detectives. Harris had to suppress whatever ill feelings he had toward Kent, though. Whether he liked it or not, he needed her. She was a big deal in the DA's office. A real up-and-comer, even if she did have to schlep and schmooze her way to the top. This rushed attempt at an arraignment by Harris must have left him a little embarrassed upon the arrival of such an accomplished attorney.

"What is this shit?" DA Kent wasted no time laying into Captain Harris. She then looked to Spencer and Carlos before realizing she was in mixed company. "Excuse us a moment." She gave them a small smile that was somehow less genuine than she had meant it to be before pulling Harris aside. Spencer and his lawyer huddled up. Kent and Harris could hear laughing coming from the two of them. Sinister laughter that faded as they moved down the hall.

Once out of the suspect's earshot, Kent teared into Harris. "You bring this in on a Friday afternoon? I was in a trial and had to ask for a recess." She was jabbing at him with the file she held. "I wasn't about to let something high-profile slip through my fingers. Not again, anyway."[16]

---

16 Marcie Kent was originally meant to prosecute Robert Durst for his murder of Susan Berman, but another attorney had flown to New Orleans to interview Durst without a lawyer present. That interview led to the trial, so it was only right that he saw the prosecution through to the end.

"Not my fault you're getting double teamed," said Harris. "Why couldn't somebody else take this one? It's just an arraignment."

"I'm going to ignore that first comment," Kent said. "But let me just say that I'll be damned before I let somebody else get their hands on this case. It's a musician, right? High-profile guy? From Ice Nine Kills?"

"I didn't think you'd go for that type of filth, but everybody's got their kinks, I guess," responded Harris. "Look, his lawyer's a piece of work. Practically dared me to arraign him, so I had to call his bluff."

"Yeah, Carlos Cochran," replied the DA. "He's a good attorney who clearly outsmarted you here. Surprise, surprise…" She looked over at Spencer and Carlos, presumably discussing the extreme lack of a case. "You can't just charge people without evidence because somebody dares you to do it. What are you, in third grade?"

"Yeah…Detective third grade, I'll have you know."

"I thought you were a captain?" Kent asked, confused at his insistence on lowering his own rank.

"That too," Harris responded. "Everything's there. You got enough to charge and we're out there looking for more. I'm expecting a phone call any minute. I mostly just want to keep this scumbag off the street."

"There's no way this is enough. It's what? A box of videotapes." DA Kent pointed to a banker's box of evidence sitting on a bench nearby.

"Hey, don't just leave that lying around! That's good stuff. You show that in there and any judge would have to be psychotic not to charge him." Kent didn't look convinced. Harris leaned in and whispered, "There's some sick shit on those tapes. Practically a confession to killing his fiancée. We got a body at the coroner's, he's the closest person to the victim, and then those tapes. We've gotten convictions with less."

"You better be right," sighed Kent. "It's your ass here, but I must be crazy to go along with this."

Harris chuckled, "We all go a little mad sometimes."

For the first time the DA noticed his appearance. He was disheveled, to say the least, unshaven and tired-looking. She hoped for her career's sake that this wouldn't be a complete embarrassment. She further hoped that he might at least make some attempt to comb his hair or tame his beard before they went before a judge, but time was of the essence.

"How bad was the victim?" Kent said, softening a bit as she tried to probe for more information on this hastily brought case.

"Pretty bad. Haven't seen her myself, but—"

"Are you joking with this shit, Captain Harris?" Kent snapped. "You haven't even seen the body?"

"I'm going tomorrow. First thing," he managed. He was back on his heels again, this time due to the strength of the questioning coming from his own side. "Kind of a Saturday morning special."

"I'm going with you," Kent responded. Before he could reply she looked at her watch, then back at Harris. "We got Reinhold. Courtroom nine. Better get in there."

Within ten minutes, the arraignment had commenced and DA Kent hoped she wouldn't need to mention the evidence. She was hoping that it was enough for the judge to arraign Spencer and hold him until trial, or at least until Harris got his act together. She had read the files on the drive over, dangerous to say the least, but necessary. As this was not yet the pre-trial hearing, she figured the judge might just allow her the arraignment and give her the weekend, but Reinhold was known for being thorough. As unorthodox as it was, the judge seemed interested in questioning the idea of this arraignment. Had Carlos somehow gotten to him before the trial even began? She felt confident enough to mention The Silence mask found at Spencer's home, which had been spotted near the scene of the crime, and also described the horrific state of the victim's body. Finally, when the judge insisted she would need to release the suspect due to a lack of evidence, she decided to take a gamble with the videotapes and asked to show one.

As soon as Kent raised the issue of the tapes, Carlos rose from his chair. "Your honor," he shouted upon standing. "These tapes have no bearing on this arraignment, or the case, and are highly prejudicial to my client."

"That's the point," said Kent. "He's a murderer and, I'm told, they're practically a confession. They depict his acting out the very crime that he is being accused of. Next thing you'll say it's prejudicial to prove he owned the murder weapon."

"Your honor, please. This is ridiculous," huffed Carlos. "There is no link to my client and whatever weapon they are alleging to have found." Carlos made air quotes as he finished his statement, before mumbling "Or planted..." Calling into question the search tactics of Captain Harris that he knew were dubious at best.

"Hold on a minute now," began Judge Reinhold. "I'm willing to see one of these videotapes before I go ahead and flush this whole thing down the toilet. What do you say, Ms. Kent? Do we have something cued up?"

Kent looked at her notes then over to Captain Harris seated next to her. She didn't usually like detectives to ride shotgun, but this case was different—and highly speculative. Besides, she felt that she would need to keep Harris on a tight leash; she knew that he often operated extra-legally and she would not want her own career to be staked on his ability to follow the rules. She looked to the back of the courtroom and nodded to a legal assistant from her office who wheeled over an older model television set with an attached VCR. Preparedness might well have been Marcie Kent's middle name.

DA Kent inserted a videotape and played through the first video that the detectives had watched previously, the one depicting Spencer as a Chucky doll and ordering the fictional decapitation of his fiancée, Nadia. A few members of the courtroom staff gasped at its gruesome conclusion. A headless fiancée does not scream innocence.

Carlos jumped up and walked to the box of evidence once the tape finished. He had been speaking to Spencer during the previous video and seemed to have some kind of trick up his sleeve. "Your honor," he started as he walked. "I would like to ask that we show one more video. One more of these so-called 'confessions,' " he said, adding air quotes.

The judge nodded his approval, he seemed to be enjoying this back and forth, hardly a regular Friday afternoon. Carlos continued strolling toward the box. After a quick perusal, he pulled out a video and held it up so his client could see. Spencer nodded and Carlos made his way to the VCR.

The video began and the courtroom watched as...

A classic 1960s Oldsmobile cuts through a harsh rainstorm and across the parking lot of a deserted, single-story motel. Everything is black-and-white. The bright, neon signs boldly announce the "IX Motel" against an otherwise dark sky, with the exception of the occasional lightning strike. The car rolls to a stop under an overhang by the motel's entrance.

A young woman played by Nadia emerges from the parked vehicle. She takes two bags and shuts the car door. Dressed in a sleek, light-colored, 1960s dress and beret, Nadia makes her way to the front door of the motel, where a bell dings upon her entering.

She places her bags down and walks across the creaky floor toward the front desk, on top of which sits a taxidermied blackbird. On her way to reception, she notices an adjacent room with an open door. An old woman in a rocking chair is silhouetted against a curtained window. Nadia then rings the bell on top of the desk and the song of the video begins.

Spencer sings as he rocks back and forth in a rocking chair wearing an old woman's blankets draped around his shoulders. The same door Nadia had just looked through shuts on its own and remains closed briefly before Spencer—now in a tan suit—reopens it and enters the lobby, smiling. He seats himself behind the desk, and she shows him a picture of another young girl with blonde hair. He shakes his head, indicating he can't help her, and instead produces a logbook for her to sign into the motel. He hands her a key, and she is soon in her room.

Nadia undresses while Spencer watches her from the window. She strips down to a white, lacy bra and panties and lies on the bed. Nadia then pulls out the picture from before and unfolds it, revealing another person on the previously hidden side of the photograph. It's Nadia herself, holding the other woman's hand; they are clearly happy and in love.

Later, Nadia tosses and turns in the bed as she dreams of her missing lover. The woman from the photograph appears in the dream, and they kiss passionately on the bed. The woman straddles her, thrusting as they continue to kiss. The sexual tension and passion between the two women is visibly apparent—true love at a time in history when such a relationship would have been forbidden.

Nadia wakes alone; her hair is disheveled, and she is disoriented. She puts on a bathrobe and exits her motel room onto the porch that wraps around the property. She makes her way down the porch, shielded from the downpouring rain that occasionally splashes onto her. She sneaks back into the lobby and toward the room in which she previously saw the old woman. She peers through the keyhole and again sees the woman in the rocking chair. Suddenly, Spencer's face fills the keyhole, and she runs away. He casually walks through the office toward the front door, which he finds strangely open. He briefly looks around before closing the door and returning to the back office. Nadia has remained safely tucked against the doorframe, out of view the whole time. She is safe—for now.

In the back office, Spencer approaches a painting that echoes Edvard Munch's The Scream but with a "IX" scrawled over the screamer's face. He removes the painting from the wall to reveal a peephole, which he immediately spies through. Through it, he watches Nadia enter the shower in her adjacent motel room. The all-white bathroom, illuminated by overhead fluorescent lights, contrasts sharply with the dark office, giving Spencer a better view as he watches her bathe. The water washes over her naked body as she cleanses herself, blissfully unaware she's being watched.

Suddenly, the door to Nadia's motel room opens, revealing the figure of an old woman, lit from behind by neon lights from the parking lot. The rain continues to fall as forcefully as the shower pouring down on Nadia, masking the sound of the door. The old woman raises a knife and steps into the room. She slowly makes her way across the floor toward the bathroom. The white noise of the water prevents Nadia from hearing anything. She cannot sense the danger approaching.

Stealthily, the old woman opens the bathroom door. Behind the semitransparent curtain, Nadia's figure continues to wash, unresponsive to the presence of another. The old woman approaches the curtain, flings it back, and raises her knife. Immediately, the camera angle shifts to reveal that Spencer is dressed as the old woman—knife in hand, ready to kill. But instead of Nadia, he finds a dress on a coat hanger, hung in the shower to trick him. From behind, Nadia seizes on his momentary confusion. She lunges at him with a knife of her own. He has no time to react and is stabbed in the neck.

Nadia throws Spencer against the back wall of the shower. She stabs him again and again, each blow sending a splatter of dark blood across the white ceramic. Spencer's mouth sputters blood, further contaminating the scene. He collapses against the wall, eyes rolling back into his head. Life drains from him as he crumples to the shower floor, his blood seeping into the pipes below.

The camera pushes into Spencer's open, lifeless eye to reveal Nadia in another room, searching for something—or someone. She quickly finds her lover in the back office, deceased and rotting away in the rocking chair. The corpse's face still bears patches of dried blood amid the extreme decay of the facial flesh as it peels from her skull. Nadia is horrified. She screams, hands flying to her mouth, overwhelmed by emotion and grief at the confirmed loss of her true love.

The band Ice Nine Kills now appears in full, performing in individual motel rooms intercut with the remaining scenes—Ricky in all white as he wails on a black guitar, Pat in black hammering on white drums, and Joe plucking a black-and-white bass—all heightening the video's emotional climax. Meanwhile, a living version of Spencer rocks in his chair, still wearing his blanket, singing the song.

Nadia imagines kissing her lover one last time as she begins to work on Spencer's lifeless body. She wraps him in a clear plastic tarp and drags him back to her motel room. There, she carves him up piece by piece, limb by limb. As she works, images flood her mind—herself kissing her girlfriend on a bed, both wearing white lingerie—while she saws Spencer's arm from his torso. Then a leg. Once finished, she packs the parts into a suitcase, cramming them in like unfolded clothes hurriedly stuffed away after a long vacation.

Back in the lobby, Nadia's key is returned to the front desk just as a police cruiser pulls up outside. Nadia then walks out to load her suitcases into the trunk of her car. Officer Noen—blonde hair, aviator sunglasses, clad in a 1960s police uniform—steps out of his vehicle, marked Fairview Police. He approaches Nadia.

"Excuse me, ma'am?"

"Oh, hello," she replies, caught off guard by the sudden presence of law enforcement.

"Have you by any chance seen this woman?" He holds up a picture of another young woman—not Nadia's lover, but perhaps one of Spencer's earlier victims.

"Sure haven't," Nadia says quickly, eager to get away. "I'm really in quite a hurry," she adds, attempting to load the final bag—the one containing Spencer.

Ever the gentleman, Officer Noen stoops to assist her. Before Nadia can object, he has the suitcase in hand.

"Now, let me help you with that...bag," he says, surprised by its weight.

"Thank you, officer," she replies as he lifts it toward the trunk.

"Jeez, that's pretty heavy," he mutters, trying to wedge it into the last corner of the full trunk.

Relieved she may have escaped detection, Nadia slams the trunk shut and heads to the driver's side door.

"Well, drive safely, ma'am," the officer calls as she gets in.

As Nadia pulls away from the scene of the crime, the officer watches her go. He pulls out a cigarette and leans against one of the posts supporting the motel roof, unaware of the material evidence he's just let slip through his fingers. The screen fades to black.

Carlos Cochran, brimming with pride, turned off the courthouse VCR machine before looking around the room. Kent had been watching Carlos and his client while the video played, and something about Spencer left her feeling uneasy. Though, if she was being honest, this take off of Psycho was right up her alley, given her appreciation for the film.

"There you have it, your honor," Carlos began, turning to the judge. "The DA's evidence…washed away." As he spoke, he made a motion with his hands as if he were playing an invisible piano and then flung his fingers off the side of it.

Kent immediately stood up. She knew they were on shaky ground, but hoped that, at the very least, this judge would give them time for Captain Harris to further unearth something about Spencer. She needed to launch into her appeal before the judge had time to consider Carlos' request, but first she had to diffuse his ridiculous tactics. "Your honor, can we have Mister Cochran cut the theatrics? It's an arraignment, not Shakespeare in the park."

"*Et tu*, DA," retorted Carlos, eliciting a slight laugh from himself and those in the room who noted his turn of phrase.

Judge Reinhold, however, did not look amused. "Mister Cochran…" he reprimanded, turning his head in disapproval.

Kent returned to her seat, satisfied that justice had been served.

Undeterred, Carlos continued, "Your honor. The DA intends to dazzle and distract in order to smear a highly respected—and I might add, Julliard-trained—musician." Carlos gestured to Spencer, who sat stoically at his defense table, staring straight ahead, showing little to no emotion.

"Bullshit," Captain Harris coughed into his hand, unable to help himself. Annoyed by this outburst, DA Kent shot Harris a glare, rolling her eyes as she did.

"Excuse me," continued Harris. He wasn't fooling anybody, and Kent worried how much of a liability he might be during this trial.

Carlos continued, "Now, the DA is going to claim that my client killed his fiancée. All because she sees some sort of patterns? In his music videos?" Carlos looked around the courtroom. The few scattered faces that littered the gallery seemed to be somewhat going along with what he was saying, but most weren't paying attention, the notable exception being a group of Ice Nine Kills fans in the back who were nodding along with his every word. For the first time, he must have gotten the slightest inkling of what Spencer might feel when on stage.[17] Carlos perked up as he continued, "Your honor, if the DA feels that life is imitating art, then I have just one question. Why is it that my client is sitting here with a pulse? When in fact, Nadia, my client's fiancée, is the one that actually kills Spencer in this video. Is this all you have, Miss Kent?

"Believe me, we're just getting warmed up," responded Kent through gritted teeth. She hated the cockiness of Cochran and wished this arraignment would end so she could begin the damage control. The first thing would be to lay into Harris for even bringing this to her without sufficient evidence in place. The next would be finding out why INK fans had already gotten word of the proceedings.

Carlos's argument was valid and Kent knew it. Perhaps sensing her displeasure, Carlos continued to antagonize the DA. "Well, I hope so," he started. "Because I'm on fire, and your case doesn't hold any water." He turned back toward the judge. "Your honor, they want to piss on your leg and then tell you that it's raining!"

"Your honor!" Kent yelled, standing back up as she did. She had to put a stop to this or at least buy some more time from the judge. They had clearly picked the wrong evidence to highlight, but surely the other videos had to count for something.

"All right, hold on now. This may be pre-empting any pre-trial hearing, but I'm inclined to take a look at these videos here," the

17 Having made frequent appearances with Spencer Charnas following the publication of my first book, I can tell you firsthand that his fans (The Psychos) are difficult, disrespectful, and downright detestable. However, they obviously love him and his music, so one can, at the very least, appreciate their passion.

judge began, looking down at a piece of paper in front of him. "Let's just see what we have on the courtroom totals, shall we?"

Judge Reinhold was not usually one for theatrics, but this case would prove different than most of those he oversaw. He held up the paper to read what was a cursory list of the horrors Spencer's videos depicted, as prepared by the defense.[18] "Eight bodies hung in garment bags, one singing ax wound victim, two bloodthirsty resurrected children, a toy train decapitation, nine zombies gunned down, one scissors stab to the face, three stabs to the chest, two in the stomach, and one in the back, not to mention the countless horror movie pun-fu, animal graveyard-fu, sadistic doll-fu, power suit-fu, and zombie-fu, just to name a few…fu."

One wouldn't know it by looking at him, but Judge Reinhold himself was a fan of horror films dating back to some of the earliest on record. He was, in a way, a student and historian of the craft. However, despite his connoisseurship, "Fu" was allegedly a term that he had been unfamiliar with at the time and was simply reading for the record. It is typically meant to signify the overdoing of something that would be considered a trope across horror films and has been used most often by a specific late-night horror film presenter over the years.

"Well, if we're gonna talk about fu's, your honor, how about this one?" Carlos retorted, using the judge's own word to make his case. "We're flushing taxpayer dollars down the toilet-fu! Shouldn't Captain Harris and his team be out there looking for the real psycho? Before this entire case goes down the drain."

DA Kent turned in her seat toward Harris. "You better find something on this guy," she whispered. "We need something to go on."

"Hey, don't worry about it, sweetheart," Harris responded

18 The list had been compiled by Spencer's record label in their attempt to circumvent censorship on various online video platforms. In this case, they had quickly been submitted by Spencer's own lawyer to show the innocuous nature of the DA's claims.

The word "sweetheart" made Kent shudder with disgust.

She returned fire. "And next time, can you shave before entering this courtroom?" She took a beat before closing the remark. "You look like the Unabomber."

Harris took it in stride, stroking his beard as he jovially said, "Hey, I'm one with the criminal."

The judge banged his gavel once more to get the attention of all parties involved. "I'd say given these series of tapes, we might have enough for an arraignment, but I'm not convinced there's a case." He then looked to Spencer's side, "I take it you're pleading not guilty?" he asked Spencer.

Before Spencer could answer, Carlos put up his hand and responded on his behalf. "Yes, your honor."

This was satisfactory to the judge who continued on.

"I'm going to give the prosecution a little more time because I do think there is something here to go on," Judge Reinhold began. "Now, I'll want The Information submitted by Tuesday and I'll take another look at a pre-trial. If, by then, it doesn't gel and isn't aspic, we may be looking at a dismissal. And a whole lot of egg on the face of the DA's office. Do I make that clear, Miss Kent?"

"Crystal," she replied before craning her neck toward Harris, throwing him another disapproving glare.

Despite the decidedly negative outcome, the judge was throwing DA Kent and Harris a life preserver, potentially saving them from drowning in an otherwise embarrassing legal defeat.

"We're adjourned until next week," the judge finished. He banged the gavel once, alerting all those that the proceedings had ended.

"All rise!" bellowed Bailiff Bosco.

The court followed his command and stood as the judge left for his chambers. Spencer breathed a sigh of relief. Kent noticed that something about him didn't scream "cold-blooded killer," but the thought was brushed aside as camera flash bulbs obscured her view of the defendant. One thing was for sure, this case would have a lot of press, and that could be very good for her career. Provided she won.

Harris' phone rang immediately after court was adjourned. He looked down to see Ophelia's name across the screen, causing him to abruptly stand up. Before answering the call, he whispered down to Kent, "No sense dwelling on our losses. Here's hoping we got something. My detective. At Spencer's house" He walked out of the courtroom with Kent scrambling to keep up.

"Hi, Captain Harris." Ophelia's voice echoed through the phone from the other end of the line.

"Where the hell are you and Dunbar?" snapped Harris as he turned the corner out of the courtroom and into the hallway, Kent in tow. He put the phone on speaker as he continued to berate his subordinate. "We're fucking drowning here."

"Did they find anything?" asked Kent, hoping they hadn't come back empty handed. Harris shooed her away as he tried to find out the answer.

"Captain, if this is about the search and surveillance, we don't have a warrant and didn't find anything useful anyways."

"Piss on the bill of rights, we got just cause!" yelled Harris—too loud for Kent's liking, given the venue.

"I didn't hear that," Kent said sarcastically.

Harris glanced at her disapprovingly, holding up his fist and making a jerking off motion.

"I'll handle this," he whispered to the DA before turning back to the phone. "Look, I need you and Dunbar at the station in a fucking hour, okay?!"

"Yes, sir. Just have to shower and I'll be right there," she said, stuttering a bit at the end.

Harris said nothing, just looked at the DA.

"Look, if you need a warrant…" said Kent.

"You stay in your lane, let me stay in mine," Harris replied.

"We need to do this by the book."

"Believe you me, sister, I know every trick in the book," Harris said before walking toward the parking lot. Kent hoped he wouldn't do anything to jeopardize the already flimsy case against Spencer.

††††

After hanging up her phone, Ophelia caught sight of herself in the mirror—mud smeared across her face and body. She had hoped to uncover more evidence but found only dirt and grime while digging in the garden and crawling through the attic of Spencer's house. A shower at home was exactly what she needed before being chewed out by Captain Harris for coming up empty-handed. A literal dirty cop, she thought, chuckling at the pun. Sometimes, she wasn't as serious as others believed. She tried to play ball, but she disliked Harris' fast-and-loose methods—his team always shot first and left the questions for someone else. If anyone in their squad was a dirty cop, it was Harris.

She was snapped from her thoughts by a sound from the far corner of the bathroom. It could almost have been a footstep behind her. She spun around—nothing. Just the antique claw-foot tub with its overhead shower attachment, surrounded by an opaque white curtain—something, or someone, could easily be hidden within it.

Feeling slightly foolish but needing to check, she took a step. Then another. She approached with the caution of a trained officer entering a dangerous scene. When she reached the tub, she flung open the curtain.

Nothing.

She exhaled, chuckling at herself for being paranoid. The bathroom was still, the kind of quiet in which you could hear a pin drop. She switched on the water, breaking the silence with the splashing and hiss of the shower.

Ophelia paused again, straining to hear whatever she thought she'd heard before. But the steady rush of water made it impossible. After adjusting the temperature, she stepped into the tub, letting the water wash over her, eager to cleanse herself after hours spent exploring the recesses of Spencer's house. The lukewarm cascade ran through her hair and down her back, helping her forget—if only for a moment—that she had to return to work in less than an hour.

Ophelia's apartment was on the first floor. Behind the wall, her shower pipes connected to a maintenance room, where the plumbing met the water heater and the building's main line. In that adjacent room—had the shower not been running—she might have heard a literal pin drop. A soft metallic ding echoed through the chamber as a small piece of metal struck the floor. This sound, however, did not reach the trained, but distracted, ears of Detective Ophelia Crane.

The pin had secured a cap on a cleanout vent normally used to prevent clogs or provide access for maintenance. Now it lay discarded at the feet of a figure dressed entirely in black. Wearing gloves and a mask of The Silence, the intruder next removed the stopper from a vial of chemical-grade acid, setting it gently beside the fallen pin. Then, lifting the vial with care, the figure poured the liquid into the open pipe.

On the other side of the wall, Ophelia continued bathing, unaware of the danger mere feet away from her exposed body. As she applied soap to her face, she felt a tiny prick—sharp, under her left eye. She flinched, then felt it again across her chest and shoulders. She tried to flick it away, but the sensation persisted.

Eyes clamped shut, she tried to keep soap from getting in—but something else was happening. The sharp, burning pain quickly overtook her entire face, spread down her body. It was unlike anything she had ever felt. She had neither the time nor clarity to identify it. She tried opening her eyes, but they felt glued shut, as if melted. As sores broke open where the water hit her face, Ophelia screamed—raw, agonized—unable to make it stop.

Her hands flew to her face, searching for the cause, but instead of relief, she found her own flesh peeling away. Wet strips of skin clung to her palms, sticking like paper to glue. The more she clawed at herself, the worse it became. Patches of skin tore off, revealing slick red muscle and bone beneath. Her screams escalated with each new handful of shredded flesh.

In the maintenance room, her cries reached through the wall as the masked figure completed the task. The acid bottle now empty, they calmly recapped the pipe and restoppered the vial. Their job done, they traced a finger across the stone wall as they slipped back into the world—Ophelia's screams slowly fading behind them.

Before the killer even exited the building, Ophelia had torn the flesh from her face, reduced her own features to muscle, bone, and blood. Her movements slowed, were no longer purposeful. Her screams fell silent. Perhaps from blood loss, or pure shock, her struggle ceased. Her body slumped forward, resting lifelessly over the edge of the antique tub.

The entire murder took place while Spencer was still at the courthouse. Despite his ironclad alibi, another life had been taken. And rather than turning up enough dirt to convict the famed musician, the case had only grown muddier.

VI

Funeral Derangements

It was early Saturday morning, and, despite having little life outside of work, the last place on earth DA Marcie Kent wanted to be was the county morgue. But time was of the essence, and Captain Harris couldn't be trusted with such an important task on his own. Nadia's family was about to take possession of her body, and Kent knew Harris had to gather every piece of evidence possible in conjunction with the county's medical examiner. They had only until Tuesday to present enough to the judge to go forward with trying Spencer for murder—but the timeline to examine the body was even shorter. Approximately three hours after Kent arrived, the undertaker from Creed & Crandle Funeral Parlor was scheduled to collect the corpse and cremate the remains. Given the state in which Nadia had been recovered—completely burned throughout—it seemed Spencer had already done half the job himself.

A few minutes before 9:00 a.m., Kent arrived at the Los Angeles County Morgue's Boyle Heights location, adjacent to the University of Southern California campus, where the 5 meets the 10. Trucks came screaming off the exit ramps at high speeds. She wondered if placing the morgue in such a dangerous location was a strategic decision to shorten the commute from the inevitable traffic fatalities nearby.

Pulling into the parking lot, she spotted Harris walking into the building with Dunbar and Nordberg. He watched her park but didn't wait for her to catch up.

Kent entered through a door reserved for law enforcement and medical personnel. Inside, she caught up to Harris as he was exchanging brief pleasantries with an imposing, yet gentle-faced, guard. Harris quieted the conversation when Kent approached.

"Fred, this is DA Kent. She's here because…well, I'm not too sure why the fuck she's here."

"I'm the one doing my job, and right now, my job is to make sure you do your job," said Kent. "Nice to meet you, Fred," she added, extending her hand.

He took it, grumbled in return.

"Isn't she lovely?" Harris asked Fred sarcastically.

Harris was clearly a regular at the morgue, which made sense for someone who'd worked homicide for the better part of twenty years. Still, it unsettled Kent how comfortable he seemed. The place gave her a chill.

"We're going up to the fridge," Harris said, nodding toward the staircase in front of him. With that, he bounded ahead, leaving the others to keep up.

The LA County Morgue was as bleak as its three-star Yelp rating suggested.[19] Stoic employees shuffled through a sterile workspace composed of cool metal and harsh fluorescent lighting. To the untrained eye, the rooms all looked the same: a viewing window (usually with blinds drawn), a metal door with a small panel of glass, and an examination table surrounded by refrigerated cabinets filled with the dead whose stories needed unraveling.

Kent appreciated the quiet atmosphere of the building, which she liked despite it leaving her with an odd sense of fear and anxiety.

19 Look it up. Only two reviews. It's said that at a morgue, the dead can speak. Obviously, they aren't using online rating sites to do so.

She wondered what it might look like to be laid out on one of those slabs. Or what if it were someone else she knew? Perhaps Harris. The thought left as quickly as it came. She wasn't a violent person, but Harris frustrated her beyond belief.

He moved purposefully down the second-floor hallway to room 45, pausing just long enough for the others to catch up and enter as a group. Harris held the door—a first. Kent assumed, probably correctly, that he only did it to watch her face as she saw the body. It was still covered, denying him that satisfaction. She smiled and tossed her hair as she stepped past him.

Inside, Kent immediately spotted Dr. Rachel Lambert in scrubs, going over notes. Lambert was the newly appointed Chief Medical Examiner-Coroner for Los Angeles County—a big title, and an even bigger job.[20] In her new role, she rarely took cases herself, instead overseeing operations from the department's central office. After thirty years as a forensic pathologist, last year she'd become, at fifty-four, the first African American female Medical Examiner to hold the post. Kent liked her from what little interaction they'd had. Lambert was direct, professional. They hadn't had a chance to work together much, as Kent had only landed a handful of homicides and Dr. Lambert's recent elevation had taken her off the front lines. Lambert being here could only mean that Kent was in for something truly extraordinary with this case.

Before Kent could ask, Harris beat her to it.

"Rachel? To what do we owe the displeasure?" he asked in a rare tone of friendliness. "They demote you already?"

---

20 Los Angeles county has recently changed the title from "Coroner," someone who is not a doctor and associated with law enforcement, to "Medical Examiner-Coroner" in order to emphasize the medically scientific responsibilities of the independent authority outside of the bounds of law enforcement. Lambert herself trained with the old guard and is said by some to still exhibit those qualities, despite her medical degree.

"No," she chuckled. "Just thought you could use some help. Heard you got dragged into court by an overzealous attorney," she said, flashing a knowing smile at Kent.

"Well, then you heard wrong from that ivory tower of yours. I've got this guy right where I want him," Harris replied, his tone bordering on flirtation.

Kent blinked. It was like seeing someone she'd never met. Harris seemed...well, almost cheerful.

Dunbar and Nordberg, meanwhile, stood nervously in the corner.

"The case is a work in progress," Kent said, easing her way into the conversation. "Good to see you again, Rachel. Congratulations on the promotion."

"Thank you. I just wish it meant I didn't have to work with this guy," Lambert said, nodding at Harris. "Sorry to see you're in the same boat."

"Easy on the cat fest here, ladies," Harris said. "Can we get back to business?"

"Might as well," Lambert replied, turning serious. "Because this is some real sick shit." She pulled back the sheet, revealing a completely charred body, almost unrecognizable as human. It resembled a museum mummy more than a murder victim. Charred flesh clung to exposed bone jutting out at wrong angles, and only the vague silhouette suggested this had once been a person.

Kent stared, holding her composure.

"Ugh!" Dunbar gagged, turning away. He immediately dry heaved, convulsing his upper torso uncontrollably over a small trash can by the entrance to the room.

"You want to take that shit outside?" barked Harris. "Ignore him," he added to Lambert. "Guy works homicide and acts like he's never seen a body."

"Not like that!" Dunbar gasped. "It looks like a beef brisket."

"Well, now I know what I'm getting for lunch," Harris said with a laugh.

Dunbar bolted. "Come on! You can dish it out, but you can't take it?" Harris called after him. "Nordberg, take notes."

Kent started, "We can probably just use the report—"

"Nordberg. Take notes," Harris repeated.

"You got it, boss," Nordberg said.

"So, what've we got?" Harris asked Lambert.

"It's bad," she said. "Most of the body has been burned beyond recognition. There's very little intact DNA. Someone really wanted to erase every trace. But through dental records, we've positively identified her as Nadia Teichmann."

"So it's definitely Spencer's fiancée?" Kent asked.

"I can handle this, Kent," Harris said curtly.

"Spencer Charnas?" Lambert confirmed, checking her notes. "Yes. He's listed as next of kin. Along with her parents. They're on their way now, I believe."

"So we're told. Thanks for the rush job," Harris said.

"No rush. There wasn't much to work with. But we recovered a few teeth," Lambert said, pointing to an indistinguishable area near the head of the table. "We matched them to records from her dentist."

"Good work," Harris said.

"But it's not the whole picture," Lambert added with a sigh. "We found multiple stab wounds, front and back—visible on the rib cage and spine. And there are strange bite marks on her neck and arms. They went deep. Through multiple tissue layers that are now mostly gone."

"Animal attack?" Harris asked.

"Human," Lambert said flatly. "Unmistakable. Like I said. Sick shit. We've pulled some impressions from what we think are the bite marks, you may want to try and match them up to your suspect. They're in that bag over there." She nodded toward a white pouch on a side table.

Harris grabbed it and stuffed it into his coat pocket. "We'll get a warrant," he said, giving Kent a pointed look.

"If it's notes you're worried about, she was right," Lambert interjected, gesturing toward Kent. "You can have these." She handed Harris a folder. "And try to get some rest. It's the weekend for god's sake."

Kent admired Lambert's clarity. Dead or alive, she could read people.

"Tell that to the judge," Harris muttered. "We need enough to charge our guy and we need it fast. I just hope you've got it here." He held up the file as he spoke.

"I'm sure Dr. Lambert's done an exceptional job," Kent said, grabbing it.

Lambert nodded. "Fortunately for you all, this is the place where the dead speak."

"Hope she's a real talker," Harris muttered. "Looks painful."

Kent leafed through the report as Lambert laid out more details.

"Luckily—if you can call it that—we believe the victim was deceased prior to the burning," she began. "It was the stab wounds that she would have had to suffer through. The ice pick you recovered? Almost certainly the murder weapon. It's all in the report." She paused, glancing at the corpse. "I don't know what went on in this girl's life, but sometimes, dead is better."

"Good for business, I guess. But we like to think keeping people alive is the name of the game," added Harris.

"In homicide, you're always a little late for that," Lambert replied.

Kent flipped through the pages. The killing, however brutal, seemed almost masterful in the artistry. Bites, stabs, fire—it was as if the killer couldn't decide on the cause of death and thus sought to confuse those who would investigate it.

She came back to reality as Harris and Lambert finished their conversation.

"Story of my life," Harris muttered. "Let's get out of this hellhole." He snatched the file from Kent's hands. "Time for some light reading. Should make for a delightful Saturday."

"Take care, Harris," Lambert said, watching them go. She pulled the sheet back over Nadia's remains. This would be her last case with Harris—but not the last time she saw the aging detective.

They found Dunbar still green and hunched over the hallway trash can.

"All set?" he asked shakily. "Can we go now?"

"Come on, numb nuts," said Harris, leading the way downstairs.

Kent followed. She had seen another side of Harris today and wasn't sure what to make of it. He seemed happy being surrounded by death, almost giddy. It made her uneasy. Just one more reason not to like him, she thought.

She made the quick decision to follow the detectives back to the station. When she arrived, she found an angry Harris screaming into a phone. All trace of giddiness gone.

"We're dealing with the case of our lifetimes! If you're not giving it your all, you better be fucking dead!"

Kent approached as he slammed the receiver down.

"You all right there, Captain? Case getting to you?"

Harris glared. "Missing officer. She didn't show up last night or this morning. She's usually pretty good about these things."

"The woman on your team?" Kent asked. "Ophelia Crane, right?"

"Yeah. We'll find her," Harris said. "What are you doing here?"

"Sounds like you have your hands full," she responded. "Consider me an extra pair. You dig up anything in those files?" She gestured toward the folder Lambert had given Harris at the morgue.

"We were just getting to it," grumbled Harris, bristling in response to Kent's micro-management. "Don't tell me you're thinking of sticking around."

"Somebody has to make sure you're digging in all the right places," she responded. "Can't have you losing any more of your people." She had wished she left it before that last part, knowing it might be too harsh.

Harris didn't respond.

†††††

For the next forty-five minutes, the entire team, Kent included, pored over the files from Lambert, looking for something they could sink their teeth into. Nordberg, Dunbar, Harris, Kent, and the others sat in relative silence as their case against Spencer decayed before their very eyes. The biggest point of confusion was the bite marks. Kent thought they were strange but wasn't sure what to make of them. Why bite somebody if you're just going to stab or burn them? It didn't add up. Nothing about this case did. And then, as if they weren't confused enough, a knock came at the door and in walked a younger, dark-haired officer with a slight build: Officer Miko.

"Captain?" he began. "This came for you." He handed Harris a yellow envelope.

Harris nodded, then ripped it open and pulled out a videotape. He looked up at his detectives, then at Kent, before turning back to Miko.

"Who gave you this?"

"Bike messenger?" Miko replied, his voice rising as if questioning his own memory of the recent incident. "He had some kind of black mask on. I didn't get a good look at him."

"God dammit!" bellowed Harris. "This guy's in the next cell over, with no phone, no internet. How the hell is he getting things delivered?!"

"Maybe it wasn't him," offered Kent.

Harris didn't respond, instead allowing Nordberg to fill the break in conversation. "She might have a point."

"I thought you were supposed to be smart. Didn't you go to law school?" Harris snapped. Nordberg nodded sheepishly. "Guess that's why you became a cop. Let's watch this thing—then I'm going to talk to that asshole."

He walked toward the VCR, ready to insert the tape.

"You'd better call his lawyer first," said Kent, condescendingly. "Oh, right. You didn't go to law school."

"Nordberg," Harris said, turning toward his detective. "Get Carlos Cock-muncher in here." He smiled at Kent. Without another word, he popped in the tape—and the video began:

Spencer stands on a lonely, desert highway flanked by a few scattered houses. With him is an older man in light blue overalls and a black jacket—farming attire, it would appear. Despite wearing a similar black jacket and jeans, Spencer looks more urban and fashionable. They both look down, silently staring at the lifeless lump of a small animal on the ground between them. The old man takes a drag from his cigarette.

"How the hell do you explain death to such a little kid?" asks Spencer, sincerely.

The man takes a second before answering. "Well, maybe you don't have to."

They sit in silence for a moment before the song begins.

Spencer's body is dragged across the rocky dirt of a graveyard, his mouth and white shirt stained with blood. Quick cuts follow: a pale boy in a white hooded sweatshirt screams into the dark night while standing in the same graveyard. Then the band Ice Nine Kills plays their instruments among the headstones, all dressed in funeral attire. Children in paper-mâché animal masks dance in a circle. Finally, the old man—now wearing a suit—faces the camera and says, "Sometimes dead is better."

In the daylight, a family is gathered at a picnic table in front of a rustic house. Spencer, the patriarch of the family, wears all light-colored denim and sits with the old man from the opening scene, who now wears a plaid shirt. The atmosphere is much lighter and more upbeat than before. They laugh and joke as Nadia, in a light summer dress, brings a picnic basket and begins to set out food. At the same table, a young boy in a bright yellow shirt and light-colored overalls turns toward the road behind him. It's the same boy who wore the hooded sweatshirt, though now far less pale. As he turns in his seat, he notices a black cat in the middle of the highway that stretches out in front of the home. Intrigued, he walks toward the cat and into the street, his blond mushroom cut blowing in the wind.

Meanwhile, a truck barrels down the same highway, farther up the road. Inside the cabin sits a twenty-something driver with a neatly cropped beard—there's something boyish about him. He reaches for a cup of coffee as he listens to music, taking his eyes off the road for a moment.

Once the young boy reaches the cat, he crouches down to play with it. Its eyes glow a menacing green, but the boy is undeterred. Distracted, he doesn't notice the truck rapidly approaching. Back at the picnic table, Spencer sees his son in the road—and the oncoming truck. He stands up and watches in horror as it careens toward his child. He screams and runs, but he's too late. The truck strikes the boy, killing him instantly. One small shoe bounces across the ground—the only evidence a child had crouched there moments before.

A funeral is held. Spencer and the other band members carry the child-sized coffin into the center of a cemetery. Once it's set down, a minister and onlookers grieve over the dead boy. Everyone wears black and white; Spencer stands in front of the group in a black suit, white shirt, and black tie, staring down at the coffin. Behind him, Nadia—now in a black dress—screams and weeps as only a mother can. The minister leads the group in prayer.

During the ceremony, Spencer begins to contemplate burying the child in the mystical ground rumored to bring back the dead. The old man warns him not to, but Spencer indicates he won't listen.

With the other mourners gone, Spencer returns to the gravesite with a shovel. He exhumes the coffin and removes his son's lifeless body. Clutching him to his chest, he mourns again. He carries the body to a circle of rocks and lays him down. Then he digs a shallow grave at the center and buries the boy, covering him with a thin layer of soil and patting the mound before departing. The boy's shoes stick out from the dirt.

Back in his house, Spencer, dirty and distraught, sits on the couch, staring blankly ahead. His tie is undone; the top buttons of his shirt are open. Nadia enters, now wearing a white blouse, her makeup still smeared from crying. She berates him, but he remains unresponsive. Finally, he looks up, revealing only the whites of his eyes. Something is wrong. Nadia, alarmed, backs away and runs for the landline. Shaking, she dials—but Spencer appears behind her. He grabs and spins her around, then stabs her repeatedly with an ice pick: first in the chest, then the stomach. She collapses, though still alive. Blood seeps through her white blouse as she struggles to crawl away. Each desperate grip of the carpet is futile. Spencer plants his foot on her calf, grinding it in and forcing her bone toward the floor. She is pinned. Finally, Spencer leans down and stabs her in the lower back.

One solid thrust—and she goes limp. The weapon protrudes from her body, its skull-shaped handle unmistakable: the Silence Ice Pick.

Under pale moonlight, Spencer carries Nadia's corpse to the cemetery. But this is no funeral. He brings her to the circle of rocks, places her at its center, and looks up to the sky, screaming over his wife's bloodied body. Then, as he did before, he digs a shallow grave and buries her, patting the mound when finished. Her head remains partially visible, a grim echo of her son's earlier burial.

Spencer returns home again—this time, he sits on the floor, not the couch. Something has changed in him. He's unraveling. He hears voices, sees visions of children in animal masks dancing in a circle. Two shadows appear at the doorway: a mother and child. A pair of small hands opens a black box lined with red velvet, revealing a sharpened scalpel.

Moments later, Nadia and their son enter the room, still wearing the outfits they were buried in. Her white blouse is bloodstained; the boy wears a white shirt and a black bow tie. Spencer recognizes them. A smile creeps across his face—until he notices their black eyes, their zombie-like appearance.

Spencer crawls toward his son, hoping to embrace him one last time. The boy approaches slowly. As Spencer leans in, the boy raises the scalpel and slashes his father's throat. Thick, dark-red blood pours from Spencer's neck and sputters from his mouth. He looks up, raising his hands in a desperate plea. Moments later, he collapses.

The undead boy and his mother drag Spencer's body to the same burial ground and cover him with dirt. He will join them now.

The band continues to play. The masked children continue to dance. There is something ritualistic—something ancient—about both. Soon after, Spencer and his undead family walk slowly through the graveyard, their fatal injuries still visible. They stop before three graves and stare down.

We see what they see: three headstones, side by side—Louis (Spencer), Rachel (Nadia), and Gage Charnas—all dead within one day of each other: July 28–29, 2001.

The video paused, and Captain Harris pulled the tape out of the VCR's slot, slamming it down on the pile of other videos they had previously recovered from Spencer's home. Kent could sense the tension in the air—Harris was clearly disturbed by the tape they had just watched.

"Killing an innocent woman is one thing," Harris began. "It's another thing to rip off the King. That is fucking sacrilege."

"Elvis? Didn't he die on the toilet?" said Dunbar, half joking.

"No. Stephen King, you asshole," corrected Kent. "That was literally Pet Sematary." The detectives all turned to look at her, clearly wondering how she knew so much about the subject. "What?" she said haughtily. "So I watch the occasional horror film. Sue me."[21]

Some detectives laughed at Kent's remark; others snorted. Finally, Harris spoke up. "All right, all right. This asshole is going to walk, and all we've got is a pile of fucking videotapes that mean nothing."

"Sorry we couldn't have dug up more on this guy," said Nordberg sadly. He was standing in the back of the room, having just returned from calling Carlos' office to request that Spencer's lawyer come down to the precinct.

"We should have dug deeper," added Dunbar.

"Yeah, well, 'coulda, shoulda' does fuck all for this case," snapped Harris. He glared at Kent as he added, "Nordberg, wait for this guy's lawyer out front. I can't question Spencer without him."

---

21 Kent's taste for horror films dates back to her college days, when a friend who had been a victim of a serious violent crime began using such films as a form of immersion therapy. Some say this was also the genesis of Kent's legal career. Regardless, her taste in films often centered around stronger female characters, from *I Spit on Your Grave* to *Scream* to *Jennifer's Body*.

Harris sat back down in his chair as Kent watched him pretend to sift through the files. She worried the captain might not be up to such a case—or that he might be digging himself deeper into a hole out of which he would fail to emerge. Candidly, she worried he might be willing to go too far, too eager to cross the uncrossable line and stretch beyond the barrier that separated criminals from the law. This was a line she had never dared to blur, but she didn't know if the same was true for Harris. She did, however, know that Harris had a moral compass that seemed to perpetually point in the wrong direction.

She would have to reorient him.

"Didn't the M.E. say they found bite marks on the body?" asked Kent, pushing for more info on the investigation. "Did you check with the lab on that?"

"We took his impressions an hour ago, just waiting to see if it was his teeth. Look, we need something on this guy," Harris said, seemingly trying to buck up his troops—or look busy for the DA. "We need to talk to his mother, his father, his priest, his…fucking little league coach. We need some dirt."

Nordberg poked his head back into the room. "Captain?"

Harris looked up, and Nordberg fully entered.

"His lawyer's here," he added, then left the room again.

Harris sighed and turned back to his other detectives. "Great. Now I get to talk to these assholes, and all I've got is my dick in my hand."

"Lovely," added Kent, rolling her eyes. "I'm going to watch from the hallway. I prefer not to face the defendants unless we're in court."[22]

---

22 As the account of this meeting is from Kent's pulled-from-the-shelves book, it can be inferred she was covering here. Had she written a truthful account, it would have mentioned that early in her career she had a brief affair with a married defendant, whom she met in the waiting area of a police station. He was there for questioning. Later, she was blindsided when he showed up in court. Her blatant attraction to him, and her memories of their tryst, eventually cost her the case. So much for a "moral compass."

She turned on the heel of her sensible black shoe and left the room.

Kent watched from the two-way mirror as Captain Harris entered the interrogation room, leaving the door open behind him. Seated at the metal table in the center of the room was Spencer, wearing a white T-shirt and black jeans, just as he had in the video. His hair was slicked back, as always. Next to Spencer was his lawyer, Carlos Cochran, who seemed out of breath from the hasty arrival prompted by Nordberg's phone call. Carlos' black suit and briefcase made him look more like a funeral director than a lawyer.

In the corner stood an officer on post for everyone's protection after escorting Spencer from his holding cell.

Harris slowly approached the table. When hunting his prey, he appeared to not go straight in for the kill but rather to briefly toy with his target first. He held a few items in his hand, which Spencer and his lawyer could not immediately make out given the bright lights facing them in contrast to the darkness where Harris stood.

"Some pretty sick shit there, Spencer. Almost as good as a confession, if you ask me." He pulled his chair close, until he was inches from the suspect.

"Yeah, well, nobody's asking you," Carlos chimed in, leaning forward. "Now, my client here has been nothing but cooperative, so if you intend on charging him, I suggest you get your dick out of your hand and do so."

"Cooperative? Why not just give me a confession?"

"The only confession my client is going to be giving is to his priest," Carlos shot back.

Outside the room, Kent turned to Dunbar—both had been listening in.

"Wait," she said, puzzled. "Aren't they a Jewish metal band?"[23]

---

23 Spencer is, in fact, a loosely affiliated member of the Jewish faith, despite what his tattoos would otherwise have you think. As a frequent attendee of AIPAC, I can tell you

Dunbar only shrugged.

Back at the table, Carlos continued, "You look like you could use some confession yourself."

Harris, clearly frustrated, had no response. Instead he gave Carlos the finger—a blatant display of unprofessionalism.

Taken aback but unwilling to yield ground, Carlos did the same.

Spencer broke the tension by offering his own thoughts. "I'm on your side, Captain. I loved her." He stared at Harris, catching him off guard.

Rarely did an actual killer seem so earnest, Kent thought from outside. Perhaps this was simply a gifted artist covering his tracks.

"I want to catch the real killer as much as you do," Spencer continued.

Carlos patted his client's back. "See? More cooperation. Have you even thought for a second that this might be a deranged fan? I mean, shit, they've got hordes of them." He gestured to Spencer. "For Christ's sake, they call themselves the 'Psycos.' Is that something you came up with?" he asked his client directly. "Is it like a PR thing?"

Spencer only nodded, seemingly pleased with the phrase.

Kent had to admit—"Psycos" was clever, even if it was deranged.

"Well, you must be very, very proud of that, Spencer," Harris said sarcastically.

Spencer paused before stating solemnly, "No fan of ours would ever do this."

"Yeah, you know what?" Carlos said, seizing on the moment. "You're right. But maybe a disgruntled ex-band member. He's had

---

with certainty, I have never seen anyone of his sort present at what I deem to be the "most wonderful time of the schmear."

to fire quite a few." He was pivoting, and Kent took note. This was what she'd be up against in court.

Harris sat back in his chair, rolling his eyes. "Ah, you mean, like, maybe a drummer? Like the geezer butler did it?" Harris' love for classic detective stories and their ridiculous tropes was on full display.

"Like a guitar player or a fucking flute player?" retorted Carlos. "Can we stick to what we're doing here?"

"Answer me this," Harris said, raising his hands for silence. "If you're so fucking lily white, how come you were covered in your fiancées blood?"

"Don't answer that, Spencer," said Carlos, not losing eye contact with Harris.

Harris tried a new tactic. "Okay, so, the killer's wearing your mask. What do they call it—the Silence? How do you explain that?"

"They sell that mask at every five-and-dime in the country," replied Spencer.

"Are you kidding me?!" scoffed Carlos. "What do you live under a rock? It's on a giant billboard on Sunset Boulevard! This is a classic copycat. And you know what else? We're done here. You've got about eight hours, Captain. The clock is ticking. Tick tock. So make your case or fucking move on."

Harris approached Spencer, sticking out his hand to offer a shake. "Thank you for your cooperation," he said, his tone disarmingly friendly.

Spencer reluctantly accepted.

Harris suddenly tightened his grip and pulled Spencer toward him.

Kent let out a small, but audible gasp from the hallway.

"Bite impressions are coming back, and I'll bet my Lakers tickets they're yours."

Kent watched the whole thing but didn't intervene.

"Excuse me!" yelled Carlos. "You want to let go of my client?" He stepped between them, breaking their contact.

"Good luck with those impressions," Spencer said flatly, impressing Kent with his cool demeanor. If he did it, he had to have ice running through his veins.

Carlos turned to Harris "Really?" He seemed appalled that an officer sworn to uphold the law could act so brazenly toward a suspect.

Kent herself was equally stunned, but she didn't want to show anybody on Harris' team how she felt; it was as if she were taking a page out of Spencer's own playbook. She had just watched as an officer of the law nearly assaulted a suspect and expected to get away with it. After the trial, she would file a report and hopefully let the chain of command work as it was supposed to, but for now, she was beholden to him and his investigative team. As hotheaded as Harris appeared, Spencer seemed equally unflappable to her, showing little emotion whether he was under pressure or otherwise. This must have been the first moment she thought it was possible that he didn't kill out of anger, as they had assumed, but had instead done it for some other reason.[24] Maybe Spencer was so dead inside that he wanted to make other people feel like he did? Kent was certain he had murdered his fiancée, but now wondered if there had been more. Perhaps he was a serial killer who liked the sport of it.[25] Whatever it may be, she was dismayed at what she had just watched. It began as an interrogation but had rapidly turned into a set of new questions for which she hadn't the first idea of how to

---

24 Kent's state of mind, as hinted at in her book and private notes, has been debated across various news media outlets. However, despite what my dear friend and colleague Geraldo Rivera has suggested, she was not, as we can tell, sleeping with Spencer, Harris, Dunbar, or Cochran at this time. Geraldo is perhaps defaulting too much to his own mindset as a former *daytime* talk show host.

25 For legal reasons, I am no longer allowed to refer to Spencer as a "serial killer" but do wish to make it known that at this point DA Kent mused that he *might* be.

answer. One thing she knew for sure. This case was going to get a lot more complicated.

"Are the cuffs necessary?" Carlos asked, feigning disgust.

"Oh yeah," said Harris. "And make it fucking tight."

Kent cringed as she heard the metallic clink echo into the hallway.

"You're such a prick," Carlos said, adding to Spencer as they walked away, "It's alright. I'll have you out of here quickly. Trust me."

Harris sat back down at the interrogation table. He was alone. Kent watched, unsure if she should enter. She wanted to scream at him. Instead, she stayed quiet.

Perhaps she needed him too much.

Perhaps she was beginning to bend the law herself.

Whatever the reason, this moment marked an inflection point in her career.

"Fuck..." Harris muttered.

He was soon interrupted by a young female officer. Kent would later learn her name was Ellie Gage.

"These just came in, Captain," said Gage, handing him a small white bag. "Figured you'd want to see them right away."

Harris opened the bag.

"Are these the bite impressions?" he asked.

She nodded.

He pulled out a set of teeth cast in clay, followed by another set—Lambert's. He held both to the light.

Kent watched from the doorway. Even to her untrained eye, they were identical.

"Yes!" Gage said. "Perfect match."

Harris looked up at her, noticing Kent in the doorway for the first time.

Kent resisted the urge to call back Carlos and Spencer. They'd need an expert to confirm the match first.

Still, this changed everything.

"We can get us a bit more if we really root around this guy's life," said Harris, speaking past Gage and toward Kent.

Kent nodded. "I'll get on that." She smiled.

As Harris drummed on the table, Kent wondered: Was this the partner she wanted through a trial? The question haunted her as she made her way to the courthouse to get the warrant.

VII
Rainy Day

LA was getting more rain in one week than it typically experienced in an entire year; El Niño was in full force. Kent's BMW cut through the relentless onslaught that beat down on her windshield, the weak wipers barely able to whisk the water away as fast as it fell. She was simultaneously attempting to follow her GPS and keep her eyes on the winding road that rose up the dangerous hill before her. Taking the incline a touch too fast had already resulted in a couple of close calls and near misses—first with a stone wall, then with a raccoon that had darted across the road. Finally, after avoiding any further brush with death from a fall into the awaiting mouth of the canyon below, she made one last acute switchback turn and arrived at her destination.

Kent double-checked her notes against the number on the retaining wall that lined the residential property, then pulled into a spot across the steep road from the house. The rain continued to pelt down on her car, forcing her to brace herself before attempting to exit. The storm had become even stronger than it had been during her drive. Kent never carried an umbrella in her meticulously cleaned vehicle—she felt that in Los Angeles, doing so seemed about as useful as a hole in the head. The weather was usually predictable...until it wasn't. She reached over to the seat beside her and picked up a folded piece of paper, stuffing it into her jacket. A search warrant.

She took one last look through the driver's side window toward the reason she had ventured out in such anomalous weather. There before her, up a steeply inclined walkway, was Spencer's mansion.[26]

Kent used her briefcase to shield her head from the downpour as she crossed the street toward the Spanish-style home. The elegant stucco walls and red-tiled roof seemed to blend perfectly with the lush surroundings at the top of the hill in this exclusive neighborhood. Everywhere the eye turned was green—a sharp contrast to the usual brown of the dry ravines that lined the street. Spencer's home contributed much of the visible vegetation: trees and shrubs in the front, a courtyard garden on the side, and ivy crawling up most of the rounded walls, woven into the wrought-iron window coverings. At least something was benefitting from all this rain, Kent thought. But, as everyone in LA knows, more plant growth meant more fuel when fire season began; the rain was a harbinger of horror for those who paid attention.

"Hey!" a voice called from behind her. Another detective? she wondered.

"He's a good kid," the man continued. She turned to see a friendly-looking Armenian man across the street, standing under an overhang.

"Just doing my job!" she hollered back, trying to shout over the constant drumming of the rain.

"I hope whatever you're looking for helps you see that deep down, Spencer isn't the man you think he is," the man shouted,

---

26 I'm using her word "mansion" here, despite understanding that the home was not the "Hollywood mansion" someone might expect when reading this description. While Kent may think differently on a DA's salary, Spencer's house is in fact a modestly large piece of property. I myself, being an accomplished and internationally renowned journalist, have certainly seen bigger.

then sarcastically added, "Good luck with your search," before returning to the shelter of his house.

Whatever notion she had of Spencer, locating anyone who had anything bad to say about him had proven difficult, if not impossible. Kent shook off the interruption and turned back toward the house. She quickly found shelter under a large, covered walkway, where she could get a closer look at the mansion. She had to admit, Spencer was doing something right with this place. Very impressive. She marveled further as her wet shoes sloshed against the soft stone of the walkway, stepping gingerly to avoid the small puddles that had formed.

Officer Leon Wesker—clean-cut, all-American—and Officer Rebecca Ashford, with short brown hair and a medium build, watched as Kent struggled to reach the house. What struck her immediately was how young they looked. Wesker was barely out of the academy, she reasoned, and Ashford not much older. Both held large military-grade weapons; they looked practically like child soldiers. She often lamented the newfound militancy of the police force, but saying so publicly would have given others fodder to accuse her of being soft on crime—a potential career-ender.

"Looks like you forgot your umbrella," said Wesker, affably. "Pretty big storm out there."

"Thanks for the weather update, officer," Kent replied. "What happened? Meteorology school wouldn't take you, so you had to become a cop?" Her attempt at a joke fell flat. She shifted from one heel to the other as she saw Wesker's grip on his rifle tighten.

"Jeez. I was just trying to make conversation," Wesker mumbled.

"Sorry. Yeah. It's been a day," she replied, apologetically.

"He's already inside," Ashford offered.

"Who is?" Kent asked, though she had a sinking feeling she knew the answer.

"Harris," Ashford confirmed. "He said you'd be coming with the warrant." She pointed toward the door, as if that somehow justified whatever Harris and his team were doing inside. "He told us it was okay."

"He shouldn't have done that, and you shouldn't have let him," Kent said tersely. She shot the officers a pained smile, attempting to reconnect after realizing her shortness with them was just misdirected anger at Harris. "It's fine. Just let me in."

Ashford stepped aside as Wesker opened the door. Kent took a few timid steps into the foyer. Behind her, the door creaked and slammed shut, cutting off the sound of the rain and leaving her in the silence of the large house.

She crossed the marble floor, feeling uneasy. She usually didn't conduct investigations of this kind—and never alone. She wasn't even sure what they were looking for, but she hoped that entering Spencer's world might help the case. Maybe she, or the detectives, would have some kind of epiphany in the accused murderer's lair.

Suddenly, from deep inside the house, she heard the clanging of items being thrown around and faint swearing. Harris, she concluded. She followed the noise into a living area to her right.

The walls of Spencer's large living room were adorned with elements from every horror film imaginable—an impressive collection, especially for someone who enjoyed horror as much as Kent. Frames and glass cases displayed bloodied T-shirts, prop weaponry, and a mélange of masks—some so obscure even she didn't recognize them. Using the investigation as an excuse, she spent the last two nights revisiting some classic horror films, but Spencer's house felt like an expertly curated museum. Her eyes settled on a screen-used knife from Scream—a favorite of hers. Her fingers ran over the case, lingering until a voice startled her.

"Stars—they're really not just like us..."

It was Harris. She turned and met his eyes, quickly withdrawing her hands.

He had entered from another door. In addition to the second entrance, the back wall held a large, mounted flat-panel television. A wraparound leather couch sat in front of it, separating the entertainment side from the museum-like side. Spencer's own private screening room, Kent reasoned.

"What part of 'wait for me with the warrant' didn't you understand?" Kent snapped.

"Easy," said Harris, holding up his hands. "We just figured we'd get a head start on the inevitable." As if on cue, Dunbar and Detective Malcolm Cortado entered the room from the same door Harris had used.

Kent glared at the three men, eyes landing on Dunbar. He held what looked like a broken fertility icon, which he clumsily tried to hide.

"And now you break things?" she said to Harris, gesturing at Dunbar. "What if I hadn't gotten the warrant?"

"Then I'd say you're doing a pretty shitty job lawyering," Harris retorted. "You did get it though, right?"

"That's not the point," Kent said, pulling out the envelope. "You can't enter a suspect's home without it in hand. Those officers should never have let you in."

"Tweedledee and Tweedledummer out there?" Harris joked. "Don't blame me for their ignorance of the law."

"Ignorance of the law is no defense," Dunbar offered.

"Shut up, Dunbar!" Harris and Kent both spoke in unison, silencing their colleague.

Kent noticed a bookshelf along the back wall filled with videotapes—relics of the past, meaningful only to diehard horror fans. "You check here yet?" she asked, gesturing.

"Yeah. A quick sweep. Why?" Harris replied, already suspecting they'd missed something.

She walked over and thumbed through titles: Halloween, A Nightmare on Elm Street (parts 1–6, plus non-canon), The Burning, Tourist Trap. Her hand stopped on a handwritten label: "Rainy Day" – Ice Nine Kills (rough cut).

She held it up. "Think this might be something, Captain?"

"Are you sure that was there before?" he grumbled, defeated. He took the tape and bagged it, failing to question how she'd found it so easily.

Just then, a familiar voice called from the foyer: "Getting to what, Captain?" It was Carlos, entering the room.

Kent stepped between the two men. "Before you start, we have a warrant."

"We know," Carlos said, holding up his phone. Spencer appeared on a video call. "He just wanted to make sure everything was done by the book—or film." He gestured to the bagged tape in Harris' hand.

Spencer's voice echoed off his own stucco walls: "Good evening, Captain. Welcome to my humble abode."

"Why is he on the phone with you? He should be in our lockup!" Harris bellowed—to Carlos, his detectives, or anybody who would listen.

"One of your guys said he could have phone privileges, on account of the search," Carlos replied.

"Nordberg…" Harris growled through gritted teeth. His anger was palpable.

Before Harris could say more, Kent interjected, "I think we can handle it from here, Counselor." She surprised even herself with her knee-jerk defense of Harris. "Why don't you go wait in the hall?"

"No, I think I—we—are okay right here," Carlos responded, not breaking eye contact with Harris. "We'll make sure nothing gets tampered with. Wouldn't want you to taint any precious evidence by pulling a Mark Fuhrman. Right, Captain?"

Captain Harris bristled at the accusation. He had worked with Mark Fuhrman prior to his famous fuckup[27] during the O.J. trial and had once publicly referred to him as an "upstanding officer of the law." Perhaps Harris was the only one who still felt that way.[28]

Harris stared at Carlos for a few seconds, then turned to Dunbar and Cortado. "Come on. Grab those other two officers out there. Let's tear this place apart."

He stormed past Carlos and Kent, rage and revenge in his eyes. Whether Carlos was aware of his limited ability to stop the search or was simply afraid of Harris' wrath, the attorney made no move to interfere with the detectives and their mission.

An hour later, Kent stood in the middle of what had become a thoroughly ravaged home. Harris and the others had rifled through everything they could get their hands on, usually leaving it dumped, splattered, scattered, or strewn across the floor. At some point, Nordberg and Movery had arrived, adding manpower to the effort. Harris used the opportunity to scream at Nordberg over his soft spot for suspects.

Kent had also overheard part of an exchange between Harris and Carlos regarding the bite mark evidence. She'd tried to insert

27 There really is no other word for this series of events.

28 To this day, Fuhrman denies ever knowing Harris. If the former's name has become synonymous with corruption in the LAPD, Harris' has somehow become synonymous with something worse.

herself into the conversation but had only caught that Carlos planned to argue the marks were the result of a consensual sexual act—rendering them inadmissible on the grounds of being prejudicial to Spencer's character. If the bite marks were ruled circumstantial, as Carlos clearly intended, then Kent would end the day farther from her goal of finding any damning evidence. Despite the thorough—and highly destructive—search, nothing had been gained. The tape Kent had discovered remained the only major break. She hoped it contained something more directly connected to the case than any of the previous videos. At this point, nothing less would suffice.

Once the house had been sufficiently searched, the detectives and attorneys gathered by the front entrance. Kent agreed to meet Harris and his team at the station to view the newly found videotape. She had briefly considered suggesting they use Spencer's own screening room but thought better of it—giving Carlos any opportunity to argue for exclusion would be reckless.

Harris led the way to the door. Kent, who had spent the search avoiding Carlos out of embarrassment over Harris' behavior, flashed the opposing counsel a pained smile before following Harris out. As she turned back to give Carlos this small conciliatory gesture, she suddenly stopped short. She had nearly walked into Harris' back—he had come to an abrupt halt.

Had he found something?

Kent followed his gaze to an umbrella stand by the door. It held three umbrellas: two black, and one with red and white stripes. Harris picked up one of the black umbrellas and handed it to Dunbar.

"Whoops, almost forgot this guy," Dunbar said with a chuckle, immediately popping it open in the hallway and then struggling to fit it through the doorway.

Harris picked up the red-and-white-striped umbrella next and inspected it, settling his hand on the handle. Kent leaned in.

"Property of Splinter Props," she read aloud. "Splinter? It's just S-P-L-N-T-R. Spelled funny."

Carlos' voice called from the other end of the hall. "Spencer usually keeps items from his video shoots. I believe that's from—"

" 'Rainy Day'," Kent interrupted, remembering the tape she had found—the one now in the pocket of Harris' raincoat. "Trophies, huh? Sounds like something a serial killer might do."

"I wouldn't go that far," said Carlos. "More like mementos."

Harris grabbed the umbrella from Kent's hands before turning to Carlos.

"Tell you what," he said. "Why don't I go ahead and keep this, then? As a…mementos."

With that, he walked out of the house. Kent looked back at Carlos, as if trying to excuse her colleague's behavior. She knew, however, that nothing could truly make up for Harris' lack of decorum. And she worried—again—that if he continued on this path, she might lose the entire trial.

The rain had finally let up, allowing Kent to focus less on the road and more on the case as she drove back to the squad room. She thought about Harris—what he was contributing, and whether he might be doing more harm than good. After all, she had been the only one to find anything useful during the entire search. She could do this alone. She didn't need his help—or, as it increasingly felt, his interference.

These thoughts turned over and over in her mind until she reached police headquarters, where a new distraction awaited: the attorney and the detectives gathering once more to dive into another of Spencer's videos.

Lightning strikes behind a large, angular glass-and-steel building that looms over the concrete jungle below. Above the entrance is a logo of a red-and-white umbrella, a red drip of blood hanging from it. The umbrella's handle is an upside-down skull with a Roman numeral IX on its forehead.

A scream echoes across the landscape as four medical professionals in white coats and black surgical masks urgently wheel a stretcher toward the building's entrance. From afar, the patient atop the stretcher can be seen writhing against some form of restraint.

Once inside, the patient is rushed down a fluorescent-lit hallway, screaming and wriggling. The doctors struggle to restrain her—and eventually succeed.

In another room, a single eye opens, first staring at the ceiling, then surveying its surroundings. The eye belongs to Nadia, dressed in a tight-fitting, all-black outfit: jeans, a tank top, and heavy black boots. She lies on a gurney, hooked up to various machines monitoring her vitals. Plastic curtains surround her like some kind of biohazard experiment. In an adjacent room, researchers and doctors observe her through a camera. One leans toward a microphone and utters a single, monotone word: "Run."

Suddenly, a female zombie with wild red hair, peeling skin, and a mouth smeared with blood bursts into the room. Screaming, she rushes Nadia. In a burst of adrenaline, Nadia breaks through her restraints, jumps off the gurney, and tries to flee. The zombie swats aimlessly, but Nadia pushes the wheeled bed into her assailant and escapes the room.

She enters an office space filled with empty cubicles. Flickering lights reveal unconscious researchers—some slumped over desks, others sprawled on the floor. Crawling down the narrow hallway between cubicle walls, she hides under a desk. The zombie enters, hot on her trail. Nadia covers her mouth, turning away to muffle her breathing. She looks toward the entrance and, for a moment, the zombie is gone. Relief washes over her—until she turns back around.

The zombie is right there.

It lunges. Nadia scrambles from the cubicle into the open. The creature follows, leaping onto her and swinging wildly. Nadia spots a pair of scissors on the floor, grabs them, and stabs the zombie in the side of the face. The creature falls. Nadia rolls, leaps to her feet, then straddles the zombie, jabbing the scissors again and again into its decaying flesh. With each thrust comes a sickening squish and a splatter of blood. She stabs until the thing is undeniably dead. Re-dead.

Exhausted, she collapses beside it.

After only a moment of respite, two more zombies appear—men in plaid shirts with rotting faces. They lumber toward her. Nadia jumps up and runs in the opposite direction, ducking into another cubicle where she finds an automatic machine gun. She picks it up, unsure at first, then emerges—only to face another zombie. This one wears a white lab coat and feasts on a corpse. His own flesh hangs in ragged patches from his skull.

Horrified, Nadia freezes—until the plaid-shirted zombies spot her. She fires. Bullets tear through their chests, and they collapse. As she turns to flee, the lab-coat zombie snarls, teeth bared.

Nadia runs toward the office exit, but another zombie blocks her path. This one wears a bag over its head, blue overalls, and wields a large chainsaw. She unloads a few rounds into its chest and bolts through another exit, pursued now by both the bag-headed monster and the lab-coated one.

She sprints down a long hallway, turning periodically to fire at her pursuers. The gun clicks—empty. She tosses it aside and keeps running. At last, she bursts through a glass door and bars it shut with a metal rod found nearby. She stands in a red-lit room, a flickering television screen casting eerie shadows. Only one exit remains: a metal door with a keypad.

Nadia rushes to it, punching in numbers at random. Denied. Again. Denied.

Behind her, the glass door shatters.

Zombies pour into the room. She's trapped. When all hope seems lost, the keypad beeps, and the door swings open.

Spencer enters, machine gun drawn.

He mows down the horde methodically, dark red blood splattering the walls. The lab-coated and bag-headed zombies enter last, but by then Spencer's out of bullets. He pulls a pistol from his flak jacket and fires multiple rounds into the lab-coated one's shoulder. It doesn't go down.

He grabs Nadia, and together they flee through the metal door.

Down another dim hallway they run, Spencer firing behind them. He eventually drops both remaining zombies. The pair reaches the building's front entrance and another coded keypad preventing them from the safety of the outside world. Spencer punches in the code—2-9-4. The screen flashes:

ACCESS GRANTED.

As they celebrate, Nadia notices a large gash on Spencer's arm. She grabs his wrist. Blood oozes from the wound.

They lock eyes.

His expression shifts.

Red lines creep across his temples. His mouth twists unnaturally. His body bends and contorts in ways that no longer seem human.

Spencer is changing.

Nadia backs away, drawing the pistol from his holster. He stares at her, eyes white. She shakes her head in disbelief. This is not the man who just saved her. She knows what she must do—yet hesitates.

Then, she fires.

Spencer flies backward, hits the wall, and crumples. Lifeless.

Nadia pushes through the now-unsecured glass door and runs into the night.

Outside, she gasps for breath. The same entrance where doctors once wheeled her in now serves as her exit. Before she can take another breath or mourn what she's done—

Spencer leaps from the shadows and bites into her neck.

Nadia falls, dead.

Almost instantly, the building spills more zombies into the streets. Spencer looks to the sky and unleashes a war cry, blood dripping from his mouth.

The undead descend on Nadia and feast on her flesh.

All goes quiet.

Then: static…

Harris pulled the tape from the VCR and slammed it down. Kent had realized early in the viewing that there was little on the tape they hadn't already seen, and she knew it would incense Harris. She was disappointed herself, despite believing in the case. Since she'd been the one to find the tape, she had sincerely hoped it contained something of value.

"Eight hours until he's back on the street, and all we've got is another fucking videotape?!" Harris hollered. Kent had predicted this. His patience was nearly nonexistent at this point in the investigation.

"The fiancée dies in this tape too, doesn't she?" asked Nordberg, trying to look on the bright side.

"Well, yeah—by a rabid pack of fuckin' zombies, but not by him," Harris said dismissively. Kent hated to admit it, but this tape would do little to move the case forward. In fact, it might only bolster Carlos' theory that the bite marks were part of a sexual act. There was something sensual about the way Spencer sank his teeth into Nadia's neck. Kent found herself uncomfortably intrigued.

"Guess that's why they call it a viral video," said Dunbar, always one to crack a joke. A mix of groans and laughter filled the room. "Wait. Is that why?" he added, genuinely pondering the logic. Then he held a closed fist to his temple and opened his fingers in an explosive gesture. "Mind. Blown." He sat in silence for a moment, processing the thought.

Kent seized the opportunity to steer the discussion. "The bite marks matched, but you heard his lawyer," she said, knowing full well they would no longer hold weight in front of a judge or jury—but hoping, nonetheless, to draw more from Harris' earlier conversation with Carlos, which she hadn't been privy to.

"Foreplay. Yeah. He's a kinky motherfucker," Harris said. Some of the detectives in the room hadn't heard this detail, and their faces sagged in defeat.

"It was the icepick that did her in. Three stabs to the chest, two in the stomach," said Nordberg, matter-of-factly.

"Yeah, but it was the one in the back that killed her," Dunbar added casually.

"I've heard this all before. I don't want to rehash it. You guys did a good job, but get the fuck out of my sight, okay?" Harris replied. Then, looking directly at Dunbar, he added, "You especially. Your jokes are really terrible."

"Humor is subjective," Dunbar mumbled, dejected, then slinked out of the room, shoulders slumped.

Kent stayed, watching as Harris paced. She decided not to leave—at least not yet. There was a nagging feeling inside her that these videos were connected. They felt important somehow. Almost like a confession—clear and yet somehow elusive. Maybe that's why Harris is so obsessed with them, she thought.

She also considered whether now might be the time to ask Harris to take a step back from the investigation. The thought scared her, but his behavior had warranted such a conversation—and more—given all that had happened.

After a few rounds of pacing, Harris began mumbling to himself. "Three stabs to the chest…Three in the chest, two to the stomach… The back…" There was a rhythm to the way he said it—almost catchy. Kent watched as he looked at Lambert's case files spread across the table.

"Three in the chest, two in the stomach, one in the back," he repeated. "Three in the…" He paused, eyes fixed on the static filling the old television screen. And then his face lit up.

Harris moved quickly. He grabbed another tape—"Funeral Derangements"—and replaced "Rainy Day" in the VCR. He picked up the remote and slid a chair closer to the television. Kent, sensing he was onto something, moved behind him.

He rewound the tape to the moment Spencer kills Nadia, skipping past the graveyard scenes and band shots. Finally, he landed on the frame where Spencer, possessed by something from beyond, uses an icepick to kill her. The same weapon used in the actual murder. Three stabs to the chest, two to the stomach, one in the back.

He watched it a second time. Then a third. "Three in the chest, two in the stomach, one in the back," he murmured again.

Kent saw it. Harris saw it. And in that moment, they both realized what they had found—the smoking gun. Or icepick, as it were.

This was enough. Enough to destroy Spencer's case. Enough to get an indictment. Maybe she had underestimated her partners' old-school detective work after all.

"That motherfucker…" Harris said, giddy. A small laugh escaped as his face lit up. "Gotcha." He stared at the screen, now frozen.

Kent claims to have felt uneasy watching his excitement. Yes, they might finally be able to lock up a dangerous criminal—but it still led back to a young woman who was dead. This crime had a victim, and Harris seemed to have forgotten that.

For Kent, winning in court was only part of it. She had always seen herself as an advocate for the dead—a voice for the silenced. But Harris seemed concerned only with "getting" the rockstar killer.

She watched him, eyes glued to the paused video. Spencer's face filled the screen in a tight close-up, his chin lowered, only the whites of his eyes visible. A demonic image. An obvious killer.

Kent looked between Spencer and Harris. And for a fleeting moment, she wondered who was more dangerous. Spencer was the one accused of a brutal crime—but sometimes, she reminded herself, those who chase monsters are far more terrifying than the monsters themselves.

VIII
Hip to Be Scared

Tuesday morning brought a packed courthouse—but not solely on account of Spencer's hearing. Los Angeles County had experienced a wild crime spree over the weekend that continued into Monday, perhaps due to the rain finally lifting.[29] Uniformed officers stood at the doorways as women and men in business suits filed in and out of the courthouse alongside their usually less-well-dressed clients; it was often possible, just by assessing outfits, to determine who was defending whom. Appearances are everything in Los Angeles.

Kent, in a neatly pressed gray skirt suit, entered the building just as Harris sauntered up from the parking area. He was as disheveled as ever and certainly looked more criminal than cop. His loose-fitting brown suit and loud-patterned tie—a color that could only be described as "vomit adjacent"—made him look borderline ridiculous. Kent was embarrassed to sit beside him and considered making him move to the gallery with everyone else, if only to teach him a lesson about proper attire.

Behind Harris, his constant lackeys, Dunbar and Nordberg, struggled to keep up with his brisk pace. At least they had made the effort of wearing proper suits and ties, unlike Harris' monstrosity of an outfit. Kent noticed Ophelia was still missing. Last she heard,

29 Or the lawlessness of a democrat-run city. I try to not be political in these writings, but sometimes, it's just too easy. And with a DA like Marcie Kent, it's hard to avoid such a cheap shot, given that she made the penalty for shootings in LA so "inexpensive."

no one had seen or heard from her since the week prior, but the detectives had assured Kent they would continue looking into it over the weekend. Clearly, their search had not been as fruitful as the investigation into Spencer; the newly discovered match between the video and the real-life stab patterns was just the boost Kent had needed going into this pre-trial hearing.

The feeling was short-lived. After walking through security and taking her seat, Kent's confidence disappeared almost as quickly as it had arrived. She was again visited by the nagging feeling that something had been missed—overlooked. Staring straight ahead as the judge entered the courtroom, a mere twenty minutes after she had entered the building, Kent remained lost in thought. In Judge Reinhold's courtroom, early was on time and on time was late, and the judge always managed to begin earlier than early. Kent should have known this, but she was uncharacteristically caught off guard by his entrance.

Being lost in thought felt safer to Kent than what she would otherwise be doing: glancing over to the defense's side and potentially catching Spencer's eyes, as she had mistakenly done when she first entered the courtroom. There was something in those eyes that she felt might make her need to leave the room—or even the case—entirely. She calls it a gut feeling in her book, but, contrary to the hunches Captain Harris would get, Kent had finally admitted to herself that she didn't see Spencer as a killer. The feeling had slowly been developing throughout the case, but now she was better able to formulate the thoughts around it. Spencer was an artist. It was possible, of course, that the killing itself was his alternative art form, but she just didn't see it adding up.

This realization blindsided Kent so forcefully that she almost missed the bailiff asking everyone to rise and was late to get on her feet. Not a good start in Judge Reinhold's courtroom; he was, after all, a man who held decorum in the highest regard—even above punctuality.

Spencer was dressed in a sharp pin-striped suit that Kent thought made him look surprisingly handsome. She had always preferred the clean-cut look on men, as opposed to the usual leather and tattooed style Spencer was known to sport the few times she had seen him.[30] His ability to dress both tastefully and stylishly was not going to help her case with a jury—or with the judge, for that matter. She needed to depict him as dark and depraved, but his current appearance presented him as an upstanding member of society, far from either of those two adjectives. The suit looked to be straight out of Carlos' wardrobe. It may well have been sourced from that very place: the Cochran Collection, as one might call it.

Judge Reinhold began the proceedings by banging his gavel and taking a brief pause to read over the papers in front of him. Kent assumed it must be the submission she had spent all Monday putting together with a team of legal assistants. It was an exhaustive list of all the physical evidence against Spencer, as well as summaries of the theories of the case. It did not, however, include anything regarding the stab patterns. Kent kept that discovery close to the vest, to be used only if absolutely necessary. She claimed she was worried it was too circumstantial and wanted to ring that bell first in front of a jury, knowing it could not thereafter be unrung.

This decision—later criticized as a potential breach of ethics—could have made sense in the moment, given the abundance of evidence already available between the videos, the bite marks (even if they might be explained away), and the brutal nature of the killing. It should at least be enough for a trial, she thought, but had been

30 Marcie Kent's dating life has been kept extremely private. There was a short time in the mid-2010s when she was linked to soap opera star and former rocker, Ronn Moss. However, those allegations were unfounded and simply a result of Moss researching a role. She was also said to have dated a fellow trial attorney but broke up with him when they landed on opposite sides of a case. Work always came first…

caught off guard days before when Judge Reinhold seemed less than receptive to her arguments. She had hoped, perhaps rightfully, that the judge had simply wanted to leave for a Friday afternoon and that he would be less thorough in his analysis during this mid-week hearing, allowing her to glide smoothly towards a trial.

To further justify burying the stab-pattern evidence, Kent later wrote that it would also give the opposition a clue as to how she intended to proceed against Spencer. This would, in turn, give them far too much time to formulate a defense. She liked to catch opposing counsel back on the heels of his dress shoes whenever possible.

Harris, of course, was upset when Kent first explained this to him, but he became more receptive after hearing her reasoning. He would have to show a small amount of patience, but she assured him it would be worthwhile. She could tell he was excited by his discovery of the connection between the videos and the real-life murder, which she promised would soon see the light of day. Appealing to his sense of revenge for whatever Spencer had done to him, she also added that this would have a greater chance of embarrassing both the defendant and his attorney in open court. Harris seemed further satisfied; it was clear to Kent by now that he was mostly in this case for himself, and not for any kind of justice for Nadia.

When Reinhold looked up from his prolonged review of the brief, he addressed the room. "Now, I had some of these videos in front of me over the weekend for the first time," he began. "And not just your summaries, Mr. Cochran." He peered sternly at Carlos over his reading glasses. "As helpful as those were attempting to be, I feel they left out the despicable depravity that your client so gleefully displayed."

Kent couldn't help but smile. If they could move this judge, what could they do for a jury? she thought.

Reinhold looked down again, inhaled deeply, and continued, "I need no further evidence presented to me in order to say that this case can proceed to trial."

Spencer dropped his gaze to the floor in defeat, though his face showed little to no emotion. Kent noted his appearance and again envied how calm he remained amid the storm swirling around him. Carlos shook his head before patting his client's shoulder.

The judge motioned to a courtroom clerk standing on the side of the room with a wheeled cart preloaded with a television and VCR. The clerk pushed the cart to the center of the room as the judge continued. "I'm going to demonstrate here what I mean by that." He turned to the clerk. "Evelyn? Would you be so kind?"

Evelyn, the clerk, hit play on the VCR...

The music begins immediately as the video opens in a chic, monochromatic apartment with '80s-inspired décor and technology. The most salient piece of tech is a silver stereo system that occupies an entire upright cabinet on one side of the room. In the middle of the living room floor, Spencer performs a series of pushups wearing nothing but a pair of white boxer briefs and a cool-gel eye mask. In the rear corner of the room stands an '80s-style speaker connected to the stereo, next to a large fern; on the other side sits a plain white couch—"pale nimbus" being the exact hue of the fabric. A telescope rests on the coffee table. Spencer continues his

pushup routine as police sirens blare outside the window, filtered through vertical blinds.

A quick flash reveals a dead businessman with spiked blond hair lying on a floor draped in white sheets. His crisp blue shirt and suspenders are splattered with blood, and a pool of the same shade of red has formed around his head, soaking into the sheets and the newspapers below him.

In a black void, Spencer sings the opening of the song. Like the deceased man in the previous shot, he now wears a crisp blue pinstripe shirt and black suspenders, but adds a red tie, blue suit pants, and a gold watch. His hair is slicked back—the perfect image of a 1980s businessman. Gordon Gecko, if he were the frontman for a rock band.

Back in the living room, the half-clothed Spencer stands up from his pushups and walks toward a mirror. There, he finds another version of himself—wearing the same cool-gel eye mask but now also a full suit and blue tie. They stare at each other until the mirror version removes his eye mask, while the real Spencer does not. Soon, the mirror-Spencer is back in the black void. The full band is then shown performing in this same space, all dressed in various power suits, mostly in shades of blue.

Moments later, Spencer theatrically waves, and the scene shifts to a cocktail bar with the Roman numeral IX lit in a marquee-style fixture on the back wall. Spencer sits among a group of businessmen who exchange business cards in this overtly corporate setting. They lounge on sofas arranged around low, round tables as waitresses dance about, serving drinks. Spencer examines one individual's bone-colored business card with raised Silian Rail lettering and becomes enraged. He abruptly stands and walks away from the table, seeking out Nadia, one of the waitresses. She wears a black-and-white cocktail uniform featuring suspenders and a bow tie.

"Patrick, where are you going?" she asks with concern.

"I'm just leaving," he replies curtly, buttoning his suit coat.

"But why?" Nadia presses.

"I have to return some videotapes," he snaps, before walking out of the room.

Leaving the cocktail bar, Spencer enters a brightly lit bedroom with white paneled walls displaying black-and-white artwork. Nadia—now clad in lacy black lingerie—greets him from a large bed at the center of the room. Alongside her lounges a strawberry-blonde woman in white silk lingerie. Spencer's shirt is unbuttoned, and his suspenders hang at his sides. He moves toward a vintage camcorder stationed in the corner of the room, aimed at the bed. The two women strike various poses as he snaps glamour shots. His shirt is now fully removed, revealing a prominent "IX" tattoo inked on his shoulder. He directs the women as he switches the camera to video mode and films their seductive movements.

In another dark room, Spencer—again in boxer briefs—walks between two rows of bodies, bloodied and hung inside clear plastic garment bags. The bags line the walls on even racks. All of the bodies are clearly visible—men and women alike, all clad only in underwear.

Back in the bedroom, Nadia reaches down to form a sensual pose, only to raise her hand, now coated in blood. She recoils in horror, letting out a scream. The woman who had previously shared the bed now lies lifeless across it, a large gash marking her skull.

Nadia runs. She flees the bedroom and ends up among the hanging bodies in the plastic bags, unable to escape. Spencer arrives behind her carrying a chainsaw, and a chase ensues.

Before the scene can continue, the tone of the song changes to an upbeat '80s melody. In the black void, the band begins dancing and playing in a more pop-like manner. Meanwhile, Spencer is now back in his mostly white living room with the businessman from the opening—alive this time, and played by Jacoby Shaddix of Papa Roach. As the man lounges on the sofa, scotch in hand and drunkenness on his face, Spencer pops the collar of a clear plastic coverall worn over his suit and walks toward the stereo.

"Do you like Ice Nine Kills?" he asks.

"Not really," Jacoby replies drunkenly.

Spencer continues, "Their early work was a little too scene for me. But when The Silver Scream came out, I think they really came into their own—commercially and artistically." He dances across the room as he speaks. "The whole album has a refined melodic sensibility that really makes it a cut above the rest."

He has now positioned himself behind the businessman, near a large ax resting against the wall, which he eagerly picks up. He raises the weapon and calls out, "Hey, Paul!"

The businessman turns toward him—only to be met with an ax to the face. The song shifts to a much heavier tone as Spencer continues his frenzied assault. With each blow, he becomes more drenched in blood until his entire face and plastic coverall are saturated.

The scene shifts again: Spencer, now clean-faced, wearing a brown overcoat and fitted black driving gloves, makes a frantic phone call from a landline in the black void. His hair is mussed, his expression desperate. Other individuals in business attire circle him as he screams into the receiver. Is it a confession? Or a cry for help?

Back in the living room, the businessman's corpse sings from the floor. Blood seeps into the white sheets and newspaper now covering the surface. Spencer and his band continue to perform as the surrounding businesspeople dance in celebration of the slaughter…

As the static filled the screen and white noise overtook the courtroom, mumbles from the gallery began to rise. Reinhold banged his gavel to silence the room before continuing.

"Seeing is believing, Mr. Charnas. And I've seen enough." He shook his head and exhaled before launching into further remarks. "Now, I'm not saying that art is the basis for a judgment. But you yourself would have to admit that, in these videos, you come off as a pretty sick guy. This is the brand you've chosen and, unfortunately, in this case, that is not without consequence."

He paused briefly, then attempted a more relatable tone with an air of folksiness. "Look, you're not Huey Lewis or some clean-cut rocker guy, despite your appearance in my courtroom today." He gestured to Spencer and his attire. "I can understand that and put it aside without any sort of prejudice. But I also have to make sure that everybody has their day in court, including the poor victim in this case—whom I gather you loved very much, regardless of what may have happened."

Spencer looked up as soon as the judge mentioned Nadia. His mouth opened slightly, as if he were trying to speak. Reinhold didn't object, instead allowing Spencer some latitude to address the court.

"I still love her. I know in these videos my behavior can be... erratic sometimes. And the album, well—"

"I don't mean to offend you here, but do your fans actually go for this stuff?" Judge Reinhold interrupted. "I'm told you have a great deal of success. I'm just curious—among whom?"

"I assume you must have researched us in some way. No morbid curiosity got the better of you? You must know what kind of fans we have and how loyal they are."

"I know. I just wanted to know if you know," replied the judge.

"It's not just the fans. New York Matinee called our latest album 'a playful but mysterious little dish,'" Spencer replied matter-of-factly.

"Mysterious—I'll give them that. But this is in no way 'playful,'" the judge said sternly. "And for that reason, as far as this court is concerned, we're going to be looking at a trial."

"Your Honor," Carlos shouted, "there is an idea of Spencer Charnas that is out there. But it's all a façade, designed to evoke certain emotions in those who listen to his music and nothing more."

"Like it or not, counselor, my mind is made up," Reinhold responded. "You'll have your time to make these arguments during the trial." The judge looked at the opposing sides, nodding to each as if requiring their agreement—despite making it clear that he certainly did not. Spencer's head fell forward in defeat as the judge began to write something down.

Kent had enjoyed watching this back and forth. Despite Spencer's appearance and his attempts to seem like an upstanding member of society, an east coast elite, who wore blucher shoes and had graduated from a place like Yale, the master of the macabre had managed to reveal himself yet again. You can take the front man out of the metal band, she thought to herself. He was showing why he was so different from the average citizen; he certainly wasn't one to blend into a crowd. Would that also lead him to break society's greatest covenant by committing a murder? She still didn't have the answer. But Harris, by contrast, seemed to have no greater conviction than that of Spencer's guilt. As Carlos and the judge spoke, he had been giddily bouncing his leg up and down next to her. At one point, she abruptly slapped the side of his knee, calming the disturbance and forcing him to let out a small yelp before catching himself and settling down amidst the open court.

After finishing whatever notes he was making, Judge Reinhold looked up from his paper and continued. "Pursuant to California Penal Code, I'm ordering the accused be remanded." He then turned his attention to Spencer directly. "Mr. Charnas, I take it you have a lot of fans around this great big world, and I could certainly see that as pointing to you being a flight risk."

Carlos stood. "That's ridiculous, Your Honor!" Then, turning to his client: "We'll get you out of there, I assure you."

"One more outburst like that and I'll have you in there with him for contempt," said the judge sternly. "Don't test me, counselor."

Kent and Harris smiled, knowing they had won the day. Spencer would be locked up for the duration of the trial, hopefully making Harris' job easier—and putting the department at ease that he would be unable to kill again. Kent, for her part, knew it was a powerful position for a DA to have a defendant locked up.

"Your Honor, one request," Carlos interjected just before court was adjourned. "May I approach?"

Judge Reinhold nodded, and both sides approached the bench, standing a few feet below his elevated platform.

Carlos began in a whispered tone. "Your Honor, my client has numerous prior engagements, with a worldwide tour set to begin in two months. Locking him up will stifle his livelihood and his ability to provide for himself and his family."

"What family? He killed his family," Kent said sharply.

"Your Honor, come on," Carlos whined. "If she's going to be like this during the trial, I would ask that you seek her removal."

"He doesn't care about his client's ability to provide for himself. He only wants to make sure he gets his legal fees," Kent added slyly.

"That's beside the point," Carlos returned.

"When does that tour begin, counselor?" asked the judge, ignoring the tit for tat.

"The tour is in June, Your Honor. It will cover most of Europe as well as Latin America. It's a grueling few weeks, but the fans there are even more eager to see their favorite band than the American Psychos—I mean, fans. Sorry..." Carlos said, catching himself in an Ice Nine Kills–based colloquialism the judge might not appreciate.

"Counselor, your client is on trial for his life here," said the judge, peering over the bench. "If he's found guilty, there's no tour, no band, no anything. Do you understand me? If there is some kind of world tour happening, he is simply not there."

"Are you presuming my client's guilt, Your Honor?" asked Carlos.

"I'm not presuming anything. Tell you what. Counselors, would you be ready to start this thing beginning of next month? There's an opening on my calendar. Murder trial should be, what? Three? Four weeks? If you win, your client makes his tour. If not..." The judge declined to finish his sentence, merely shrugging at the implications.

Carlos looked to Kent, who shrugged as well.

"That would be acceptable, Your Honor," said Carlos confidently.

It was on. The trial would happen sooner than expected, and Kent was certain she would be victorious. The defense was gambling away its preparation time in the hopes of making a European tour. It was almost too easy. She was waiting for the other shoe to drop.

"There's just one more thing. The big tour is in June, but Spencer has a concert scheduled for a few weeks from now. It's my understanding that it would be an important international display of camaraderie. It's in conjunction with the Slovakian Consulate here in Los Angeles. Go figure that one. Apparently, the Slovaks really go crazy for Ice Nine Kills, and the ambassador in Washington, D.C., has a daughter who's a fan and lives out here for school. So, it would be close by. We'd just ask for a compassionate release for this show, given that it was planned months ago—long before my client ever thought he'd be framed for a murder." Carlos was trying to insert his argument wherever he thought possible.

"Did I not make myself clear?" asked the judge. "I feel as if my mask of sanity is slipping right now, counselor." He took a deep breath, creating a silence that hung over the courtroom—tension on every face in the gallery. "Look, if this is coming from higher up in the State Department, then get me the paperwork and we'll see what we can do. He'll need a court-appointed liaison and chaperone, so to speak. That means armed officers escorting him to and from the show. And there will need to be a representative from the DA's office as well. This is complicated—not to mention expensive—and he'll be the one paying for it. If I allow it."

"Understood, Your Honor," said Carlos, attempting to contain his glee. "I'll get you all the requisite documents." He flashed a smile at Kent, adding a taunting wink for good measure.

After receiving Carlos' gesture of ill will, Kent turned back to the judge. "I guess we're just letting murderers come and go as they please now?" Her tone shifted, though, as she continued, "As long as it's just this once and the paperwork is in order, we have no objections. I'll even go myself to make sure your client behaves." Kent saw an opportunity and took it. A chance to see Spencer in action. Maybe something in his shows would be of value to her. Or maybe these few hours of reprieve would be enough of a temptation during which he couldn't help but kill again. It was worth trying, even if she knew Harris would make it a point to attend as well.

"Well, if that's all, then...?" Both counselors nodded, and Judge Reinhold banged the gavel, breathing life back into the rapt courtroom. Reporters ran to submit their stories. Various onlookers tried to take pictures despite Bailiff Bosco's objections, and Carlos walked over to the defense table.

"Guess that just means we'll be seeing each other sooner than we thought," he said cockily, then added sarcastically, "Nice work with whatever you did here to get this to trial. I'm sure it was all very aboveboard—seeing as you're both such upstanding members of the legal system."

"Save it, Cochran," responded Kent.

"What? Can't take a little praise for the win? I'm just trying to say good job. Too bad you got the wrong guy—and whoever did this might strike again..."

"The compliment was sufficient, Carlos," said Kent, rising as she spoke. "We have to review some videotapes." She gestured for Harris to get up. Slower on the uptake, he struggled to his feet and followed Kent toward the gallery behind the attorney tables. Just before she reached the swinging gate separating the two areas of the courtroom, she turned and addressed Carlos. "We had the evidence. Your client did this to himself when he chose to murder his fiancée. Premeditated."

"We'll just have to see how that works out for you," Carlos replied. "My client can be very persuasive when he's in front of an audience—be it concertgoers, a jury, or even a DA who thinks she has it all figured out. See you in court." Kent turned and left in a huff.

Entering the hallway of the courthouse, Kent and Harris heard whispering among groups of stragglers still milling about after the hearing. Fans and members of the press alike gathered around their phones and looked up at the DA and the detective—as if they knew something the two didn't. They both immediately switched on their phones, which had been off during the proceedings. Harris had multiple missed calls from his fellow detectives—Dunbar, Nordberg, and others. Kent also had a number of calls from her office, but it was a news brief notification that caught her attention first:

LAPD DETECTIVE FOUND DEAD
IN GRUESOME APARTMENT SCENE

Kent looked to Harris, realizing what this might mean. Ophelia had been found. Given the timing, it may not have been a coincidence. They quickly walked out of the building and got into their cars. Other than Harris dialing his fellow detectives to liaise on the scene, it was a long and quiet drive for each of them to Ophelia's apartment—each trying not to picture the horrific sight awaiting them.

Ophelia's building was a classic Spanish Revival stucco structure with four units—two on the top floor and two on the bottom—centered around a staircase, courtyard, and flanking parking areas. The lawn in front was riddled with police and emergency personnel as Harris and Kent pulled up separately, parking on the street. Ophelia's apartment was on the second floor, right side. Kent immediately noticed the heaviest police presence was around that particular staircase and hallway. Neighbors watched from doorways in the building and from down the block. If it was this much of a spectacle outside, what would it be like inside? Kent and Harris, trailed by Dunbar and Nordberg, raced up the stairs, prepared to confront the inevitable. Ophelia was gone.

Harris knew exactly where to go. Just days before, he had been at this very building while looking for Ophelia, but, seeing no signs of entry or a struggle, he left emptyhanded. This time, wishing he had been more determined during that earlier encounter, he entered first. The smell hit him before he even opened the door. The stench of rot was so strong he had to choke back his vomit. He turned to Dunbar and Kent and, in a rare act of mercy, said, "You two better stay out here." Then, perhaps sensing his vulnerability, he added, "I don't need you, especially, puking all over the place," gesturing to Dunbar.

Before Harris could finish, Dunbar caught the odor too. It was no use trying to keep him out. He pushed past his captain to see what the bathroom held. He was stopped in his tracks. Lying halfway out of her tub was their colleague, Ophelia—her brown hair hanging down onto the floor, pieces of green skin scattered around her. One arm was draped out of the tub, a clump of maggots weaving through the decaying flesh. Blowflies buzzed through the room, feasting.

As the three got closer, it was impossible not to notice the heavy swelling in her limbs. Decomposition had set in. Fluids had built up—her right forearm looked like a water balloon about to burst. In other areas, where skin had peeled away, her body looked lumpy and barely human. Her face was the clearest sign of rapid decay: all the skin had been stripped away, revealing raw muscle and bone crawling with larvae. Kent turned away in horror, unsure if she had ever seen anything so gruesome in all her years in the DA's office.

Dunbar took another step forward, then recoiled. "Jesus, fuck," he muttered, shaking his head.

Nordberg approached from the front of the apartment. "I'll call the M.E., Captain. We should get her out of here before more press show up." With that, he pulled out his phone and left the room.

Harris paced for a few seconds before growling, "This was Spencer. I fucking know it. It had to be him. We've got a serial on our hands."

"He was in your custody when she disappeared," Kent replied—surprised at herself for defending Spencer, but knowing she was right. "There's no way—"

"It's him, goddammit! Or his goons. Those damn psychos. The way they follow him?" Harris was working himself up. "He ordered this."

"I just don't understand. Why her?" Dunbar choked back tears.

"Because he's a murderous little shit, that's why. She was a good cop, and we're not gonna forget it. We're going to get this guy." Dunbar nodded in response. Harris could see this was hitting him hard. "Come on. Let's go back out front."

Kent followed, stealing one last glance back. How could Spencer have done this in such a hands-on way from a jail cell?

The air cleared once they shut the bathroom door. Whether it hadn't yet fully reached the living room or their senses had simply adjusted, the stench seemed to fade.

"What are you going to do about this?" Harris asked Kent. "He clearly had a hand in killing one of my officers!"

"I'm going to put him on trial in front of a jury of his peers for the murder we know he committed and..." Kent trailed off, for once at a loss. She regained her composure. "That's all I can do—for now."

"And for Ophelia?" Harris shot back.

"Why don't you worry about finding out who did this, and I'll worry about what I do in the courtroom," Kent said, her tone defensive. "There's no way this was Spencer. Or at least not alone. Looks like you're at square one, Captain. Better get busy."

"If he didn't do it, he damn well ordered the hit—and then leaked it to the press as soon as we left court," Harris said, conceding her point but unwilling to absolve Spencer. "He's got a type, it seems. Ever think of that, Counselor?"

Kent remained silent.

"Petite, attractive women. Some in law enforcement?" Harris continued. "You could be next..."

"Are you saying I'm attractive?" asked Kent, giving the argument her best cross-examination while seizing a chance to embarrass Harris.

"No, I'm just saying Spencer might think that way is all," Harris stumbled. "I'd be watching my six if I were you—or doing my damnedest to keep this guy in a cell where he belongs."

Dunbar continued to stare at the closed bathroom door. "I loved her, you know," he said. "Ophelia. We never said anything, but we were going to tell you—"

"Are you fucking kidding me right now?" snapped Harris.

"What?" asked Dunbar, his voice cracking.

"This is not the time for deathbed love confessions," Harris barked. "We've got a killer on the loose—" He turned to Kent. "Could be serial. Could be a copycat. I need your head in the game. Snap out of it and get to work. Talk to Lambert as soon as she gets here. We need to get cause of death and see if we can pull any prints."

"Sounds like you've got your work cut out for you," Kent said, seizing an opening. "And I have a trial to prepare for. Let's try to stay out of each other's way until then. What do you say?"

"Don't tempt me with a good time, sweetheart," Harris replied with a laugh.

The idea of having Harris off her back while he buried himself in this alternative investigation elated Kent. If it led back to Spencer, fine. If not, she'd make sure the murder of Detective Ophelia was handed off to another assistant district attorney. Let them deal with Captain Hardass and his merry band of idiots. For all the control Kent usually exhibited, she was finding it harder and harder to maintain her composure. The trial hadn't even started yet, and she was already approaching a tipping point—one that would change the trajectory of her life forever.

It would come during the impending trial. And she'd have Spencer—and Captain Harris—to thank for it.

IX

Take Your Pick

DA Kent slammed the steering wheel of her light blue 2022 BMW 3 Series sedan. Traffic was backed up for miles—and it was only 7:15 a.m. She was due in court by nine for jury selection in the Spencer Charnas trial. Plenty of time for an ordinary day in court, but in Judge Reinhold's punctual courtroom, there was no margin of error, despite LA's infamous traffic. She checked the GPS but quickly realized it would only lead her to an overcrowded local street filled with clueless tourists and lost Angelenos trying to get off the freeway.

During one particularly elongated standstill, she clicked through her phone, trying to find some answer as to why the backup was happening. Apparently, an accident in the Figueroa Street tunnels was causing delays all the way onto the 5. That was her exit—and now, her problem. She sighed, picked up a file from the passenger seat, and began to read as the traffic refused to budge.

An hour and a half and many perused documents later, Kent arrived at the Los Angeles County Superior Courthouse. The grounds teemed with reporters and curious onlookers eager to get the inside scoop. Hordes of Ice Nine Kills fans clustered around a perimeter fence, with police officers stationed in front of the barricades. This was going to be a zoo, she thought, as if it wasn't already. Arriving early might have helped her avoid all this, but there was no use dwelling on what might have been.

As she turned into the reserved attorney lot, she noticed several fans wearing Silence masks—evidence they still needed to link to Spencer. The masks were so ubiquitous, it would be difficult to connect the one found at the scene to him specifically. She could practically see Carlos Cochran pointing outside and telling the jury to just look out the window for their reasonable doubt. Fortunately, courtroom nine was on the far side of the building. Still, the scene felt like an ominous sign of things to come.

Making her way toward the blocky, Moderne-style courthouse, Kent was met with jeers from Ice Nine Kills fans lining the path. In addition to Silence masks, some wore costumes from various horror films. She recognized characters like Jason Voorhees and Michael Myers, but others were beyond her knowledge. One group, clad in work coveralls and vintage gas masks, particularly disturbed her. If the outfits were from a film, she couldn't place which one. She shook her head and climbed the courthouse steps, entering through the glass doors.

Inside, the hallway leading to the courtroom was narrow and crowded. The low ceiling and packed bodies gave the space a claustrophobic feel. Kent lowered her head and pressed forward, a woman on a mission. She eventually entered the courtroom, where Drew Feldmann, one of her legal assistants, was waiting.

Drew, a shorter man with neatly cropped dark hair and glasses, had a nerdish look. He'd graduated at the top of his class at UCLA School of Law and brought both eagerness and energy to the team—occasionally too much of both. Kent couldn't recall ever being as on top of things in her early days at the DA's office as Drew was now. At just twenty-six, he was already impressive, if a bit green. A savant at jury selection, he could swiftly analyze jurors' backgrounds, mining data to determine whether they leaned toward the state or the defense.

He also excelled in forensics, a subject Kent admittedly struggled with. Despite limited murder trial experience, around the office, he was known as the "Wizard of Blood." He understood the science and could explain it in layman's terms—a valuable skill for a jury trial as gruesome as this one. Kent was glad to have him on her team.

As Kent headed toward the attorney's table, Drew rushed to keep up beside her.

"I thought I was going to have to ask for a continuance! What happened?" he whispered, panic in his voice.

"Traffic," she replied curtly.

"Well, glad you made it," he said, his tone softening. "Sounds like the judge wants to start jury selection right at nine."

"If I know Reinhold, it'll be 8:58 at the latest. Let's hope we get a good pool. Do just what we discussed."

"Size them up for their ability to understand the evidence," Drew said, as if reciting from a textbook.

"But not too much ability," Kent corrected. "No lawyers or anything like that. But not some Virginia coal miner type, either. We need people we can chip away at with what little we've got to connect Spencer to this case."

"It does feel a bit flimsy," Drew said reflexively.

"Tell that to Captain Harris," Kent muttered, pursing her lips. "He's not here, is he?"

Drew pointed toward the back of the courtroom. Kent turned to see Harris sitting in the front row—on the defense's side, not her own. He waved in an exaggerated manner. She had hoped he'd be out finding more evidence, not wasting time watching her. Maybe seeing jury selection up close would finally drive home how thin their case was.

Harris hadn't turned up anything more on Spencer in the intervening weeks. Even worse, he'd made no progress on the murder of Detective Ophelia Crane since they found her following the pre-trial hearing. Kent was not immediately attached to that particular case, as she was able to pawn it off onto ADA George Fisher, another attorney from her office who was known as the corpsegrinder for his years of hard work specializing in murder cases. Kent had, therefore, been free of Harris for a greater amount of time than she had previously been accustomed to; it was just the mental vacation she needed as she prepared for this trial. It was only through the grapevine of the DA's office that she heard what little progress was made on the Ophelia case. While they had confirmed that severe trauma and loss of blood from acid burns were the cause of death, that was work done by the M.E. and not Harris.

The lack of a suspect, or any other leads for that matter, was baffling, especially given that the victim was one of their own. Kent had even heard that the FBI was getting involved, which would undoubtedly embarrass Harris to a certain degree. As she sat at the attorney's table, she felt Harris creeping up behind her—an instinctive reaction she hadn't missed since the last time they were together.

"Long time no see," Harris said with a jocular tone that didn't quite mask his discomfort.

"And whose fault is that?" Kent replied. "If you'd dug deeper on your suspect, maybe I wouldn't be going into jury selection blind."

"Hey, we got enough. Just make your case and nail this son of a bitch."

"If we win, it's very little thanks to you and your team," she snapped. "You were the one saying Spencer was ordering hits and killing your officers. Weeks have passed. Not a peep since Ophelia."

She looked back down at her notes. Harris stood there awkwardly.

"I'm working on that. I'm sure he's involved. You stay in your lane, I'll stay in mine," he said, seating himself beside her despite her obvious displeasure.

"How is sitting with me staying in your lane?" she asked, giving him a sharp side-eye. He got the hint and moved down a seat, leaving space for Drew.

At 8:58 a.m. sharp, the courtroom stirred as Spencer Charnas and his attorney, Carlos Cochran, entered. Cameras clicked and fans cheered. Spencer posed for selfies and flashed grins at the press. Celebrity trials, Kent thought, were always circuses. She detested the attention but relished the opportunity to remind the world that no one was above the law. And, of course, the notoriety wouldn't hurt her either.

"All rise! Court is now in session," shouted Bailiff Bosco. His voice echoed, silencing most. Spencer, however, kept whispering to Cochran.

Judge Harlan Reinhold entered. Kent noticed denim peeking out beneath his robe. *A Canadian tuxedo?* she scribbled on her legal pad and passed it to Drew, who stifled a laugh. She handed it to Harris as a peace offering, but he merely shrugged. She remembered Harris' appearance at the previous hearings and realized that he wouldn't object as forcefully as she did to the casual nature of the judge's outfit.

Reinhold banged his gavel. "We've all seen the media circus. But let me be clear: this courtroom is not a zoo. That said, let the games begin," he added with a wry smile.

Groups of potential jurors were sworn in for their service, and the selection progressed without much of a hitch. Voir Dire, the procedure during which attorneys for both sides ask questions of the potential jurors to uncover any bias and assess the ability to serve, went forward as it did for any other trial. Many jurors were dismissed on grounds of their typical consumption of media or having a direct, verifiable conflict in their schedule. Some, however, were even dismissed on grounds of being fans of the band. There seemed to be an alarmingly high number of fans in the jury pool, but Kent chalked it up to the popularity of Ice Nine Kills and nothing else. Besides, finding the obvious fans only made it easier to throw out those who might be biased toward Spencer.

Drew had been passing her notes on multiple prospective jurors. For most of the potential jurors, he had been able to unearth a decent amount of information, though for others, there was little to dig up. This was not to say the potential jurors would be biased, but simply that many of them didn't live their lives online, something that may help the prosecution. Of those jurors eventually selected, many had seemed amiable enough, even without much information to go on and, therefore, passed the test from each side.

During the process, Carlos Cochran had objected to a number of jurors, even ones that would have seemed amenable to his client, from women-hating, incel types to those who were obviously soft on crime and more willing to forgive a defendant. DA Kent wasn't quite sure what he was up to, but there had to be a strategy here. Nevertheless, she didn't fight him on what she knew would surely help her convict Spencer.

The first seated juror, Eli, made Kent uneasy—he held her gaze a beat too long. Still, he looked like he'd be the type to convict, so she buried that feeling.

The next two chosen jurors both coincidentally worked with school-aged children, a fact the DA liked for different reasons. Juror 2 was the number assigned to a thirty-something, third-grade teacher named Tom. His career potentially meant that he could use reason and compassion to make his decision, hopefully for her side, and that he also possessed a nurturing nature that would be more likely to empathize with the victim. Tom was followed by Juror 3, a retired bus driver named Al. Twenty-eight years on a bus full of bickering ten-year-olds had forced him to become numb to the ills of the world. He was weary and hardened, just enough for the DA to be able to get across all the gory details, but not so much that he wouldn't convict. He was perfect, she wrote on her legal pad, smiling and tapping the page so that Drew might share in her celebration.[31]

Two women—Mary L. and Mary H.—were empaneled as Juror 4 and 6, despite Kent's objections. They looked like metal fans, but appearance wasn't enough for Reinhold to immediately dismiss for cause. Kent further declined to use her peremptory challenges. She hoped their shared youth with Nadia would sway them toward the victim, toward a conviction.

Between the two Marys was Shinji, a Japanese-American programmer from the Bay Area, who became Juror 5.

Before midday, Jurors 7 through 9 were selected: George, a part-time Canadian hockey player; Clive, a British expat and restaurateur; and David, a chemistry professor. All three expressed support for law enforcement. Kent noted that George and Clive's worldly perspectives might help when dealing with a celebrity defendant. David seemed to live under a rock (even if he could

31 Kent's legal pad was recovered as part of a later investigation into this entire affair. Initially held by the police, it was eventually cleared and given to the press. The pad was notable for the numerous disparaging remarks about Captain Harris in the margins. A personal favorite is when she called him a "conniving cunt of a cop."

presumably tell you its chemical makeup). By lunch, they had these nine jurors selected and the court was dismissed for a break.

Judge Reinhold called for the recess and departed for his chambers. Kent whispered to Drew to keep researching and darted out, eager to avoid Harris.

"Hey! Kent!" Harris called after her, turning to Drew. "What's with her?"

Drew only shrugged.

††††††

The DA made a left out of the courtroom and strode quickly down the tunnel-like hallway toward the back of the building, peering occasionally over her shoulder as she went. She left the main corridor packed with people and descended a marble, U-shaped staircase into the basement. This hallway was much narrower than the one above, but it was empty, making it feel somehow wider—yet confining at the same time. What made it seem even more like an enclosed space was the fact that there were far fewer doors on this lower level. Immediately at the bottom of the stairs, she was confronted with the open door of a clerk's office. She peered in, but no one seemed to be working. With the other three doors on this stretch of hallway all shut, she concluded that she was alone.

Finally reaching the end of the first hallway, Kent made a left-hand turn to follow the square-shaped path that wound around the perimeter of the building. This next segment of the corridor was slightly dimmer. She might have reasoned that it had been darkened to save energy in favor of the air conditioning that kept the courthouse cool—or perhaps she allowed other, more sinister explanations to enter her mind. What may have furthered those ominous thoughts was the fluorescent light above that flickered as she passed under it. Off, then on. Back off. Back on…

As she moved past the light, Kent's cell phone vibrated in her jacket pocket, startling her. She jumped at the sensation of movement near her right hip before quickly settling herself to answer. It was Harris. Her peaceful lunch would have to wait.

"Where are you?" Harris' voice echoed through the hallway as he shouted on the other end of the line.

"Downstairs..." she said reluctantly into the phone.

"I'll be right down. Need to talk to you, but don't get your panties all in a twist," he replied.

"Sounds good. Just give me a minute," was all she managed to say. Kent hung up immediately. She hadn't meant to sound so weak with Harris—and perhaps wanted to regain some power by hanging up on him.

She continued down the hallway and beneath the flickering light, sliding her phone back into her jacket as she walked. She looked behind her but felt silly about it—and was glad no one was around to see. Upon turning back in her original direction, she slammed into a body. The collision forced her to drop her briefcase and files. When she regained her composure, she looked up to meet the eyes of Juror 1, Eli. They seemed to bulge out of his head like a frog's. It was unclear who was more startled. She had noted his strange stare in the courtroom, and now she was confronted with those same eyes looking down at her from his six-foot-three, lanky frame. He blinked a few times before either of them said anything, as if he were also trying to place her.[32]

"Sorry—excuse me," she managed to say, stopping to pick up her papers.

---

32 It is important to note here that, unsurprisingly, this interaction is omitted from Kent's book. We know from Harris' notes that she did see Juror 1 in this hallway, later claiming it was mere coincidence and that it had no bearing on the case. In seeking to preserve the highest order of journalistic integrity, I am inserting a string of innocuous dialogue here that would not reflect negatively on any of the parties involved, despite the fact that, in this case, all are guilty. More on this encounter later...

"My mistake," the juror replied, bending down to assist her. "You're—"

"Not supposed to be speaking with you," Kent interrupted. She gathered her papers before standing up.

"See you around, counselor," said Juror 1, continuing down the hallway. "Good luck on the case."

Kent tried to shout after him as he turned a corner, "You're supposed to be sequestered this way!" Her attempt to redirect him landed only on deaf ears. But in a building like the courthouse, someone was always listening. She stifled any further attempt, realizing the hallways went all the way around the building and he would eventually arrive at the correct destination.

"Kent!" she heard, coming from behind her. Turning around, she saw Harris at the other end of the long hallway, back toward the staircase she'd used earlier. Kent waved him forward before entering the break room to her left. She leaned against the wall and sighed.

Harris entered, asking, "What was that about? Isn't he one of our jurors?"

"I have no idea what he was doing down here," she lamented. "But I'm not about to have a mistrial on day one. Let's just eat and go over the next batch."

"I won't tell, if you don't," Harris replied. She shuddered at the idea of being ethically aligned with him—even for a second.

The break room was a relatively sad affair, decorated in shades of beige and brown, primarily thanks to the yellowing wallpaper and cheap wood paneling. Various posters displaying workplace safety messages and legal notifications adorned the walls—some faded, others peeling away. A fridge sat in the corner. Kent could only imagine what horrors it held after years of abandoned lunches. She walked toward the wooden table in the middle of the room and took a seat. Harris stared at her.

"What?" said Kent, reacting to his look.

"I just didn't take you for a rule breaker, is all," replied Harris, impressed with the new information about the DA.

"You saw what happened. He bumped into me," said Kent defensively. "No rule against being clumsy."

"All I saw is, I come around that corner and you're talking with one of the jurors. Big no-no, if you ask me. But hey, if it gets our guy, I'm all in."

"I don't need to cheat to win a case. You, on the other hand—"

"Ouch," replied Harris, feigning injury. "Doesn't matter how you get the fucking results, sweetheart. You just gotta get it done."

"Can I eat in peace, or did you have something to discuss?" said Kent, changing the subject and pulling out a smashed sandwich from her purse. "Dammit."

"That juror did a number on your lunch, huh? Well, that's what you get for breaking the rules. Instant karma," laughed Harris.

"You're not even using that term right," Kent retorted. "The sandwich is fine. But it's turkey. I asked for roast beef."

"I should've known you were a red meat kind of gal. Let me guess—a little pink on the inside?"

"Keep it up and I'll bite your fucking head off. How's that for red meat?" snapped Kent.

"Kinky," he said before taking out his own lunch. "You sound like our boy Spencer there." Kent glared at Harris before leaning forward to start eating her disappointing sandwich.

"Remember? The bite marks?"

Not getting the reaction he'd hoped for, Harris unwrapped his own sandwich. Kent immediately noticed he had roast beef. Had Drew switched up the orders, or had the detective just stolen her sandwich?

Harris shifted in his chair. "Look, the reason I came down here was to let you know we got the affirmative on the stab patterns. Our expert did a recreation of the crime scene and compared the wounds on Nadia's burned remains—barely discernible, by the way—with how Spencer stabs her in the videos."

If Kent was excited, she didn't show it. Instead, she offered a matter-of-fact, "Good. We needed that." She then shifted her tone. "But that's all you got? Nothing new?"

"We're working around the clock on this thing. Plus the Ophelia case. I'm sure they're connected. You'd know about all this if you bothered to answer your damn phone."

"I'll answer my phone when you bring me something worth listening to—instead of the same tired evidence I helped you find over a month ago," Kent replied.

Just as Kent reached the peak of her anger, a maintenance worker wearing a blue jumpsuit entered the room carrying a nail gun. "'Scuse me, ma'am. Sir," he said, nodding to Kent and Harris in turn. He spoke with a slight accent, European or Canadian, Kent couldn't tell. "Won't be more than a minute. Carry on as you were." He looked around before spotting the peeling posters on the wall. "Just need to get these back into working order."

Kent watched the man as he set about his work, periodically checking over his shoulder at the DA and the detective. Something about him made her uneasy. She questioned why he would bring such a large tool for such a small job—not to mention how he didn't seem entirely sure why he'd come into the room in the first place. Harris seemed unaware of anything out of the ordinary, choosing instead to focus on his lunch.

After a few seconds, he broke the silence, picking back up their previous conversation. "The evidence may be…what did you say?

Tired? But they don't know that. You just pick a good jury up there, and I know they'll go for it. This Spencer guy's as good as gone…"

Kent clocked the maintenance man shifting slightly at the mention of Spencer. Realizing she couldn't take any chances, she picked up her phone. Barely looking at it before speaking, she said hurriedly, "Wow, look at the time. I need to be getting back upstairs. And you should get back out looking for whatever you can. I can handle things here."

"I haven't finished eating," said Harris, roast beef exploding out of the sides of his full mouth.

"Then you do that. I need to go," Kent said, cleaning up her things and heading out the door.

With the lunch break finished, jury selection back in the courtroom continued much as it had for the previous few hours. They had three more selections to make, plus two alternates.

Scott, a bed-and-breakfast proprietor from Altadena, became Juror 10, and shortly after, both sides agreed on Samantha. Sam, as she was known, was sixty-five and newly retired from a career running a year-round camping program for children in Tennessee. Recently, she had found a retirement job working as a baker for a friend's shop. Her maternal presence and flexible schedule made her a shoo-in for Kent, who wanted to shift the jury away from being as male-dominated as the first nine picks had been.

Bernie, a retired doctor who lived in Brentwood, would be the last of the empaneled jury—Juror 12. His knowledge of medical science might have initially made both sides nervous, but he was too jovial to reject: a sweet old Jewish man who seemed harmless, to say the least.

DA Kent breathed a sigh of relief as the last juror was selected. They still needed two alternates, but she felt confident in the jury she had chosen. She could practically see the case being won before her very eyes. Carlos, however, looked less than enthusiastic. He seemed distraught over the selections—but maybe that was just his act. Spencer, as always, looked his usual unflappable self.

For the alternates, a surfing instructor named Katrina was selected, along with Jonathan, a short-order cook. Earlier in his career, Jonathan had worked at a Waffle House. This may have desensitized him to horrific violence, but Kent still felt positively about him, given his seemingly strong moral compass. With these two alternates, jury selection was complete.

Kent sat beside Drew and Captain Harris as Judge Reinhold thanked the jury pool and both sides of the case. He then banged the gavel to dismiss everyone for the day. She looked over at Spencer, who returned her gaze, staring at her until she had to look away.

He was confident, collected—and she often had to remind herself that he was a killer. Nevertheless, she had her doubts, even as the trial was about to commence. Her job, it would seem, would be to suppress those ideas, forcing them so deeply inside her they would never see the light of day.

She further remembered there was also a victim who would never see the light of day again herself: Nadia. And then, of course, there was Detective Ophelia—which only raised her level of anxiety. Maybe Spencer was still actively killing, even if through some kind of surrogate.

What if Harris' words from weeks ago were something to be taken seriously? Did this alleged killer have a type?

She had to get a conviction. Her life might just depend on it.

X

The Box

If you've made it this far, you've watched as we unpacked the days and weeks leading up to the Spencer Charnas murder trial, albeit slightly out of order, but often as depicted in Kent's book. As she began in the middle of the trial and used frequent flashbacks, I have here attempted to do the same. We now return to the day where this story truly began—the day America was welcomed to Horrorwood during the opening act of this real-life courtroom drama. As Kent keenly recognized in her own writing, it was necessary first to lay the foundation of knowledge as we ventured deeper into what could easily go down in history as the trial of the millennium.

So, after the now-lengthy discussion of the investigation, arraignment, and jury selection, we've reached the point where one thing was clear (and it certainly wasn't the innocence or guilt of our favorite metal front man). The only thing entirely clear—at least according to Kent's book—was that the relationship between Kent and Captain Harris—DA and detective—was irreparably strained. She hated the very essence of the man, from his demeanor when dealing with others (especially women) to the way he conducted his investigations (barely on the right side of the law). This was evident not only in her writings on the subject, but also in her behavior in court and her body language during that first press conference following day one of the trial.

A discerning reader might assume it all stemmed from Kent's momentary lapse in judgment—where Harris may have caught her in an inappropriate run-in with a member of the empaneled jury. But that would be missing the forest for the trees. The devil, in this case, lies not in the details, but in that big picture.

And so, we journey forward into the trial itself, where hell's ninth circle takes the shape of a courtroom.

The first day (previously discussed in chapter one) had largely been a success for DA Kent, despite a few initial stumbles. What clearly irked her most was the press conference—particularly Harris' behavior as they were peppered with questions from the media. For someone so brazen and cocksure, he seemed to have no idea where another one of his own officers was. Dunbar was missing. And if he had met the same fate as Detective Ophelia, it would devastate both the case and the entire team working it.

Morale was already low, but if the officers were now sitting ducks for a serial killer? Worse still, with Spencer in lockup, it would be easy for anyone—including the jury—to immediately rule him out as a suspect. As much as she hated to admit it, Kent had confided to Harris that she felt like she was missing something and needed more evidence from him and his team.

Harris, however, kept coming back empty-handed.

Toward the end of the press conference, Spencer was escorted by a team of sheriff's deputies back to his awaiting jail cell. Harris made sure to publicly taunt him during the process—yet another reason Kent viewed him as a liability. Once the media circus ended, Kent needed a moment to catch her breath after enduring the hot lights of the cameras—and, worse still, doing so beside Captain Harris.

But all that agony was nothing compared to what was happening across town.

Unbeknownst to either Kent or Harris, Officer Grant Dunbar sat just a few miles away in the corner of a dimly lit, damp-feeling warehouse. He was not alone—and certainly not safe.

†††††††

The constant drip of a leaky pipe punctuated the unrelenting seconds of the minutes Dunbar had been held captive. There was little inside the abandoned warehouse where he was held, save for an older-model television. From its outdated screen, the press conference with Kent and Harris cast a flickering light over the room, including onto Dunbar, who lay only a few feet away, writhing against a pair of restraints cinched tightly around his wrists.

His arms were pulled behind his back and wrapped around a metal pole in the center of the room, denying him any movement. Metal clanked against metal as he struggled, echoing through the cavernous space and drowning out the low volume of the television. Only seconds earlier, he had woken up in this unfamiliar place, disoriented and unsure of what had happened.

He tried to scream, but immediately found that something restricted the opening of his mouth. A sharp stinging, like pinpricks across his lips, told him all he needed to know. It had been sewn shut with heavy thread. Each attempt to open his mouth became more painful than the last. The threads refused to budge. As the TV continued to broadcast the press conference, Dunbar struggled even harder against his restraints, so much so that cuts began to form on his wrists and ankles from the friction he created.

Aside from the television and Dunbar, the industrial room contained two mannequin-style dress forms—one headless, the other wearing a Silence mask—shoved into a corner beside a workbench scattered with papers. At the far end of the bench hung a bulletin board covered in photographs. From his position on the floor, Dunbar could make out the faces: Harris, Kent, Ophelia, and himself, a red "IX" marked over the last two.

Behind him, a set of scaffolding reached to the ceiling, where a sliver of light crept in through either a skylight or an escape hatch. The room had no windows and only metal walls, making it difficult to determine whether he was above or below ground.

He caught flashes of the press conference out of the corner of his eye, but his attention remained on survival. Still, the sounds from the broadcast gave him one slim hope—his absence would not go unnoticed. He had to believe his fellow detectives would find him, just as they'd found Ophelia.

A stiff collar restricted the movement of his neck, limiting his view. But he could hear Captain Harris bragging about some newfound evidence. Then, his name came up in a journalist's question. They knew he was missing. Hope surged—until it didn't.

A figure in a cloak stepped into frame, blocking the TV's light. Dunbar recognized the mask instantly—The Silence. This had to be Spencer. But he was at the trial. A copycat? A partner?

Had they all been wrong?

The Silence approached the table on which the television sat. In front of the screen, an array of weapons gleamed under its glow: a skull-handled ice pick, an ax, assorted knives, and surgical tools in various states of decay. The Silence lingered over each item before finally selecting a red, metal gas can.

They walked across the floor and placed it beside Dunbar. Then, crouching low, they brought the blank eyes of the mask inches from his face. From beneath their cloak, they pulled out a piece of cardboard with a message scrawled in thick black marker: What's the evidence?

Dunbar shook his head. He couldn't give them anything. Even if he wanted to, he couldn't speak—his lips were still sealed.

Almost as if on cue with Dunbar's thoughts, the Silence pulled out a pair of scissors and cut through the air a few times, as if to practice the procedure they were about to perform. They then brought the scissors close to Dunbar's face, slowly and methodically. At first, he wriggled against it, worried of the pain that was about to overtake him. But, The Silence soon held his head still and began to cut away at the threads surrounding his lips.

SNIP SNIP SNIP.

Dunbar's feet kicked against the ground as he writhed in pain from The Silence's every cut. The threads that held Dunbar's mouth shut soon fell away and he tried to let out a terrible scream. Instead, he gurgled and coughed as blood that had built up inside his mouth gushed out and onto his shirt. Finally, he managed to let out a half-yell kind of noise followed by a whisper and mumbles of a few unintelligible words. The Silence seemed unfazed by the noise Dunbar was making and just kept looking at their prisoner, who soon realized that he would need to give an answer in order to get anywhere with his masked captor. Dunbar's head bobbed to the side as he winced from the pain and managed to form his first words since waking up. "I...don't know...shit."

The Silence continued looking at him for a few seconds. Finally, they stood up, still brandishing the scissors which menacingly passed in front of Dunbar's face. They moved toward the gas can and picked it up.

Dunbar panicked, his mind racing between the possible outcomes of what would happen next. "Hey!" he yelled "What are you doing with that?" The Silence continued undeterred, opening the cap to the gas slowly as their prisoner went on. "I told you I don't know shit!" he pleaded. It appeared that his cries fell on deaf ears as The Silence began to pour out the liquid gas around Dunbar.

"Dude, come on!" continued Dunbar. "Stop!" At this request, The Silence began to pour gasoline on Dunbar himself. Dunbar responded by stepping up the intensity of his screams. "Okay, all right!" Dunbar cried. "All right! Okay!" He stopped thrashing. He needed to change tactics. "Okay…" Dunbar said, cautiously. "If you let me go, I'll tell you."

The Silence paused.

"If you let me go, I'll tell you?" he repeated, confirming his offer. A slight nod followed. The gas can was set aside. Now he had to deliver.

"We know Spencer's stab pattern," he said, breathless. "It's the same as in the video. Three in the chest, two in the stomach, one in the back."

He hung his head, ashamed.

"That's how we were able to arrest him."

The Silence watched Dunbar, almost disapproving of how weak he was. Dunbar stopped fighting against his handcuffs, knowing he would live to see another day. All it took was disclosing this small secret. The secret, he reasoned, would have come out in the trial in the coming days, so it wasn't really a secret at all—just something unknown to Spencer's team and the general public for the time being. He relaxed, having convinced himself that he would survive this ordeal and that his betrayal wasn't really a true betrayal at all. It had limited consequences. A win-win, he must have thought.

Dunbar, further loosened up as his fears of death subsided, returned to his old joking self, even with such a deadly interlocutor as The Silence still in front of him.

"That's also how we were able to remember it. It's kind of like a song." He breathed in before launching into a country-style rendition of the sing-songy way in which he would remember the stab pattern. "Three in the chest…two in the stomach…one in the back…yeah, yeah," he sang.

Over and over again, he was lost in song as The Silence reclaimed the gas can and moved toward the exit. Dunbar didn't notice as they continued to pour the liquid in a straight line toward the door.

"Hey!" Dunbar yelled, having noticed The Silence continuing their task. "What are you doing?" He started to struggle against his restraints again. "Hey, man, we had a deal," he said, now more urgently.

The Silence continued pouring, not listening to Dunbar, who continued to struggle. "We just had a deal, man!" he screamed. He waited for a response. Nothing.

Finally, The Silence produced a Zippo lighter and flicked the cap open, igniting a small flame from the top. Dunbar immediately recognized what was about to happen.

"Oh no, man, come on. You can just stab me," he said, resigning himself to his fate and wanting it to be as painless as possible. "Just stab me…I'm right here."

The Silence failed to acknowledge his offer with any kind of response.

"You can just stab me, man. That can be part of our deal now," he continued pleading. "New deal! You can just stab me! Please don't!"

The Silence raised the lighter higher, each elevation matching Dunbar's voice as it became louder and higher-pitched; he was growing more desperate by the second.

"Please don't do that. Come on, man."

The Silence, unwavering in their determination, dropped the lighter from over their head. It landed on the ground, instantaneously igniting a burst of flames.

"No! NO! NO!" screamed Dunbar.

The flames danced their way across the floor and toward the officer, following the same line The Silence had taken when pouring the gas. Within seconds they were right in front of his feet, and he frantically stomped in a desperate attempt to extinguish them. He should have been more careful in how he stomped, because he himself had gas on his shirt and pants, but luck was certainly on Officer Dunbar's side—even if her presence was ever so brief. With all of the gas on the floor lit and burned off, the fire diminished, eventually fizzling into nothing but smoke and a lingering odor. The gas had not been distributed all the way to Dunbar, and that small gap proved enough to prevent his fiery demise.

He breathed a sigh of relief, gasping for air. A smile came across his face. He had just had his closest brush with death, but The Silence seemed satisfied. They walked away toward the exit, just as a small red light located on the collar around Dunbar's neck lit up. The light, just below the left side of his jawbone, was unseen by Dunbar himself—but even if he had seen it, he might not have recognized it to mean the device around his neck was now armed.

The Silence then raised their hand to reveal a small remote with a similarly sized green light and a small push-button trigger. The gloved thumb of The Silence pressed the button, starting a high-pitched beeping noise and causing the red light on Dunbar's collar to flash.

Watching them leave, Dunbar called after The Silence, thankful that he would be spared. "Ugh, for a minute there I thought I was dead meat," he said, relieved.

But before he could finish his sentence, a giant explosion came from the collar around his neck. In a split second, Dunbar's head burst outward from his body, and pieces of flesh and muscle and organs rained down around the room. His right cheek was quickly smeared and splattered all over the television screen still showing the press conference. His left cheek and eye socket didn't travel as far—they broke away from his neck and fell into his awaiting lap. Dunbar was done for. But, like a chicken still rushing around after decapitation, blood continued to gush from his carotid artery for the few seconds during which his body failed to keep up with the speed at which he had unceremoniously lost his head.

The Silence never turned around to admire their work. Instead, they quietly disappeared into the shadows—just as they had entered the room in the first place.

It would be days before Dunbar was found. Meanwhile, Kent continued with the trial, undeterred by what might have happened to another of Harris' officers.[33] In her book, she has a tendency to brush past the extreme violence committed during this killing spree and move right on to more mundane matters. Thus, to give you a taste of her writing, I intend to do just that. But, we're not ready to lay Dunbar to rest just yet. More on that later…

Following the first day of opening statements, Carlos was given his chance to lay out the case for reasonable doubt. He did just that, effectively planting the earliest ideas of a seed of innocence in the minds of the jury. Cultivating that seed and bringing it to harvest would be a longer process, but it would have to wait until the state presented their arguments. Day three held Kent's first witnesses as she began to unfold her theory of the case to the jury. The first set of testimony was given by none other than Spencer's fellow bandmates from Ice Nine Kills. This batch of witnesses would eventually eat up two more days of the trial. If they were to convict and hold Spencer accountable, the jury and courtroom audience

33 Anyone reading this far would have undoubtedly consumed much of this trial in real time, whether through the (often) lying mainstream media or another source. Therefore, it would be an effort in redundancy for me to reprint it here. However, I will go into some detail regarding certain aspects of the trial that I believe hold a special purpose for understanding what ultimately would happen with Spencer Charnas and his case.

needed to be introduced to the cast of characters, and Kent felt it would be best to meet them head-on, face-to-face, as she painted a picture of Spencer's depravity.

Joe Occhiuti, the bassist, keyboardist, and vocalist, was the first bandmate to take the stand. Anyone who was in the room would concur that he took the proceedings the least seriously of the group. It was not a good start for Kent or her trial. Joe simply offered one-word, cryptic answers that often seemed to contradict each other. Even his name was difficult to pin down, as Kent asked him, "Is it Joe 'Oh-cutie' or Joe 'Oh-Chootie'?" His response was a simple: "Correct." In true form for the multi-instrumentalist he was, Joe seemed to be playing the prosecution like a fiddle—or a harp, or whatever else he could get his hands on.

Ricky Armellino, who next took the stand, was the most nervous of the bunch. He was often seen moving around in the hard, wooden witness chair as he attempted to get comfortable; his movements were to no avail. Ricky's answers were long and drawn out, yet difficult to follow. To a jury, Ricky must have seemed like he could have committed the crimes himself (he had an alibi, of course). Shifty, unfocused, overexcitable—hardly a useful witness for the prosecution. Kent knew that he was not helping her case in the slightest, and so decided to move on as quickly as possible. It was difficult to get him to finish his long answers, but she eventually interrupted him and dismissed him from the witness box.

Dan Sugarman came next. Calm and collected, he seemed as relaxed as Spencer had been in all of his interviews. Kent saw this opportunity to use Dan as a warm-up for when—or even if—Spencer took the stand in his own defense. Dan spoke mostly about the music and how he and Spencer had put together some of the guitar parts for an upcoming tour. Hardly helpful to the actual case at hand, but perhaps fun for a fan who might have been watching the trial.

Finally, Pat Galante. Pat, the drummer in the band, gave candid and helpful remarks throughout. He painted Spencer as somewhat closed off, someone who would disappear for periods of time only to come back looking disheveled and "off" (his word). As Pat told it, Spencer could have easily been a killer who was able to hide it from most of those around him—but not necessarily everybody. This character witness was perhaps the most damning to Spencer, but it was decidedly not enough to convince a jury of undeniable guilt.

On cross-examination, Carlos opened the door to the possibility that, with such different pieces of testimony by the members of the same band, any one of them could have killed Nadia and then used Spencer as the fall guy; any one of his bandmates could have been lying this entire time. It was as if none of them had the same image of this singer, and so, Kent feared, the jury might also come to such disparate conclusions. The alternative theory of a bandmate being the killer seemed to land with certain members of the jury, namely Jurors 4 and 6, the two Marys, both of whom seemed more smitten as each successive bandmate took the stand. Kent was interrupted from watching Carlos question Pat by Drew tapping her on the shoulder. He pointed down to a yellow legal pad where he had written: "fans?" Kent must have felt confident enough in her position at that point, because she quickly wrote on the pad, "absolutely NOT," the latter word appearing in capitals.

Following the testimony from the band members themselves, the days of the trial ticked by as Kent put forth one witness after another. Outside of court, Harris seemed to be making no progress whatsoever on Ophelia's case. As the parade of various forensic scientists and experts took the stand, it became clearer and clearer that this case was one of the most opaque Kent had ever put before a jury. All of the evidence was circumstantial at best, with Carlos refuting each and every piece of it. However, one witness—a forensic scientist who had analyzed both the stab patterns on Nadia and Spencer's music videos—appeared to score the most points with the jury.

Cotton Barker had spent a number of years with the Navy before settling down and taking up a professorship in criminology at the University of California at Irvine. His testimony during the trial had the jury hanging on every word as they nodded along. Kent would certainly have noticed this and thought she was finally making headway with the panel of Spencer's peers. Finally, they seemed receptive to something: the idea that Spencer had practically shown in his music videos how he would commit a crime, and then actually committed it not long afterward. Kent had initially been playing the stab pattern evidence close to the vest, but when it had somehow leaked to the media a few days prior, she had to scramble to find this witness and prepare him for the stand. Carlos, of course, tried to play the copycat card, but it appeared to fall on deaf ears. Kent would undoubtedly have felt at this time that she was winning. But despite this sense that the pieces of the puzzle had been assembled in just the right order, it wasn't over yet. She rested for the prosecution feeling in command of the case, but what Carlos would do in defense of his client was anybody's guess.

The only other piece to mention regarding the prosecution's case—and why I specifically acknowledged that she was making headway with the jury—is that, in this writer's opinion, Kent put forth the best prosecution she possibly could at the time. It never felt as if she were throwing the game, so to speak. She had the case exactly where it needed to be in the eyes of the jury and in the eyes of the public. Perhaps this is why the eventual outcome was such a shock.

Carlos began his side of the case—the defense of Spencer—by refuting evidence piece by piece and reminding the jury that, as a public figure, Spencer could easily have been framed by any number of bad actors and deranged fans. He trotted out experts who used far-flung theories to try to refute the evidence introduced by Kent, but these arguments didn't gain the same traction with the jury as the videotapes had. However, it wasn't until the day Spencer took the stand that things really opened up—for Kent. For Carlos, conversely, it was as if Pandora's box had opened right there in the courtroom, unleashing the evils of the world onto him.

Trial attendees will doubtless remember the unseasonably cold Tuesday in February when Spencer took the stand. For those present, the tension was palpable. Everyone in the courtroom was on pins and needles, wondering what Spencer would say as he addressed the court from the witness box. While his strong stage presence came out during performances with his band, Spencer's dealings with the press and during fan Q&A sessions seemed far less effortless. His demeanor was not nearly as forthcoming and direct as his onstage persona would suggest. He was an enigma wrapped inside a riddle, all placed into a tightly sealed container.

Spencer's testimony was a spectacle in itself. The crowds in and around the courthouse were massive that day, spilling into hallways and onto the surrounding lawn. A separate viewing area was set up for overflow, allowing many more onlookers than could fit into the courtroom a chance to hear what Spencer had to say. Protests on the lawn—between those who believed he was innocent and those who believed he was guilty—had quieted. It felt as though the world itself had stopped to listen rather than shout.

After all the buildup, the testimony was, regrettably, less than remarkable.[34] Spencer answered questions about his personal life and career—nothing that couldn't have been gleaned from any magazine interview or panel at one of the many conventions he appeared at. He insisted numerous times that he was innocent, that he loved Nadia with all his heart, and that he couldn't possibly have done something like this. Carlos then pointed to the alternative theories—yet again. A fan did it. Or maybe a copycat killer (inspired by the videos, but not because of them, the defense attorney clarified). It could even have been a former bandmate, Spencer suggested, recalling difficult musical relationships from the past. Kent had called current members of the band to the stand, but none of the former ones. Carlos was more than happy to exploit this oversight.

To give an example of the testimony we all witnessed, reprinted here is a segment from DA Marcie Kent's cross-examination of Spencer Charnas, as recorded by court stenographers Ryan Kirby and Brandon Saller. Note the interjections and objections by Carlos Cochran throughout. I hope this excerpt gives some sense of how the case unfolded for both sides—without reproducing the entire trial transcript:

MR. CHARNAS: I loved her. Why would I kill her?

DA KENT: That's what we're here to find out, Mr. Charnas. (Mr. Charnas adjusts his chair, attempting to get comfortable.)

MR. CHARNAS: I didn't kill her! I did not! This is what I've been trying to tell everyone, and they just don't get it. You just don't get it, though, do you? We're on the road maybe two-thirds of the year. Do you know what that's like? It's great to play music for a living. Don't get me wrong—it's a pretty sick gig when all is

34 I hate to be the contrarian here, but the talking pinheads from the various national news stations tried to make this testimony seem more than it was, which was straightforward and, frankly, quite dull.

said and done. But it's hard to be away from people you care about. It can make you go a little crazy.

DA KENT: And did you go a little crazy?

ATTORNEY COCHRAN: Objection, Your Honor. Argumentative—not to mention prejudicial to my client.

DA KENT: Withdrawn. How did it make you feel to be away so much?

MR. CHARNAS: I love the fans. The shows. All of that. It's great. So that makes it a bit better, you know? But at the end of the day, you just want to be home—in your own bed, your own house. That kind of thing.

DA KENT: And Nadia?

MR. CHARNAS: She didn't like that I was gone so much either. She'd come on the road sometimes, but I think she wanted to be home too. She didn't sign up for this.

DA KENT: Did you ever fight about it?

MR. CHARNAS: Sure. Maybe once or twice.

DA KENT: Did it ever get violent?

ATTORNEY COCHRAN: Objection.

MR. CHARNAS (laughing): It's all right. I'll answer that. No. Not at all. Like I said—I loved her. Why would I kill her?

DA KENT: Sometimes love makes us do crazy things.

MR. CHARNAS: What would you know about love? Let me guess. A lifetime of being single—by choice, right? Waiting for that perfect man, but no one waiting for you to come home to. Just a cold bed and a cold dinner in front of a cold blue television set. Right, DA Kent? (The district attorney stays silent for a moment, staring at Mr. Charnas on the witness stand.)

DA KENT: I'm not the one on trial here.

MR. CHARNAS: I think I struck a chord…(The district attorney turns to the judge, backing away from the witness.)

DA KENT: Objection, Your Honor.

ATTORNEY COCHRAN: She can't object! It's her cross!

JUDGE REINHOLD: He's right. It's your witness, Miss Kent. Redirect if you can, but you can't object to your own line of questioning. (Kent becomes flustered.)

DA KENT: Right. Of course. I'm sorry.

Court was dismissed soon after this exchange, and Spencer was excused from the witness stand. To the untrained eye, Kent appeared to be letting him off, as if unable to make headway in an attempt to enter his psyche. However, I would argue that this was exactly what she wanted: a show of vulnerability from herself, and a chance to unmask Spencer's cruelty toward women in a public setting. The real question was—would it land with the audience of twelve?

When court was adjourned for the day, Spencer picked himself up from the witness chair and turned to Bailiff Bosco, holding out his hands and saying, "Drag me back to hell, Bailiff." The jury laughed. He was charming, poised. This wouldn't bode well for Kent's case, she must have felt. Here she was trying to show him for who he was—a cruel sadist wrapped in the body of a rockstar. Instead, he was proving himself to be downright likable.

Interestingly, this portion of the trial is barely mentioned in the manuscript of Kent's book—reduced to a single line noting that the defendant took the stand, with nothing more specific. Still, something about the exchange stuck with this writer.

As I've stated before, Kent was attempting to garner sympathy from the jury by making herself vulnerable, but this went farther than she had likely bargained for. First, it showed the usually composed DA Kent quite literally back on her heels as she moved away from the witness—caught off guard, something that rarely happened to her in court.

Second, and more importantly, there was something in the way Kent stared into the eyes of the accused—who, in this instance, was also the witness—that made it painfully clear something else was at play. While this cannot be read in the transcript, those who were there (and I have spoken to many) could feel it in the room. Kent appeared to understand Spencer more than she had before. She seemed to sympathize with him. It could well have been her vulnerable moment of weakness, opening her mind to this emotional shift. Rarely does a prosecutor show such signs of compassion and empathy for the person they've put on trial. There was almost a shared understanding between the two. And yet, when he shifted the questioning back onto her, it was a quiet rage that welled up inside of her. Even if only fleeting, it was significant.

Of course, Marcie Kent didn't include this in her writing either, but it was evident to anyone in the courtroom that day. And yet, for whatever reason, nobody was able to connect the dots in real time—this writer included. It's much easier to Monday-morning quarterback this situation; hindsight being 20/20 and all that. But it stands to reason that had someone present been able to fit the pieces of this convoluted puzzle together—and link this exchange to what would happen next—it might have prevented further tragedy. None of us is innocent. Not the prosecuted, certainly. And now, it would appear, the prosecutor herself held some modicum of anger. The squeaky-clean DA Marcie Kent had another side, and soon, we would all learn what it contained. I believe it can most easily be traced to this moment. Each of us present in the courtroom had, in our own way, failed to notice the box had been opened—and what came out could never be put back inside.

XI

F.L.Y.

Following Spencer's testimony, the defense rested. Carlos seemed to feel that this was the most positive takeaway a jury could have been given: his client telling them he didn't do it and how much he had loved the victim, Nadia. Not to mention the awkward exchange with the DA, as discussed in the previous chapter, which showed her to be seemingly entranced by the singer, if not also incensed. Whether or not anybody was talking about this new phenomenon—and they weren't—it must have been felt by the jury and was clear as day to a few of us in the press pool.

Spencer had served as a nearly perfect witness in his own defense. There was nothing in his voice that appeared to feel contrived or concocted. And to those who were there on the day, he did seem to be telling the truth. That's not to say that he was innocent, nor is it to suggest that he actually was telling the truth during the entirety of his questioning. As with many artists, the outward, world-facing persona is rarely the reality that lurks beneath. They have a kind of dual identity. That is why I say "nearly perfect" and not simply "perfect": his very being exudes something that is inherently untrustworthy.

As mentioned before, many of the ins and outs of the trial are known to readers here, whether through the endless reporting, the podcasts, or the litany of YouTube videos[35] and various other media on the subject. I do, however, want to expand upon something I have touched on briefly thus far, and which I feel was missing from practically all of those primary sources: the feelings in the room. I will now attempt to recreate what it was like to be a fly on the wall as the closing arguments commenced, giving you an inside experience of what it was to sit in that room and hear those speeches and see the faces of the jurors, the lawyers, and, of course, Spencer himself.

Closing arguments came after the weekend following the defense resting its case. On the surface, the closings went as one might expect in a high-profile trial full of uncertainties and doubts. Each side felt they were winning—that much was clear. DA Marcie Kent had boasted about this feeling of invincibility in both an interview given just after closing and through page after page of her unpublished memoir; I have spared the audience much of this content. For Carlos, the feeling of confidence was easily deduced through the slightest glance at his face. To say he was giddy, gleeful, and gloating would be an understatement. Only one of the two attorneys could be correct about their chances, but both were, curiously, right to be confident. How is that possible? That will become evident soon enough.

Kent had an interesting weekend, to say the least, and one which was not fully dissected until after the trial had concluded. It involved her seeing Spencer and Ice Nine Kills perform live. Yes, you read that correctly. She attended a concert for the man who was on trial. Now, she had only been there as an officer of the court, supervising his release, but that's not to say she didn't thoroughly enjoy herself during the judicially mandated outing.

35 Many of the official videos that show Spencer's depravity are linked throughout this book, but there are countless fan videos online as well. Far too many of these celebrate the sickness of the singer, in my humble opinion.

Additionally, the weekend turned up the body of Officer Dunbar, who was found by Harris and his team, resulting in an emergency regrouping of his staff. Harris was present in court for the closing arguments, but not at the attorneys' table and not as his usual casual, callous self. These two weekend occurrences are something I will go into in the subsequent chapter, but for now, I wish to keep us in the courtroom and with the trial itself.

Kent began her closing arguments by simply reciting the facts of the case by rote. "Passionless" was the word used by Buddy Neilsen of the El Lay Times,[36] although perhaps "sterility" would be more apt. It felt as though she were simply going through the motions. "Spencer did this," "he wore this when he killed," "here he is on stage," etc. It was nothing the jury hadn't heard before, but it was also hardly being sold to them as interesting or important. She spoke of Nadia's body from a clinical perspective, hardly touching on the fact that she was stabbed, mutilated, and then burned—although not while still alive, horrific nonetheless. Certainly no mention that she had once been a living member of society, young, vivacious. Kent discussed Nadia's murder as if she were reading from a high school physics textbook, listing the various findings from Dr. Lambert, the medical examiner, rather than building empathy with her twelve-person audience.

One other curious element of her closing was her discussion of Spencer as an artist. She seemed to sympathize with his case far more than any prosecutor should; this was evident purely through her descriptive admiration of his music and stage performance. No doubt this had been born out of the recent weekend's activities. At the time, many of those covering the case felt that she was

36 This is not a typo. The *Los Angeles Times* did cover this case, but in such a dull manner that many readers found more exciting coverage in such indie publications as the *El Lay Times*, an online newspaper put out by ex-members of the pornography industry. "The Valley's Stickiest News Source" first came to prominence during the Presidential Erection of 1997–1998 involving Clinton and Lewinsky.

trying to portray him as a showman and liar, a skilled performer capable of a maddening level of duplicity. She insinuated that he was simply hiding in plain sight. By employing horror in his music, Spencer was therefore free to carry out such horrific acts in real life without even the slightest suspicion of those around him, including the authorities. However, her discussion bordered strikingly on adoration, elevating Spencer to the level of a god—a level of idolatry customarily seen only in his fans. Had she somehow been converted to a Psycho over the weekend break? Most of those in the courtroom would have concluded that this was highly unlikely, but the truth was not so far off.

Kent's newfound admiration for Spencer was shrouded so carefully that it is only obvious to those of us who have the benefit of looking back. That is to say, it was not as salient in the moment as I am now making it out to be. At the time, Kent was hanging her argument on the idea that Spencer's gifts and talent on stage could also be brought into the courtroom—and that he was not to be trusted. Unfortunately for her, only the jury could decide whether Spencer seemed trustworthy, and with her last-minute pivot from her previous arguments to this new one, she risked being given that untrustworthy label herself. From the outside, what had seemed like an open-and-shut case now looked more like a jury still undecided between Spencer the man and Spencer the monster. Of course, for the sake of her own career, Kent needed them to choose "monster," but her tone on that final day was not nearly as convincing as it had been in the preceding weeks.

Kent's voice shook and her hands trembled during much of her closing argument. One might have concluded nerves were at work, but she had certainly tried large cases before—even if none were as "make or break" as this one. Something else must have been at play; it was as if she were experiencing some kind of loss that preoccupied her mind, something unknown and from beyond the courtroom. This split concentration (there are numerous theories as to what it was) would later be blamed for the outcome of the trial, but I do not believe that was the whole story. Kent had a lifetime of good schooling and greater successes that had led up to this very point. She would not have simply crumbled under pressure. Her body language, much like her voice, appeared closed off—not as warm as her usual self. She often connected with juries, bringing them into her heart as much as to her side. Here, however, she seemed somehow distant from them, as if speaking to them from another realm into which she had passed.

After simply reciting the case point by point, she closed by saying that the jury had an important decision to make. She felt the case was clear (she didn't say in which way, I might add) and repeated the judge's earlier instructions that their decision would affect many lives. The pressure was on, to say the least, but no one knew which way the jury would lean—or if Kent herself was the one doing all the breaking.

Of course, there are those who feel this case was argued perfectly, even up to the final words of the closing arguments. They want to blame Spencer and his team for what would ultimately be, in the eyes of many, a miscarriage of justice. Judging by the contemporary news clippings written that day, almost no one believed the jury wouldn't choose to convict.[37] So it's fair to say that Kent wasn't "throwing the case" if all of these outlets felt that she had done her best work and driven it home. She was, however, holding something back. That's my opinion, but it was also mentioned in a few of the articles at

37 Almost every piece of contemporary commentary surrounding the day of the closing arguments felt the jury would convict. Sure, some cases favored the famous, but this appeared—on its surface—to be an open and shut situation. Only one journalistic outpost covering the case, BloodyDisgusting.com actually appeared to have seen the writing (or blood splatter) on the wall. Spencer's innocence was professed across the pages of their website. Were they in on this great conspiracy too? Hard to say…

the time and often attributed to her having "an off day." And while, admittedly, I didn't write about this myself at the time, in returning to the case, I was able to see the interconnected web of it all. Kent let the case die, at least plausibly in the eyes of the public, and we would soon know why that was.

DA Kent finished her lukewarm closing and walked back to her seat, avoiding eye contact with Harris, who watched from the first row of the gallery. As soon as Kent sat down, Carlos popped up, his bright white smile flashing at his client and then at the jury. He walked toward them, turning his head slightly toward Kent and nodding as he went—a gesture of camaraderie not previously seen during the trial.

If Kent's closing argument was unimpressive, Carlos' began almost equally so. He spent most of the opening discussing his client's various accomplishments in the music industry—hardly material that could prove innocence. It was beginning to feel like some kind of orgiastic praise-fest, all leveled at Spencer. The jury was not there to decide the merits of the music of Ice Nine Kills (an acquired taste at best, if you ask me), but rather to consider the facts of the case and the murder of Spencer's fiancée, Nadia. It's all too easy to forget the victim when one gets wrapped up in the cocoon of spectacle and drama. However, after Carlos finally mentioned the case and moved into the heart of his conclusions, things looked slightly better for the lawyer and his client.

Carlos refuted DA Kent's arguments point by point, weaving a tapestry of doubt through every element. It was confusing, to say the least, but that must have been his aim. Dazzle and distract—the Cochran way. Could it have been a fan? An angry ex-band member? An escaped orangutan? Mr. Goldblum with the lead pipe in the conservatory? Nearly all were suggestions the jury had heard before. This time, however, he even brought the missing detectives into the narrative, citing the fact that Ophelia had been murdered while Spencer was in custody, and that Dunbar's time of death (newly discovered) coincided with the first day of the trial. If Spencer had ordered the murders, that was one thing—but it was clear to everyone that he was not physically present to commit them.

Kent, of course, objected to the introduction of this new evidence, and it was stricken from the record.[38] Before it could be removed, however, Carlos also accused the DA of committing the murders herself—a desperate tactic or a glimpse of inside knowledge? Regardless, it was a hypothesis that would later be tested. Though the comments were stricken from the record, those of us in the room took note of Carlos' words and the jury's reaction. It appeared the argument might have made some headway, even if only in the most microscopic of measures.

Carlos also emphasized that his client had a clean record prior to Nadia's death. Another reason he may have added the detectives' murders was to link them all together—as if a serial killer was on the loose and it couldn't possibly be Spencer. By connecting the three murders and ruling Spencer out for the latter two, Carlos aimed to make it less likely he had committed the first. He wanted the jury to sense this connection and ask themselves: why would a serial killer appear out of thin air after a lifetime of good behavior? Well, in Spencer's case, mediocre behavior. Carlos further muddied the waters by avoiding mention of Spencer's previous case in Massachusetts. It was a kind of "my client never killed anyone in this state" defense.[39]

38 Because of this action, one would not see any of this in the transcript of the case and the jury was told to disregard. But, once the monkey is out of its cage, it can be impossible to put him back in.

39 This writer, of course, has his own thoughts on the subject—which are expounded on thoroughly in The Silver Scream, available wherever books are sold. Spencer had previously killed people in the Commonwealth of Massachusetts, despite being let off on all charges, and it's possible that he killed again. I am legally required to tell you that "It's also possible he was set up in both cases."

This was no longer just about one body; it had grown far beyond Nadia. And Spencer couldn't be blamed for all of it—regrettably, I might add. The jury nodded during both closings, but more in polite acknowledgment than agreement. Despite Carlos' limited ability to connect with the jury, Kent still appeared green with envy—or illness. It was hard to tell in moments like this.

Carlos returned to discussing the evidence in relation to his client's role—or lack thereof—in the murders. "A conviction would be unwise in this instance because of the preponderance of evidence suggesting it could have been anyone off the street. Hell, it could have been you," Carlos said at one point, gesturing to the jury as a whole. Though he did not single anyone out, he appeared to be pointing in the general direction of Jurors 3 and 4.

Kent stood up and objected once again. "Your Honor, counsel cannot continue accusing people in the room of this crime when it is so obvious his client was involved." It was the most forceful objection she had raised all day, but she stopped short of saying "murder"—and Carlos picked up on it.

"Involved? Or guilty?" he asked, snidely. "Which is it, Ms. Kent? Because if he was only involved, then why is he on trial for his life? And what is the level of involvement? Certainly, now that we're here, we're all involved, aren't we?"

The DA glared at Carlos, unwilling to engage.

Judge Reinhold banged his gavel. "Now hold on just a minute," he said. "You are both dancing on the edge of the thinnest of webs. Best tread carefully before you fall through. Jury will disregard."

Kent sat back down, and Carlos resumed his closing argument. There was still some fight left in Kent, but it wasn't clear whether it was genuine or simply for show. Something seemed off. It's easy to say now, looking back. Maybe the trial had taken its toll. Maybe the Marcie Kent who flew in like a hurricane on the day of the arraignment was no longer the same woman who now sat across from defense counsel, reprimanded alongside him as he made outlandish claims.

From the outside, Carlos didn't appear to be making much inroads with the jury either. Even if the stab patterns were identical, he argued, the video had been publicly released and could have been copied. This line of speculation did not resonate with the jury, as evidenced by two separate eye rolls from Jurors 9 (David, the scientist) and 5 (Shinji, the software programmer). Or perhaps the eye rolls signaled their irritation at being flippantly implicated by Carlos in the very crime they were judging.

From Carlos' arguments, it appeared the battle now being waged in court was less about the actual facts and more an existential debate between art and science. Which would win out? Was it that Spencer's art was copied by the killer? Or was there enough evidence and hard facts to prove he had crossed the line—killing his fiancée and possibly others? The first scenario presupposed that he was free to create whatever he wanted, regardless of how extreme the content, so long as it didn't spill into real life. If others had acted on his behalf or in response to his videos, would he be implicated then? That question might belong to another trial. After all, inciting murder and committing murder are two very different things—unless you're the deceased party, in which case, death is death.

One particular portion from the end of Carlos' closing stands out—primarily for Kent's reaction to it. "Do we follow the science? Or do we follow the art?" Carlos asked, turning his attention to each juror in succession. "This is the fundamental question we've established here. Spencer may have killed someone. Ice Nine Kills slays every night." He chuckled to himself. One or two jurors did the same. "I submit, however, that Spencer did not kill anybody and is simply being targeted for his sick, depraved, and downright disgusting displays of disembodiment and gore. But just as a great horror film allows us to experience the evils of the world for one glorious, fleeting moment before being returned to the safety of our couch or bed, Spencer gives us the same escape through his music. It's that brief period between fear and safety that we all crave."

The jury hung on every word.

"You see," he continued, "horror is never about the kills—it's about those who live. And my client, Spencer Charnas, is here in front of you. Living. Don't throw away his life simply because society believes that anyone who depicts killing must also be a killer. This kind of small-mindedness has overtaken small towns across America and locked up multiple teens simply for looking a little different."

The two Marys—Jurors 4 and 6—both countercultural in their own way, nodded along. He had reached them; anyone could tell. But there were still ten others who needed convincing.

"The thrill of horror is in the survival of the ordeal," Carlos went on. "We make it out alive on the other end. And I have no doubt my client will do the same. Not only because he is innocent, but because you, too, understand what it means to go through hell and come out the other side. Transformed. Improved. The amount of time and energy he puts into the band would make you puke. He's built something greater than himself—and it has such a big following that if he stopped today, it might still live on. You've seen the people in masks outside, no doubt."

He looked at DA Kent, who wore a small smile as though she were enjoying the performance.

"It's cult-like. But not in a bad way," Carlos added, smiling at the jury. A few smiled politely, but most seemed stoic—either unimpressed that he would make light of the situation or deep in contemplation of the words delivered by a clever, silver-tongued lawyer.

Carlos continued, though with less philosophical flair. By the time he finished, he had laid out several carefully crafted conclusions that may have left some in the public uncertain about the case. Unfortunately for him—and his client—the public would not be deciding anything. Unlike the laypeople of Los Angeles, the jury held the pages to a different story. They had spent weeks listening to multiple witnesses, poring over evidence, even visiting the crime scene.[40]

Now, the jury would be sequestered for the night in a hotel, where they would remain until deliberations the following morning. The judge believed the case had grown too complex to allow full freedom. When a verdict would be returned was anybody's guess—but at the time, all signs pointed to a conviction. The mainstream media saw it the same way, and nearly every major outlet reported as much.

But, oh, how wrong we were.

---

40 The jury had visited the place where Nadia's body was discovered. It was not that eventful of a day as they were bussed to the top of a canyon only to look down on a pile of rocks and dead trees. With the body gone, was it really still a crime scene or just a place for tourists to take selfies?

XII
Worst Vacation

PLEASE NOTE: While we do not have a complete and corroborated account of the events from the weekend preceding the closing arguments in the Spencer Charnas murder trial, DA Marcie Kent's contemporaneous notes and portions of her book serve as the basis for the following account. In the interest of full transparency, there is some speculation involved—but not solely on the part of this author. It would seem that Kent herself fabricated some details of what happened during this interim. This is evident, given that we also have a conflicting account from Captain Harris, among others. However, because nobody really likes to see how the sausage is made, I will treat each morsel—whether real or fabricated—as fact, presenting them all together in what it would appear is the timeline Kent wanted us to see, thereby taking the DA at her word. This will hopefully give you, the reader, an idea of what Kent was trying to do in the closing days of the trial and will set up for what was really going on behind the scenes. It may also shed some light on why things ended as they did. Like aiming a blacklight at a hotel bed, it may not always be pretty, but at least we'll all sleep easier knowing the truth.

If you'll allow us to step back in time slightly, we will now take a look at the events that occurred on Saturday—the day after the defense rested its case but prior to closing arguments (which we have already discussed). These events are out of order because of the way Kent structured them in her book, and I wanted to honor that in hopes of offering a brief vacation into her confusing mind.

On Saturday evening, DA Kent arrived on the Westside of Los Angeles around 7 p.m. It took her a few minutes to park, which she only began to attempt after locating the small venue that was to provide the night's entertainment—if one could call an Ice Nine Kills show "entertainment." Kent was still unsure what exactly to expect from her murder suspect's performance that night, but as an officer of the court, she was there in a legal capacity. Morbid curiosity and a desire to learn more about the defendant had presumably propelled her to volunteer for the weekend assignment. She braced herself and stepped out of her car, instantly hit by a breeze that had picked up earlier that evening, forcing her to pull her black leather coat closer to her neck in defense against the frigid air.

Spencer and Ice Nine Kills had played everything from small bars, VFWs, and basements in their early days, but this venue seemed on the dicier end—especially given that they had recently started performing in front of arena-sized audiences. Tonight, the band would be returning to their roots at the "King of the Swing," an aging club just down the road from the Slovakian Consulate. The foreign government would often use this venue for external events. On this night, the Slovakians had worked with Ice Nine Kills to develop a show that would coincide with a holiday typically celebrated back home in Eastern Europe. Truthfully, the event was really an excuse to celebrate the birthday of the consul's daughter, Natalya, a big fan of the band.

Kent approached the door to the venue just as a large, bald-headed bouncer was forcibly removing an intoxicated-looking patron.

"Be careful!" the patron shouted to Kent as he was being dragged past her. "You can spend all your money in there! Crooks!"

She watched as the man was shoved toward the street, where he adjusted his jacket and continued on his way. She wasn't sure what his warning meant, but it was already an ominous sign for the evening.

After watching the bouncer reset himself at the front entrance, she pulled out her court ID and handed it to him.

"DA, huh?" he asked in a thick Slavic accent, sizing her up. "You're here about Spencer, no?"

"Correct," she replied, respectfully. "Anything you can tell me about him?"

"He's got two officers with him in the green room, and now you are here? All I can say is, he is great—number one guy!" the bouncer said, overly giddy for a man his size. "And he didn't do any of those things you say he did."

Kent was once again encountering the recurring theme from everyone who had ever met Spencer. He was a nice guy—she got it by now.

"Thanks for the advice," she said, grabbing back her ID and walking past him.

"Any trouble in there, you let me know. Just because I like him doesn't mean I can't also help you." He struggled to formulate his next phrase before deciding on: "Two things may be true at once. Yes?"

She stopped for a second to contemplate this unexpected philosophy lesson from a foreign-born bouncer at a divey nightclub in the no man's land between Westwood and Santa Monica. She wondered—could two things be true at once with Spencer? Could he have another side she wasn't seeing? Things with Spencer always seemed so black and white: he was a bad guy, killed his fiancée, bragged about it in his videos. Or maybe none of that was true. But it was still a binary outcome. With how far she had gone trying to make the case, she hoped she wasn't mistaken. She had to come out on top.[41]

Once inside the club, Kent encountered a crimson-red hallway leading from the front door toward the larger venue. The narrow passageway felt like it was filled with smoke, despite the practice of smoking in bars having been outlawed in Los Angeles decades earlier. Nobody was smoking, aside from the occasional vape pen being surreptitiously used, but that didn't explain the cloud that hung over the area like a thick fog. It could have been the remnants of a time gone by, or perhaps simply a smoke machine. Or maybe it was the air of mystery that comes from stepping into the unknown.

Kent still had no idea what to expect at the show. This might also explain her feeling that the hallway was narrowing as it reached its end—like the alleyways used to herd cattle through progressively smaller channels before they arrive for the slaughter.

At the end of the red hall, Kent immediately saw the room explode with energy. Lights and bodies swirled around as an opening act performed onstage. It was here she first felt overwhelmed by the sheer force of it all. Like an out-of-body experience—as if an avatar were in her place and she was watching it all from above—Kent felt the rush of the crowd, her heart skipping beats with each rhythmic pulse of the double bass drum hammering away onstage.

Spencer hadn't even begun to perform, but she could already sense the passion of the fans—their rabidness was palpable. She didn't catch the name of the group playing onstage at the time, but we now know they were called The Quarantinos. They finished almost as soon as she had arrived. The crowd went wild as the opener's set ended and the house lights punched upward, illuminating the room.

41 It has to be reiterated here that this is the mindset Kent displays in her book but was more than likely not her true pattern of thought. Sometimes what goes on behind closed doors is the last thing anyone would dream of.

This was Kent's first chance to take in her surroundings. Perfect timing, she must have thought to herself. She could see a large bar that ran along the right-side wall and a smaller one on the left. In the middle of the venue, right in front of where she was standing, the floor dipped down, and hundreds of people were crowded in, facing away from her and shoving toward the stage. They cheered and hollered as a banner with the words ICE NINE KILLS dropped from the ceiling, confirming what they already knew: Spencer would be playing next.

The crowd was mostly made up of younger people—metalheads, scene kids—dressed primarily in black. She felt out of place in her smart-casual leather jacket, but at least she'd gotten the memo on color. Tattoos also appeared to be the norm here; what might make someone stand out in the polished setting of a courtroom would certainly go unnoticed in the sea of ink that washed over this club. The crowd, however, did not appear to resemble what one might expect from an official event hosted by the consular delegation of an Eastern European country. "Were there even any Slovakians at the Slovakian Consulate's party?" she wondered.

††††††††

The ceilings were high in the main area—much higher than they looked from the outside—and there was a second tier of people standing on a mezzanine that wrapped around above her. Despite being underneath most of this upper level, she could see the far reaches of the audience gathered behind retaining railings at the two ends closest to the stage. She couldn't quite make out the individuals, but she could have sworn one of them looked familiar. It was a face she had been staring at for weeks—and the one she had run into in the basement of the courthouse that first day of jury selection. Eli.

However, her mind would have had to quickly dismiss the possibility. He was a juror on a case set for deliberation in a few days. He wouldn't be so stupid as to be seen at the concert of the defendant, even if he was a fan. She hoped she was wrong.[42] She did nothing at the time to confirm whether or not it was him, but her book later revealed that her suspicions were raised. Maybe he slipped away too quickly for her to snap a photo and report him to the court, or maybe she simply stopped caring so much about the case and wanted to enjoy a night away from it. A drink would take the edge off. That's what she needed.

The bar was busy, but Kent managed to squeeze into a small opening on the side nearest the entrance. Quickly getting the bartender's attention, she ordered a house cocktail—something with gin and schnapps, she would later recount. It went to her head almost immediately. She realized she had forgotten to eat before arriving. This was a far cry from the hors d'oeuvres-filled parties she was used to. She looked around for something to quell her hunger. Nothing. She stopped searching almost immediately after the house music faded and silence enveloped the venue. Spencer was about to take the stage.

Kent would later write in her book that "Ice Nine Kills has a lot of multimedia in their shows. It's an experience as much as a concert." A cold description of what was undoubtedly a spiritual experience for her. One could not infer this from the text of her writing, but rather from her later actions. To her, being there must have been intoxicating.

With the stage in darkness, an opening voiceover warned the audience of explicit content and even seemed to mock the trial

42 It has been argued and later proven that Eli, Juror 1, was present at this concert that night. Although not explicitly against the law—there is no evidence he had any contact with Spencer—this could have easily tainted the case had it been brought forward earlier. Kent, however, sat on this information.

Kent had worked so diligently to prosecute. But was she offended or enamored? It was anybody's guess. She took a place near the door and at the end of the bar. As fans rushed into the main pit, her position afforded her a slightly elevated view of the performance.

Spencer took to the stage in shadow, though just enough light revealed he was wearing a striped button-down shirt, dark dress slacks with suspenders, and a Silence mask with the bottom removed for easier singing. He also wore black leather gloves—reminiscent of another famous LA murder trial Kent was loath to recall. As Spencer began singing, the attorney saw another side to him. His voice had a softness absent from the courtroom. The music was more melodic than expected; it humanized him. Did this edgy rockstar have another side to him—or was it all an act? she must have wondered.

Soon after, the crowd roared as Spencer raised a large knife. Slowly. Theatrically. It was high art. And yet, the sheer size of the blade was almost comical. Still, Kent had to consider: Where did the comedy end and the tragedy begin?

Almost immediately after the knife reached its apex, the guitars, drums, and bass kicked in. The music was raw and powerful. The crowd loved it. One had to see the show live to fully comprehend it. Perhaps now that Kent was doing just that, she would see what the fans saw: true artistry, witty irreverence, and a penchant for parodying horror films.

Songs were punctuated by voiceover and video reels combining horror-film clips with intros about the band, including references to Spencer's legal troubles.[43] Costumes changed from

43 There have been reports that even yours truly, Roy Merkin, was used in some of these "introductions." While my newscasts are public and therefore legally utilized, I take great offense to this kind of behavior. I had to see for myself once and attended an INK concert in the Boston-area during Spencer's Silver Scream Convention. I have never seen such a sick showcase of depravity. I would encourage anyone to go one September and see for themselves the disgusting display.

suits to clear plastic jackets. One song parodying Stephen King's It featured Spencer in a clown wig and Ricky in a yellow raincoat. There were actors onstage for several songs, acting out horror scenes. Alongside Spencer, they cycled through a virtual armory of prop weapons: an axe, a chainsaw, a drill, and, of course, an icepick. Each scene mimicked the videos Kent had introduced as evidence in the courtroom only weeks earlier. And yet, she wasn't offended. She was having fun. At least until she wasn't.

About halfway through the set, Ice Nine Kills played a song parodying Psycho, the Hitchcock classic—and a personal favorite of Kent's. Spencer brandished a large knife. The performance culminated in an actress being "killed" behind a semi-transparent shower curtain. Only their shadows were visible, mimicking the black-and-white imagery of the original film. Kent rose on the toes of her thigh-high black boots to get a better look over the crowd. She was loving it.

Then—a tap on her shoulder. A chill ran down her spine. She turned around and was confronted with Harris' angry face. Had he seen her enjoying the show? she wondered. As the thought hit, the music echoed Psycho's infamous shower scene—discordant, tinny, mimicking a stabbing. Coupled with Harris' presence, it was a jarring reminder of the reality she would face on Monday.

Harris shouted over the music, "Having fun?"

Kent forced a pained smile.

"Bunch of sickos, am I right?" he added.

"It's almost like a confession," she shouted back, half-heartedly but aware that there might be some truth to the statement.

Harris nodded and turned to the stage.

They stood silently for a moment, unsure what to say next.

A song or two later, the band was now wearing full suits and sunglasses, except Pat the drummer, who would be too restricted in such a coat. "So much energy," Kent found herself commenting to Harris, admiring the stamina of both the band and the audience.

"How do they see with those things on?" he managed to ask, confused at the band's choice of eyewear, not privy to the fact that a few songs before they had all been wearing large masks of various horror icons.

The next song began with an actor in a leather apron and rust-colored shirt. He wore what looked like a latex cap and carried a large surgical knife. The lyrics began in German, and the crowd chanted along. More staged "kills" followed, so bloody and graphic that Kent had to have felt a certain awkwardness as she watched them unfold before a crowd that labeled it as "entertainment." This was potentially a real-life killer onstage, she reminded herself.

She glanced at Harris and caught him chuckling to the sight of the staged beheading of a young actress. Disgusting. She again wondered how he'd ever become a cop. At this point, Spencer had shown more ethical qualities. At least what he was doing was art. Harris' response only confirmed her hatred of him. She hated a hypocrite. That felt worse to her than someone who was honest about their darker nature—even if that honesty included murder.

Kent was about to address Harris—perhaps to excuse herself—when she spotted another familiar face across the room. Mary. Juror 6 (or 4—she could never keep the two younger jurors straight). She was sure of it this time, tipped off by an unmistakable tattoo of a Brazilian Fila Mastiff on the woman's left forearm. Similar to a bloodhound but a rarer breed, the dog on the tattoo caught Kent's interest on the first day of jury selection, having grown up with one of these mastiffs herself. Even from across the room, she would have recognized this inked image that held a deeper meaning for her. Harris followed Kent's gaze, just as the tattooed woman at the bar turned, narrowly avoiding detection.

"Friend of yours?" he asked, joking.

"I thought it was one of the jurors," Kent said without thinking. "One of the Marys."

"Wouldn't that be nice. Slam dunk. Juror tampering..."

"Or a mistrial," Kent corrected. "You want to do this again? Public sentiment's shifted. We might not even be able to charge him."

She was right. Crowds outside the courthouse had grown, calling for Spencer's release. The LAPD was not exactly popular—especially with this crowd. She suddenly felt unsafe. Would a fan recognize her?

"Better hope it's not her then," Harris said.

"Not who? Me?" Kent asked, distracted.

"What?" Harris scoffed. "No, the juror. With that eye makeup and black clothes, any girl in here could be a juror. Some of the guys, too."

He laughed as an androgynous man in his twenties passed them on the way to the restroom. Kent frowned at the attempt at humor. When she looked back to the bar, the woman was gone.

Pushing past Harris, Kent headed to the opposite side of the venue. Harris followed as they made their way around the back aisle that connected the two bars. Upon arrival, she searched for the juror. Had Spencer invited them? Was he tampering?

She realized she might never find her. Everyone looked the same in the sea of bodies. They could wait at the exit—but there were several. And she dreaded spending more time with Harris.

She turned to suggest they call it a night when the current song ended. The crowd cheered and quieted. From her elevated vantage point, Kent had a clear view of Spencer.

As the bass drum continued, he addressed the crowd.

"Ladies and gentlemen, we have two very special guests tonight!"

The crowd roared.

"All the way from the LA County Courthouse..."

Kent froze. A spotlight illuminated the bar area where she stood.

Fans began shouting and swearing. Then: a chorus of boos.

She searched for the nearest exit. Harris reached instinctively for his service weapon.

"Wait!" Spencer shouted. The room stilled.

"They're just doing their jobs. Isn't that right, DA Kent and Captain Harris?"

Kent nodded, eyes on the crowd. Harris grumbled and tightened his grip.

"Let's give them a warm, Psychos Only welcome," Spencer added. "We all look forward to my full exoneration later this week."

The crowd went wild. Whether for Spencer or her, Kent couldn't tell. But somehow, she had survived. Spencer had made sure of it. Unlike in the courtroom, however, the power—and her life—was in his hands.

As the next song began and the spotlight disappeared, the bouncer approached.

"My boss says it's not safe," he warned.

"We'll be the judge of that, big guy," Harris snapped.

"You want to take chances with crowd? Be my guest."

A glass bottle smashed against a nearby column.

"Get us out of here," Kent said. "Harris, we need to go. The other officers can handle Spencer. I've seen enough."

"Lead the way, Andre the Giant," Harris muttered.

The bouncer glared but complied. Along with two others, he guided them through the crowd. Kent couldn't see much on the way out. But she heard the audience chanting in unison with the band: "From way below."

They were unified—visually, sonically, spiritually. And she was being evacuated from their midst.

One last oddity: in the margins of Kent's manuscript, next to this portion of the concert recap, was a handwritten note: "J3 by entrance."

Juror 3. Tom, the schoolteacher. Had she seen him, too? If so, why omit it?

The question of when Kent crossed a line in her pursuit of Spencer has long been debated. But we know from this account that something was off. It was no longer about winning or losing. It was about surviving. And Kent was determined to survive.

XIII
Ex-Mørtis

The weekend between the end of the trial and the beginning of closing arguments held more excitement than just DA Marcie Kent's first time seeing Ice Nine Kills live. She found the show interesting, to say the least. Contrary to her expectations, she thoroughly enjoyed both the music and the production value. The depictions of horror films were likely what did it for her. As she had lately been reconnecting with her favorite horror films of the past, she realized the quickest way to her heart might be a knife through someone else's.

In the courtroom, Kent was a killer—but that's where it ended. This week was a prime example: she had an obvious bloodthirst in her desire to win the trial. She would do anything to make that happen, though it was now out of her hands. She was a woman who wished to be on a mission but instead had to sit idly by until the verdict. She had vowed to use her Sunday to decompress and quiet her racing mind in order to enter the week with a clear head. And yet, she couldn't escape two things. The first was the music of Ice Nine Kills. It clung to her like a fog, the songs stuck in her head like the proverbial earworms they were for many fans. The second, as she later indicated in her book, was the matter of the jurors. If she had seen just one of them at the show, she might have doubted herself. But several? That couldn't be a coincidence. She made notes about them in various places, though not all of it made it into her book.

Sunday morning, Kent's plan to bury herself beneath the covers and shut out the trial was thwarted. Thoughts of Spencer, the concert, and the jurors burned holes in her mind, like the ringing still present in her ears from the night before. That alone would have been enough to keep her awake. But then her phone rang at 10:30 a.m.

Kent was staring at the blank wall beside her bed, the covers pulled tight around her head, when her phone buzzed on the nightstand. She ignored it until it stopped. Relief. Then it started again. Someone clearly needed to reach her. She threw off the covers and crawled across her queen-size bed to the opposite nightstand. It was Harris. She rolled her eyes. He should've known better than to bother her on a Sunday. She couldn't wait for the trial to end. She answered.

"What?" she said sharply. "It's Sunday morning."

"And a good morning to you too, sunshine," Harris replied—not exactly chipper, but far more awake than she was.

"Can I help you?" Kent asked flatly.

"Gonna need you to get to Downtown," Harris said, then paused. "We found Dunbar. I'll send you the address."

And just like that, he hung up.

She could tell from his voice that Dunbar must be dead. It was only fitting: another death connected to the case right before deliberations. Who would be next? Her? The thought had crossed her mind. Someone was picking off those associated with the case. She wouldn't wish harm on anyone—but maybe she'd make an exception for Harris, especially if it meant saving her own skin. She hated that she thought that way. But she wouldn't miss him.

She dragged herself out of bed and stepped into the shower. The warm water enveloped her, a rare moment of calm she wished she could savor. This was supposed to be her day—no Harris, no courtroom. But her thoughts returned to the jurors. Her best thinking often happened in the shower.[44] If the jurors had been at the show, and if they had seen her, she'd clock it first thing Monday. She could usually tell when someone was hiding something—even if she didn't know what it was. She made a mental note, later written down, to attempt eye contact with each juror the next day.

Maybe it was thinking of Ophelia and how she died, or the urgency of Harris' phone call, but Kent left the shower quicker than she would have on a lazy Sunday. Whether it was fear or that time was of the essence, she quickened her morning routine. She dressed comfortably in leggings and an oversized sweater—something she could pass off as workout attire if questioned. The shower would have otherwise revealed that she hadn't rushed out the door immediately after Harris' call.

Within twenty minutes, Kent was on the road. Fifteen minutes later, she arrived at the address Harris had texted—not a bad turnaround given the circumstances. She wasn't in the habit of visiting crime scenes. But this one was different. This was one of their own. She used the drive to collect her thoughts. She had no issues with Dunbar. If he was indeed dead, she'd miss his humor most of all. Not that he was particularly funny, but his jokes annoyed Harris, and that had always been enough.

The scene in the warehouse was gruesome. I've detailed what happened to Officer Dunbar elsewhere, but picture the horrific, head-exploding carnage and add time: decomposition,

---

44 This has been somewhat documented in files that came out after the trial through the Human Resource Department of the LA County DAs office. Allegedly, an intern had once been requested to come to Kent's house and take notes from outside her shower (with the curtain drawn) while she mused about a case. While this behavior may be expected from Hollywood producers, it was not usual to see this spill out to other industries.

stench, staging. An old newsroom adage goes, "If it bleeds, it leads." This would become front-page news for weeks. Blood covered the floor as well as the centrally located cement column. No one could hope to clean it. The building would have to be condemned—just as Harris must have hoped whoever did this would be.

There was, however, one person they had to immediately rule out. Spencer. He had been in custody for the duration of his trial. For someone Kent once believed guilty as sin (wrath being the operative sin), Spencer now looked like the wrong suspect. Two dead officers, in addition to Nadia. All connected to the case—but not to him.

As for the body: pieces of rotting flesh, muscle, and brain were strewn in a circular pattern. Dunbar's lower half was intact at the center. A metal device had been affixed around his neck and detonated, sending remains up to twenty feet away. Some fragments of his lips remained tethered to the device by the threads previously used to sew his lips shut. Kent could barely look at first. But after a few moments, she adjusted, recognizing the significance of the murder. If Spencer had somehow orchestrated this from a jail cell, it had a theatrical flair only he might have conceived. There was creativity in the brutality. She hated that she thought like this. Something had changed in her—and not for the better. Maybe that's what happens when a murder case becomes this high-profile. To catch a killer, you begin to think like one. She certainly was.

Putting aside the twisted beauty, Kent couldn't recall a time Los Angeles County had witnessed such a grotesque scene. She was convinced of its severity after watching seasoned members of the Medical Examiner's Office gag in a corner. These weren't rookies. They were professionals—nauseated by something she observed with morbid awe.

†††††††††

The trial reconvened on Monday, where Kent gave her less-than-enthusiastic closing. Jury deliberations then began the following day. After Carlos mentioned Dunbar's death, she knew the jury had been exposed to new information she hadn't had the opportunity to refute. So much for being sequestered—the jury seemed to be in the dark about nothing. She had initially considered introducing Dunbar's death herself but quickly realized it would hurt her case.[45] Spencer couldn't have physically committed the murder, so the information would only add to the deluge already before the jury. She needed them to stay focused on the path to conviction; piling on new, unprovable allegations would only risk derailing that effort.

Court proceeded relatively normally throughout that Tuesday morning. For nearly two hours, Judge Reinhold gave jury instructions—a particularly long reading for a judge known for his brevity. But given the complexity and profile of the case, it made sense that he would want every detail to be clear. The jury was then led out and into their deliberation room. Suddenly, it was all out of Kent's control. The fate of the case—and perhaps her career—was now in the hands of twelve people. Spencer's life, the memory of those lost, and maybe even the jurors' own reputations would all be shaped by what happened next.

Kent's notes indicate that she wrote down "Dunbar killing to Jury?" and it was then crossed out so violently that the pen ripped through to the paper below on her legal pad. She was obviously going through a lot during the closing days of this trial.

Within thirty minutes, Judge Reinhold called everyone back. There was a jury question. Often mundane, these interruptions are part of the process. This time, the presiding juror, Eli, asked whether a conviction could carry any penalty more severe than life

45 Kent's notes indicate that she wrote down "Dunbar killing to Jury?" and it was then crossed out so violently that the pen ripped through to the paper below on her legal pad. She was obviously going through a lot during the closing days of this trial.

without parole. The judge reminded them that the death penalty was not on the table and that no harsher sentence could be imposed.

Eli appeared shaken. He dropped a hardback binder, which hit the floor with a loud thud. He scrambled to pick it up as the jury was led out again. The question seemed like a good sign for Kent. However, she didn't appear to think that way, barely looking up and instead typing intently into her phone.

Not twenty minutes after the first interruption, the judge called everyone back into the courtroom again. But this time, something was wrong. Anyone in the courtroom could tell. The look on Reinhold's face was not that of a judge merely entering the courtroom for another brief jury question. His was a face of defeat, regret; he was not his usual stoic, yet folksy, self and instead wore his heart on the sleeve of his judge's robe.

There was some whispering between the judge and his clerk before he looked over to Kent. She sighed, seemingly knowing something bad was about to come.

"I received some interesting communications only a few minutes ago," Reinhold began. "Counselors, will you approach?" He put his head down as Carlos and Kent made their way to the bench. Whispering soon ensued. Both parties looked concerned, Kent only slightly more than Carlos.

"You may return," Reinhold said, loud enough for all to hear.

We will never know exactly what was said in that sidebar conversation, but it seems pretty obvious given what happened next.

When both attorneys had returned to their tables, Carlos looked over at Spencer and grinned. Spencer gave a small smirk. Kent herself smiled, but almost as if in disbelief before her expression again returned to one of regret. Was it possible she was happy? Relieved, maybe.

"Ladies and gentlemen of the jury, counselors, Mr. Charnas, and members of the court," Reinhold began, addressing the entire room, "I received some disturbing news today."

He looked directly at the jury. "Some members of our jury have not been fully forthcoming during this trial. Are there among you fans of the band Ice Nine Kills?"

Several jurors looked down, most notably Eli (1) and Mary L. (4).

"We have the pictures," Reinhold continued, now facing the gallery. "Some jurors appeared in the background of music videos featuring the defendant. As extras, I'm told. Others were seen at his concert this past weekend—alongside members of this court." He fixed his eyes on Kent.

An audible gasp rose up from the gallery spectators and members of the press. This was followed by whispering and low chatter before the judge silenced them once again.

"In all my years on the bench, I've never seen such blatant disregard for this process," he said. "If you thought this would bring you closer to fame—or to the defendant—you may have succeeded. But in doing so, you weakened the integrity of our justice system."

He turned back to Kent. "And you, Miss Kent—how you failed to ask basic, pertinent questions during voir dire is beyond comprehension."

Kent looked down.

"I have no choice but to declare a mistrial." The judge took a breath before continuing. "Mr. Charnas, you're free to go until if and when the state decides to retry you." He glared at the defendant, then took one look at the jury before swiftly exiting the courtroom. He was red in the face and mad as hell; he looked like if he didn't get out of there quickly, he might end up a defendant himself.

The courtroom sprang to life. Cameras clicked, journalists shouted into their phones, and fans cheered. Spencer put his head down into his hands and breathed a sigh of relief. Carlos immediately stood up and threw his fist in the air, further exciting the crowd. Some members of the jury awkwardly got up, as if they were unsure if they could, or should, leave. It seemed as if the whole world around them was moving except for two people: Kent, at her attorney's table, and Harris directly behind her. Both stared in disbelief. All the work they had put into this case, the lives they had otherwise buried in order to put Spencer away for the rest of his life was gone. They had nothing to show for their efforts. Well, not exactly nothing. Kent may yet have a silver lining, and the small gleam in her eye would have let a discerning onlooker know that something was yet to come for the Assistant District Attorney.

Spencer also had a new life breathed into him, like a phoenix from the ashes. Kent looked directly at him. He was not the Spencer she was used to seeing in the courtroom, but rather Spencer, the showman—the one she had seen in the performance over the weekend. He held up his arms and the courthouse audience cheered. As Judge Reinhold had already vacated the bench, there was no one there to silence them; they were free to do as they pleased. For Spencer this was especially true. He relished in the moment, presenting a victorious front for his adoring fans. He had won the day and would continue to live as a free man. For now.

XIV

Farewell II Flesh

I began this book by saying that some of the chapters would be based more on speculation than the recount given by Kent in her memoir on the case. This chapter is the most speculative of the bunch, relying less on the meat and bones of her book and more on interpreting the spirit and essence of what happened to Kent—both before and after the mistrial. It is not entirely an autopsy, but rather an exploration of the life, and afterlife, that this trial would have in store for her, Spencer, and the others involved. So, for the time being, we bid farewell to the facts and branch into a certain type of factually informed fiction to try to discern what changed in Kent from just before the trial to the final tribulation.

It was widely reported—by the media and Kent herself—that she gave her all to this case and continued to fight for a conviction until the bitter end. I, however, submit that she most certainly did not. Therefore, we have to go back to the beginning again. Although this time, we will inspect the murder weapons more closely. Each dagger laid throughout this book marks a turning point—a moment where Kent wrote that she had done one thing, but in fact, may have done quite another.[46]

46 You'll find that these symbols † are not mere markers, but something that cuts a bit deeper. More in a moment.

As Marcie Kent would have us believe, she spent the day after the trial feeling despondent. She had failed to convict in the highest-profile case of her career. Sitting in her living room alone, listening to soft piano music, she reflected on how, in every criminal proceeding, there are winners and losers. Many winners go on to legal greatness, while the losers face one of two fates: obscurity or reinvention. Some resurface through book deals, media appearances, or lesser-known podcasts. Her greatest hope now, she imagined, might be to score a sponsorship deal from a mattress or web design company, offering the promo code "DOOMED DA" at checkout.

This, she says, was when she dreamt up the idea of turning her story into a book—a path out of eternal damnation in the DA's office. She knew she would struggle to show her face there again. It might be time for a clean break. But the idea of becoming a public figure, of becoming queen of her own hive, had taken root long before she ever stepped foot into that courtroom.

Each part of this trial had been her setup to become something more than a DA. It was the result of a dream to be someone the public revered—or feared. She wanted that ever-elusive quality that draws so many to Los Angeles: celebrity. And she would find it, through the music of Spencer Charnas and Ice Nine Kills.

Up until now, I have given a relatively straightforward account of what Kent wrote in her book. But it's only in reading between the lines that we can piece together what Kent actually did to achieve what she was really after. And what better way to slice open the subject than with the sharp edge of a literary knife. I invite you to look back on the daggers scattered throughout this account. With each one, the lies deepen and Kent's path becomes more dangerous.

†

When I say that Marcie Kent was not chosen to take this case by accident, I mean she clearly jockeyed to get herself onto it. Many might assume she was just chasing a high-risk, high-reward opportunity. But I believe she selected this case long before it ever reached trial. She used Spencer and his band to boost her own notoriety, while offering Spencer the publicity he eventually gained. That's right, she knew Spencer before this entire affair began. They had lived in the same building in Los Angeles for a time—proximity is often the root of the deepest relationships. From that poisoned root grew a poisoned tree, which bore the fruit of my theories. Together, Kent and Spencer crafted the narrative surrounding Nadia's death. Her job was to sell the prosecution's side, and she did—with arguments that appeared strong, tailored perfectly for the media. She would later bolster the same narrative within her book. It was clear she often had second thoughts along the way, but she persisted, murdering her own career for a chance at something bigger.

It may sound far-fetched to claim the DA was engaged in such duplicity, but her subsequent actions during the case support the theory. This was only the first dagger in a series of clever moves. She played a virgin in the light, but was a killer in the night.

††

When it came to working with the insufferable Harris, Kent played her role to perfection. She hated him, obviously. But she used that hatred to inform her character and to make her performance more believable. This performance, it must be said, would be laudable for any actor in Hollywood, but it was particularly distinctive in the fact that she had no formal training, beyond that of a lawyer. The way she managed the press while seeming to pursue justice was equally impressive. Spoiler: she wasn't trying to win the case. Or maybe sometimes she was—it's hard to say definitely.

That's the brilliance of it. Because win or lose, she came out on top. Either she'd be the woman who put away a killer or the one who almost did. Fame works both ways. Once you have it—positive or negative—you can do just about anything. Just ask Lorena Bobbitt, who later started a nonprofit against domestic violence.

†††

Harris being the lead investigator wasn't just a happy accident for Kent. She deliberately chose him as well. Go back and read how she referred to him. All of this is based on her own words. She knew he was the most erratic, rabidly self-righteous detective in the LAPD. Which made him perfect for a case full of holes—and not just the stab wounds. That body (soon to be discussed) was placed where it would be found by the right people. Harris being on vacation at the time? Also deliberate. It left him unprepared and forced his team—especially Nordberg—to scramble. Kent planned to throw them under the bus later. Harris was collateral damage. Although, based on how much he irritated her during the trial, maybe not so collateral. She noted his record: most citizen complaints, overzealous prosecution, brutality, and a slew of overturned convictions. Perfection.

††††

Dealing with Harris proved more useful than Kent had imagined. He was reckless, a loose cannon, and a nightmare to work with. But for Kent, he was a tool. After the first day of trial, she wrote that she was home, regrouping. But her phone records place her at The Green Bar in Burbank, just off Cabrini Drive. She went there not for its proximity to her home, but because it had become a home base. It housed a group she'd just been introduced to—the innermost circle of The Silence.

It happened just after Detective Ophelia Crane was killed. Kent met with Ophelia's killer hours after the murder. Hard to say exactly who it was, but we know where they met and that they were among this group. In the basement of The Green Bar, there was a large open space, lit by candles and adorned with altar-like structures. It felt like a church—and, in some ways, it was. A gathering place for Ice Nine Kills loyalists. With Spencer under arrest, the group lacked a leader. Kent saw an opportunity.

She arrived late, threw on a ceremonial robe she had been instructed to procure, and descended the stairs behind the bar. It was like a reverse speakeasy—alcohol out front, secrets in the back. In the basement, a dozen or so robed figures stood in a circle, chanting. She joined them. Hoods went down. Faces were revealed. Sarah, Carson, Domingo, Kelly, Robert. Familiar names she had heard Spencer mention, now connected with faces. A few members recoiled or moved toward the door. Steve, the closest thing this group had to a leader, stepped forward, welcoming Kent. "Wait!" he shouted, trying to keep his group intact. "She's a friend. Sent by Spencer himself." This was all part of the plan.

Kent exhaled and stepped forward. "I'm not here to harm you. We're all working toward the same goal." She looked around the room and spotted a few jurors—still unsequestered in those earlier days of the trial and free to attend gatherings, just not ones like this. The group relaxed, and Kent was welcomed. She immediately sensed their weakness: too trusting. She'd have to change that if she wanted to survive the trial.

†††††

Looking back on Kent's account of the trial, it becomes clear she was actively sowing reasonable doubt into her own case, the idea being that she could later pin the blame on Harris and his squad—or on an ignorant jury—when the verdict didn't go her way. The bite marks on the victim were one such piece of evidence that she deliberately had planted and came up with in conjunction with Spencer. These were a match to his teeth, obviously, and had been made by him placing his mouth over the victim prior to her death and biting down. It would show his animalistic tendencies, rile Harris up, and convince him that he had a clear piece of evidence. However, it was easily argued that he was just engaging in foreplay with his fiancée, confusing any jury. When Kent came up with this part of the plan, it may have just been the spur of the moment. She could have been at Spencer's house and witnessed him bite down on an apple, say. It was that motion that she then might have zeroed in on, leading to the idea that prior to killing his victim, Spencer would bite her. This way it would leave a lasting impression that was sure to muddy the case. Kent enjoyed creating a massive gray area in which to work.

††††††

During jury selection, Kent engaged in her finest subterfuge of the entire trial, completely undetected by the masses of spectators and press. To ensure the result she wanted, Kent had to make it possible for the majority of specific jurors to be selected. The first step was rigging the jury duty system so that Spencer's own people, even had a chance of being picked. When she later attended that first meeting in the basement of the Green Bar on Cabrini Drive, she would see some other rejected jurors who didn't make the final cut. Having a pool of handpicked jurors was easier than one might think: it simply involved swapping out the paperwork of real citizens called for jury duty in favor of Spencer's list of psychos. The real potential jurors were more than happy to be excused, and his people took their place.

This was made possible by a courthouse intern home from college. He was new to the job, but in the brief time Kent had known him, he had always struck her as a bit of an incel. A small amount of flirtation was all it took to gain his cooperation. She was not above using her sexuality to get what she needed, provided it was used sparingly and never went further. When he left for the semester and the trial began, she was rid of him and no harm was done. Well, except the complete undermining of the entire California legal system.

Once her jurors were introduced into the pool, she sent them an anonymous package containing information that coached them on exactly what to say and how to manage their internet presence so that Drew wouldn't detect anything that might jeopardize the plan. She even planned to use him as a fall guy if things went south. Of course, when things eventually did, Drew had already resigned from the DA's office to take a job at a firm that primarily defended musicians accused of misconduct with underage fans—a dream come true for the legal wizard, and a veritable cash cow with the frequency of these instances.

At the end of jury selection, DA Kent was able to seat six of her own jurors. Not exactly a majority, but enough to make a play in the room and perhaps sway the others. The judge had disqualified two potential picks through what Kent considered unnecessary questioning, and another juror, Jonathan, was seated as an alternate. Six wasn't half bad, though, and if all else failed, she could always expose the plot and trigger a mistrial. As the case wore on, this increasingly seemed like the best option. It would leave Spencer vulnerable to future prosecution, thereby increasing the power she might have over him. It would also give her more material for a post-trial book.

Kent's encounter with Juror 1 in the basement was no accident. She and Eli were able to exchange paperwork and notes on the jury room's inner workings. They continued to meet as the trial progressed. Eli claimed he needed a private bathroom in the basement for religious reasons, allowing him to slip away from the deliberation room guard and meet with Kent. He also maneuvered himself into the role of presiding juror, giving Kent—and by extension Spencer—a massive advantage in securing the outcome they wanted: a very public, very unexpected acquittal (or the next best thing and what eventually happened—a mistrial).

Dunbar was collateral damage, plain and simple. Kent actually enjoyed watching him irritate Captain Harris, but he had to go. He was too competent despite his clownish demeanor, and his love for Ophelia would only motivate him to uncover her killer. Kent found his death regrettable, but after witnessing his visceral reaction to Ophelia's body, she knew what had to happen.

She used a member of the inner circle of Silences[47] to lure Dunbar to an abandoned warehouse under the guise of a lead. Once there, he was subdued, tied up, and subjected to coercion. The goal was to extract information about the stab patterns. Kent already knew this information but needed it to leak to the media. Dunbar's death offered the most plausible delivery mechanism. She couldn't risk doing it herself, so she let it appear to come from an anonymous source. Investigators might eventually land on the Circle of Silence, if they dug deep enough, but she never feared her own involvement would be uncovered.

47 Because the name of the group Spencer and Kent formed, or had formed around them, was never disclosed, I will give them one. Hereafter, they shall be known as "The Circle of Silences."

By this time, Kent had complete control of the group and their unwavering loyalty. In Spencer's absence, they had lacked leadership, and she provided it. She used Spencer's freedom to manipulate his followers, ensuring they understood she held the power to keep him out of prison. Some jurors, including Eli, attended their meetings, giving Kent further control. If the Circle of Silences was ever exposed, she ensured the blame would fall solely on Spencer. No one would ever suspect her. Not in a million years. She held his life in her hands—in more ways than one. No honor among murderers…

††††††††

Kent attended the concert not only as the lawyer prosecuting the band's lead singer but as a fan. Since aligning herself with Spencer, she had started listening to Ice Nine Kills and liked what she heard. The concert was the culmination of her fandom. She could enjoy the music and revel in the horrorcore theatrics.

It can be argued that she was in love with Spencer. There was definitely some attraction, but she remained all business—especially that night. She needed to look like she was there in an official capacity, standing quietly in the back, interacting with no one. When she spotted Eli on the balcony, it wasn't by chance. She was there to meet him. She wanted a read on the jury heading into deliberations. Things looked promising, but she still snapped a photo of him—something she would later deny. LAPD's Computer Crimes Unit would eventually find photos of both Eli and Mary H. (Juror 6) on her phone. The photo of Mary was blurry, likely because Harris startled Kent, causing her to jolt the camera. She also photographed Tom (Juror 3) outside and casually asked about the jury's leanings.

Kent's notes didn't reflect that she had seen the jurors after the concert—they were written beforehand, detailing where and how she would interact with them. Everyone missed that detail the first time around. A discerning reader might wonder why her notes were included in the manuscript at all if they were just reminders. I submit that she had been writing her book before any of this even happened—creating a story first, then shaping reality to fit it. An interesting way to live, to say the least.

She didn't fail to photograph the jurors or report them—far from it. The photos were her insurance policy. Only two jurors had previously appeared in Ice Nine Kills videos. If the judge disqualified them, two alternates remained, only one of whom she controlled. She needed more compromising photos. And where better to get them than at a concert headlined by the accused?

Finally, the presentation of Kent and Harris to the crowd was unplanned and caught her off guard. Video evidence confirms this. She may be a good actress, but she still had her own emotions. Spencer was sending a warning. Perhaps he believed Kent was overstepping in leading the Circle of Silences during his absence. He wanted to remind her who held the microphone.

†††††††††

When Eli dropped his binder, signaling that an acquittal was no longer assured, Kent made the boldest move of her career: she triggered the mistrial. Using a burner phone, she leaked the concert photos and video evidence of jurors appearing in music videos directly to the judge. Kent herself drove the final dagger into the case.

There may have been a brief moment in the courtroom when she realized she had argued the case so well—despite not wanting to win—that maybe she should have let it all play out. Perhaps she thought, "Job well done," and considered allowing the jury to reach a verdict. Her people were trying to do their part to block a conviction, but she must have swayed the others too well. Even when trying to lose, Kent was a natural winner.

Allegedly, in the final moments before the mistrial was declared, Kent stood in the women's restroom, staring at herself in the mirror and repeating, "I can do this." Five times, according to an eyewitness. And she did it. "It" just wasn't what the public expected. She was psyching herself up for the loss of a lifetime.

What happened after the trial can be even more confusing. I'll attempt to explain it in the next chapter, through the simplest lens available: Captain Harris. Knowledge can be a blessing or a curse. For what promises to be a pileup of betrayals, backstabs, and bodies, why not approach it with Harris' ignorance, just to get the full effect? Even those in the know never saw it coming—Spencer included.

So before we move on to our grand finale, I leave you with this: a question that may never be answered—why did Kent throw it all away? Was it Spencer? The music? The power she held as de facto head of the Circle of Silences? This author chalks it up to the magnetism of Horrorwood. Once you start dreaming of it, you'll wake up in a nightmare.

XV
Meat & Greet

KNOCK KNOCK KNOCK. The banging on the door ricocheted through Detective Harris' head as he rolled over on his couch and out of his drunken stupor. He looked around before getting his bearings and realizing it was someone at the door—and that he'd been asleep in the cramped living room of his Westwood bungalow. If he wanted the banging to stop, he'd have to answer it.

He got up, kicking aside food wrappers and empty beer cans as he shuffled to the door. "I'm coming! Hold on!" he shouted. The knocking started again. "I said shut up!" he hollered, even louder. The noise stopped.

Harris hadn't been to his cabin since the case, instead remaining in his sad, small home on the west side of town. It was nice enough, when he kept it clean. The last few months, however, saw little cleaning. Little of anything, besides drinking and wallowing as he finished out his final days before retirement from the force.

After avoiding a few hazards around his cluttered floor, Harris finally reached the door. He clumsily unhooked the chains that were secured to the wall and opened both deadbolts. Flinging open the door, he was greeted by a messenger from a courier service standing on his front stoop. The messenger's red hat was pulled down so far toward the front of his face that Harris could barely make out any of his features. He was clean shaven, that's about all he could see.

"Who the fuck are you?" Harris barked.

Without a word, the messenger shoved a videotape into Harris' hand and leapt off the step. He ran across the browning, unkempt lawn and disappeared into the darkness.

Harris studied the tape in his hand. It was a relic from another time. Although only a few weeks had passed since the trial concluded, it felt like an eternity given the weightiness of the verdict, or lack thereof. Harris was again confronted with another videotape. Spencer still haunted him.

He closed the door and returned to his living room. There, in the soft light from his television set, he noticed a small note attached to the tape: "Let this Meat & Greet be another Hello… and not Goodbye."

He wondered what this could mean and whether or not it had even come from Spencer. He barely knew what was real versus fantasy these days. Unable to tell night from day, up from down, or hello from goodbye, in this case. How could he possibly analyze something as cryptic as this?

Harris was himself a certain kind of Luddite and didn't mind videotapes. That is, until Spencer had soured them for him. But, fortunately, he had a VCR attached to his TV and would be able to play it. Though less fortunately for him, he was a beaten man, broken and this felt like another twist of the mortal blade that he had recently suffered under. Ever the detective—or masochist—Harris had to do it. He had to see what was on the tape…

The sound of a guard over an intercom echoes down a long hallway lined with prison cells and cold, fluorescent lighting. At the end closest to the viewer, the barred metal door leading to the outside world slides open at the push of a button from a nearby guard, who watches security footage on a bank of monitors. Through the door walks the prison warden—suit and tie, slicked-back hair, and a look of fatigue on his face. He leads a woman into the cellblock. It's Nadia, dressed like Clarice Starling in her gray checked blazer, white blouse, and black pants. Her dark brown hair falls just to her shoulders, and she clutches a brown purse at her waist. Piano music begins just before she walks through the door.

She is stopped by the warden, who turns to her with instructions: "He's in the last cell. Stay to the left."

"Thank you," Nadia replies, barely listening.

"Don't get close to the glass," the warden cautions, adding, "And be careful."

Nadia continues walking, undeterred by his warning: "If he smells your fear, he'll eat you alive."

She walks slowly down the corridor past the cells, each containing a member of Ice Nine Kills playing an instrument. They wear matching blue jumpsuits and move as if possessed. Reaching the end, Nadia turns to approach the farthest cell. There, she encounters Spencer, also in a blue jumpsuit, but more composed and deliberate in his movements. He turns around, sensing her presence. His hair is slicked back, and his arms are tucked neatly behind his back—the quintessential Hannibal Lecter posture. He begins singing behind the glass as Nadia watches.

Spencer's cell is lined with books and drawings and appears more lived-in than the others. Eventually, he offers her a seat. She declines and instead shows him a sketch artist's rendering of The Silence, complete with scarred mask and hood. Nadia's eyes roll back; she looks dizzy, as if in a trance.

Suddenly, she is transported in rapid succession to three places: a ballroom where she dances with Spencer, the bottom of a well where she begs for her life, and a room where another version of Spencer dances in women's clothing and a blonde wig, channeling Buffalo Bill. Before her mind returns to the cellblock, she sees Spencer in the ballroom, his face morphing into that of The Silence.

Spencer continues speaking to her through the glass. She appears to fade in and out of consciousness. The video cuts between the ballroom, Buffalo Bill's room, and the well, where Spencer now sits above her, holding a small, fluffy white puppy. Back in the cellblock, Nadia listens to Spencer as Lecter for a few more moments before running out of the prison.

Next, Nadia is seen holding a gun as she enters an abandoned-looking garage, accompanied by uniformed police officers. Suddenly, the lights go out. Unable to see, she aims her weapon randomly, hoping for a clue. Instead, Buffalo Bill appears, donning night-vision goggles to stalk the room unseen. He fires his weapon, killing the officers one by one.

Meanwhile, Spencer is wheeled out of his cell on a gurney by armed guards. He wears the iconic Hannibal Lecter mask with bars over the mouth. Drugged, he lies still. Lights flicker as the guards push the gurney down the corridor.

Back in the garage, the officers accompanying Nadia continue to be killed until only she remains. Using his night-vision goggles, Buffalo Bill reaches toward her in the dark, attempting to stroke her hair. Instead, he cocks his weapon, alerting her to his presence. She spins around and fires, hitting him point-blank. He falls, writhing. The lights return. His twitching hands and goggles resemble a dying insect.

Spencer, now imprisoned in a large cage in the center of a room, wears all white and stands calmly. Two officers bring his dinner. They cuff him to one of the bars, then enter the cage. One guard stands watch while the other carries a tray of steak to place on the lone table. But the table is occupied—Spencer's drawings and the sketch of The Silence rest atop it. The officer must move them, bringing him too close. In a swift move, Spencer reveals he has escaped the cuffs, restrains the officer with them, and attacks the second. He bites the guard's face, killing him, then turns to the cuffed officer and beats him with a nightstick. Slow, methodical, rhythmic—he enjoys it.

The song ends and the screen cuts to black. It returns to show Spencer in the barred cell, two dead officers at his feet. He stands over the table, The Silence sketch and a tape recorder before him. He presses play. Classical music pours from the speaker.

Later, Nadia and a group of officers enter to find the cell door open. One officer has been artistically arranged like an angel, hanging from the bars. Nadia steps inside and approaches the table. There she finds her sketch of The Silence, with Spencer's Hannibal-style mask placed over it—an eerie confession that he was The Silence all along.

The video ended, and Harris angrily chucked his beer can at the screen.

"Oh my god…how many more of these piece-of-shit videos is this S.O.B. gonna make?!" Harris mused aloud, despite sitting alone in his living room. Unable to answer such an open-ended question, he ejected the tape from the dated cathode-ray television set and began flipping through the channels of his basic cable package. After a few ads, he eventually settled on a news update from American Case File's own Sethley Ferber.

Sethley was reporting on a medical emergency involving nudists wearing coverings made of rodent fur. Harris chuckled at the idea that these scofflaws had gotten what was coming to them—at the hands of their arch-nemesis, clothing. The report then pivoted to the hottest story still dominating the 24-hour news cycle, even weeks later: Spencer's mistrial and release.

"Jesus Christ!" Harris shouted, slamming his hand on the arm of the couch. "I can't get rid of this troglodyte!" Onscreen, more footage played of Spencer walking free. It was as if Sethley Ferber were personally torturing Harris.

The report explained how various jurors had been revealed as Ice Nine Kills fans, compromising the integrity of the trial. Some had even appeared in the band's music videos. Harris had access to all these tapes during the investigation. If he hadn't been so focused on Spencer alone, he might have noticed the overlap between faces on those tapes and faces in the courtroom. Not just present—prominently placed.

The news cut to two specific jurors. Eli, Juror 1, appeared in a split screen: one side showed him in court; the other, with a fake "IX" tattoo on his forehead in a video shoot. Then Mary L., Juror 4, seen in court and, in another clip, fully made up as a zombie in the "Rainy Day" video. Harris could only shake his head, wondering how he and his team missed something so obvious.

Then came the moment he feared. "The state has decided not to pursue new charges at this time. Meanwhile, the person police have dubbed 'The Silence Killer' is still at large," Sethley said with veteran gravitas.[48]

This was too much. Harris hurled his beer can at the television again. "Jesus Christ, it's Spencer, you fuckin' idiots!" he screamed. Now they showed Carlos Cochran taking a victory lap and replayed a previous press conference that made Harris look like the LAPD's biggest fool. Retirement was no longer a choice. He would be fired—and lucky to keep his pension.

Just then, his phone rang. It was DA Kent. Impeccable timing. He snatched it up and answered with a curt, "What?"

---

48 Despite my repeated mistreatment by the folks at American Case File who have been VERY RUDE AND NASTY TO ME due to my political beliefs, I respect Sethley as a journalist and find his temperament to be acceptable.

On the other end, a tired-sounding Kent asked, "Get any interesting mail lately?"

She must have received the video too.

"Yeah, I just suffered through the last fucking video," Harris replied, unsure where she was going with this.

"Can you meet me? I want to go over the case."

"Are you kidding me?" Harris said. "After the way you Marcia Clarked this case up?"

"I've got him," Kent said, coolly.

"Oh, now you've got him?" Harris scoffed, leaning back into his sagging couch. "What makes you so sure?"

"You want this guy, don't you? What else do you have going for you right now?"

She knew exactly where to dig.

"Well, Miami Vice doesn't come on for another hour," he admitted.

"Maybe it's time to get the old band back together. 713 East Temple Street. It's an old warehouse," she said. "We can't meet in my office."

"All right," he said, and hung up.

Harris was reinvigorated. The idea of putting Spencer behind bars—or worse—gave him new life. He felt betrayed by Kent, though he didn't know the full extent yet. Still, if it meant catching Spencer, he could trust her—for now.

He picked up his LAPD-issued Glock 22 and aimed it at the television set. "Fuck yeah," he muttered, cocking the weapon. "You're going down, killer."

Images of the news report flickered across his face as he laughed maniacally. Maybe justice would be served. Or maybe he was fantasizing about what he'd do if he met Spencer outside the legal realm. The bullets in Harris' Glock had one name written across them: Spencer Charnas.

Given that it was nighttime in Los Angeles and traffic was light, Harris arrived at the warehouse about twenty minutes after the call. He pulled into an alley and got out of his ancient tan sedan, pulling out a pair of binoculars to survey the scene. After a cursory check, he tossed them back into the car. If petite DA Kent had walked in alone, how dangerous could it really be?

He dialed her number to confirm the location. As it rang, he whispered, "Come on, Kent."

By the fourth ring, he gave up—and just then, gunshots echoed from within the building. He instinctively drew his weapon and approached a metal door. It opened easily, too easily, he should have thought.

Inside, a dark, narrow hallway stretched ahead, lit only by the faintest glow at the far end. Gun drawn, finger on the trigger, Harris advanced. Once he was through the tunnel, flickering orange light danced across his face. Candlelight.

He stepped into a larger space, lit almost entirely by wall sconces and the aforementioned candles. It resembled a religious ritual, but something darker and more occult than the Catholic masses of his youth.

In the center of the room, tied to a chair and hooded, was a figure. A spotlight made this person the room's clear focal point. "Kent?" Harris whispered. No answer.

He advanced, heart pounding. "Kent?" louder now.

The figure was male, bound to the chair with tattooed arms. A white pillowcase marked with a spray-painted "IX" covered his head. He mumbled unintelligibly.

Harris yanked off the hood. Spencer. Bloodied, dazed, with a rag tied in his mouth.

"Spencer?" Harris slapped the singers cheek. "Where's the DA?"

"Get me out of here," Spencer croaked. Blood trickled from his lips.

"I'm not falling for that bullshit," Harris muttered, stuffing the rag back in and starting to replace the pillowcase.

Suddenly, the spotlight died. Only candlelight remained.

Harris called out. "Kent? Kent!"

From the shadows, something struck him. His gun clattered to the floor. He turned, dazed, as the lights came back up. A hooded figure in a Silence mask stood before him, gun raised.

Harris raised his hands in surrender. The Silence turned and shot Spencer in the chest. Spencer slumped. Dead.

"What the fuck?!" Harris cried. "Who the fuck are you?!"

More Silence-masked figures emerged, encircling him. Then, the central figure removed their hood and mask.

Harris was dumbstruck. "Kent?!"

Here she was, the woman who had prosecuted the case alongside him for all these months. The woman who had failed to lock Spencer up. The woman who now appeared to control some kind of militaristic force of his fans. And she just killed Spencer in front of Harris' very eyes. He stood confused, scared, and, quite frankly, a little turned on. He remembered the gun still pointed at his head and tried to reason with his unlikely captor. "What did he do to you?" knowing full well how these kinds of cases could go to someone's head but wanting to find out from her just what he needed to say to stay alive.

Kent didn't respond. She only smiled as she kept her gun fixed on Harris. Nervously, he continued, hoping that in some way conversation might buy him more time in this life. "Look—we can cover this up. He pulled a gun on you. I mean, or—"

"You can't get it through your fucking skull, can you, Harris?" she interrupted. "I did this. We did this."

"The Silence did this..." she added quietly, feeling the full weight of the army supporting her with their silent presence.

"You mean..." Harris began, trying to piece it together. "You blew the case so you could join that wackjob and these fucknuts?"

Kent laughed. "There was never a case, idiot," she snapped. "Just a dime-store Dirty Harry with a grudge against a band because they used a little blood and guts in their act." She whimpered as she spoke, mocking Harris' perceived prudishness when it came to horror. Her voice then became harsher, more pointed as she asked, "I mean, come on, did you even bother to listen?"

"Listen to what?"

And then Spencer's voice: "Listen to the silence..."

He stood up, pulling off the pillowcase. "I'm not dead," said Spencer. He held up a discharged squib showing how the fatal gunshot had been faked. He then delicately took the gun from Kent and began to walk away from Harris. "But it sounds like the silence is killing you." Spencer turned like a gunfighter in an old western film and fired into Harris' stomach. Harris staggered.

"Meat and greet. Meat and greet," Spencer chanted. Kent joined. The Silences joined.

Spencer raised a hand. Silence.

"It's amazing what you can do with a bigger effects budget." Spencer proceeded to fire round after round from the handgun into Harris' stomach. With each shot, Harris stumbled further back. Kent laughed, thoroughly entertained by the image of her colleague's murder. But Harris was, somehow, okay.

"Don't worry, Captain, they're only blanks," Spencer conceded, throwing down the weapon with a theatrical flourish.

"So that's how you did it?" Harris exclaimed. "Hundreds of Spencers? Oh my God, that's how you did it!"

He was starting to understand. This was bigger than any one man.

It was a movement. A conspiracy.

"What can I say?" Spencer said, twirling to acknowledge his followers. "We've been building quite a following, huh guys?"

"Ugh, you've got to be kidding me," Harris said, barely believing the absurdity of the situation. "Not the old cult trope." Whether he was sincerely unimpressed or simply trying to survive was anyone's guess.

"You know," Spencer said, flicking open a knife, "that's just what the Weinsteins said about Halloween 6 and the Cult of Thorn. Look what happened to them."

His horror-film knowledge impressed Kent, who smiled and nodded as if listening to a prophet.

"So, you're a murderer," Harris snapped, pointing. "She's a murderer. And all of you—" he addressed the crowd, "you're all fucking murderers!"

"I mean, is he really?" Kent said in a whiny tone. She and Spencer pressed their heads together, a deranged display of unity.

"What, are you representing him now?" Harris asked in disbelief. "So much for the state bringing new charges." Kent only smiled, prompting Harris to remember Spencer's previous attorney. "Whatever happened to that weasel Carlos Cockring—or Cockroach, whatever the hell his name was?"

Unbeknownst to Harris, Carlos was in Panama. After winning the case, Spencer had rewarded him with business-class tickets to the Central American country. But Carlos had since secured a string of high-profile (and mostly guilty) clients. At that very moment, he was riding in a limo from the airport, barking orders to his assistant over the phone about his newly acquired private jet. So much for business class.

"Hey, dónde está, motherfucker?" Carlos pulled the phone down from his face to yell at the limo driver through the glass partition. "Did I tell you to stop?"[49] He ended the call, trying to reorient himself.

Back in the warehouse, Spencer resumed the scene. "Why don't we check in on old Cockring," he said, controlling the moment. "Maybe kill two birds with…one phone?" He dialed. Kent chuckled. The call connected almost instantly.

"It's for you, Captain," Spencer said, handing the phone to Harris.

Harris looked at the screen. It was Nadia.

"Here's the big reveal," she said. "She's alive!"

Harris blinked, thinking it had to be a trick. Her hair was two-toned—blonde and brown—and she held a long-barreled pistol.

Carlos' voice came through the phone: "Why the hell are we—? Shit!" Nadia turned the phone's camera to reveal Carlos in the limo, finally spotting her.

"You're supposed to be dead!" he exclaimed.

"See? He never believed you, baby," Nadia said to Spencer.

"I never said that," Carlos protested. "Who is that? Spencer?" He grabbed the phone. "Spencer, my favorite client, man."

Spencer turned to Kent. "Looks like we're having some old friends for dinner after all." She laughed, catching the reference.

Carlos, now nervous, said, "Wait a second…what did I ever do to you?"

49 Carlos' newest assistant, an older woman named Hester, only caught this portion of the conversation before the call ended. A talkative woman, the rest of her testimony was not entirely helpful and she seemed to have a thing for her boss. The Cochran charm was alive and well with this one.

"You tried to sell my story rights to Shudder," Spencer replied. "But this, counselor—this is a studio picture."

Nadia raised her gun. "And here's your establishing shot."

"Shit!" Carlos yelled just before a gunshot rang out through the phone and across the warehouse. Glass shattered. Carlos was dead.

Spencer hung up and turned back to Harris.

"But we found her body," Harris said. Even if it wasn't Nadia, someone had died.

"Right…three in the chest," Kent began in a sing-song voice—Dunbar's line.

"Two in the stomach, one in the—" Spencer joined in.

"Whatever the fuck," Kent said, cutting him off. She added, "You know it's amazing—with a little bit of fame, people will die for you…"

"And it was an INK fan who gave the ultimate sacrifice," Spencer whispered, hands in prayer.

Kent let out a mocking whimper. "And when we got done with her—"

"Whoever the fuck she was…" Spencer continued.

The two finished each other's sentences now.

"You couldn't tell the difference between her and morgue meat," Kent giggled.

"You can't buy the kind of publicity this trial got us," Spencer said. "All of us," he added, eyeing Kent.

How long had she been in on it? Harris wondered.

"Marcia Clark got a book deal after O.J., didn't she?" Kent said, bouncing with excitement.

Spencer nodded. "Time's up, Captain. You've got your answers. Take them to your grave."

On cue, a Silence behind Harris grabbed him and shoved him forward.

"Bye bye," Kent said sweetly. Spencer echoed her with a tiny wave.

Harris' eyes widened as he was led toward a long banquet table now revealed at the far end of the room. Silences joined in clearing it off and sliding Harris across it until centered. Ropes tied him down.

Kent removed her coat, revealing a sleeveless black crop top and ribbed white undershirt. Gloves still on, she watched as Spencer picked up two electric turkey carving knives and slowly approached. The Silences parted to allow him through.

"I thought you guys said you weren't murderers!" Harris shouted.

"Oh, we're not," said Spencer, taking in the whole room. "But I can't speak for the rest of the psychos." He pulled the triggers, and the blades began to whir.

"Are you kidding me?" Harris asked. "Turkey carvers?"

"Oh yeah," Spencer said proudly. He stepped forward—but the blades abruptly stopped.

Spencer turned to see Kent playfully dangling the unplugged cord.

"What the fuck are you doing?" he said sharply. "Plug it back in!"

Kent turned away. "You're no fun..." She picked up something unseen and spun around, swinging a black police-issue nightstick into Spencer's face.

Spencer dropped. Blood streamed from above his eye. Harris laughed.

"All right, DA!" he shouted.

Kent stood over Spencer. "Sorry, sweetheart," she said darkly. "You've lost your touch." She beat him repeatedly, channeling years of rage.

"Domination and annihilation! Ha!" Harris cheered.

"He was cute," Kent said, catching her breath after the beating. "But you know what they say about rock stars…they're worth more dead than alive."

Two Silences brought her coat. She slipped it on.

"Well, at least we agree on something," Harris said. "Look, look, will you untie me? There's just too many crooks in this kitchen."

A Silence handed Kent a chainsaw. Harris panicked.

"Whose side are you on?" he asked.

"My own," Kent said. "Spoiler alert: you're gonna die next." She teased him as she approached.

"And then you're going to pin it on me? Fat chance!" He scoffed, afterwards pausing in search of a reason why she shouldn't kill him. "Look, I'm a highly decorated officer! I've only had 132 complaints in 34 years!"

Kent leaned in. "Aw, don't worry, Captain," she said sweetly. "We'll tie up all the loose ends and the plot holes—in the book. Or the film adaptation. Because all of this?" She began to circle the table. "This is too fucked up for YouTube."

"Well, at least will you just split me in two like they did in that Terrifier movie!" Harris begged.

Reaching the far side of the table, Kent lifted the chainsaw and pushed her Silence mask up like a baseball catcher's. "When the house lights go up in Horrorwood…" She pulled the mask down. "They're gonna love what they saw!"

She revved the chainsaw. The Silences lined up along the table. Kent drove the blade into Harris' stomach. Blood and viscera sprayed. She was in control now. The Silences lived up to their name and stood silent, witnessing their new god at work.

XVI
Afterword

History tends to be written by the victors, whether or not those victors happen to be mass murderers hellbent on cleaning up the messes they've left behind. And so, Kent immediately set out to write a book about her "ordeal" in the case of Spencer Charnas. This book, published under the title "Only in Horrorwood: A Crooked Cop, A Misjudged Musician, and the DA Who Saved the Day," was momentarily a best seller, until it was pulled from shelves and almost every copy snatched up in the largest buyback in the history of her publisher, Bare Nerd Books.

Kent had positioned herself as the hero in the story. The person who took down Harris and exonerated Spencer. She was, as I am telling you here for the first time, not that at all. We may, however, never know the full extent of her villainy. Following her first book signing at Wardenbooks, Kent was driven away in a limo. The car was later found in a ditch with the driver and Kent both killed inside. Some say it was an accident, despite their throats being slashed, others reportedly saw a person in a Silence Mask driving the car as it pulled out of the parking lot. Whatever it was, Kent was gone and her secrets buried with her.

For his part, I believe Spencer to be innocent in almost all of these dealings. He was originally contracted by Kent and swept up into her fantasy of becoming famous. She almost made her own dream a reality, even potentially dying a martyr. Instead, around the same time she was killed, Kent was exposed for being the fraud she most certainly was. Much of her book was fabricated and this is the first time that anyone has made an attempt to unweave her web of lies. In doing so, I have used many of her own words against her. Words can be a powerful tool, whether in a novel, film, or even song lyrics. I have made my best attempt to choose mine wisely.

As they say, every saint has a past and every sinner a future. I believe that Spencer would have had a future had the DA not gotten to him like she did. There are some who say he was put into a medically induced coma and is still alive and well and rocking out. Others say he died and has been replaced by some kind of AI-powered look alike. I, of course, fall into the latter camp. What you see as Spencer, is not the man he is claiming to be. I believe that Spencer is dead, and we are all responsible. Our Silence killed him.

Goodbye from Horrorwood,
Roy Merkin